Fault Lines

A NOVEL BY REBECCA SHEA

Fault Lines

REBECCA SHEA

COPYRIGHT

This book is a work of fiction. Any resemblance to any person, living or dead, any place, events or occurrences, is purely coincidental. The characters and storylines are products of the author's imagination or are used fictitiously.

Createspace

ISBN-13: 978-1975712280 (paperback)

ISBN-10: 1975712285

ISBN-13: 978-0986428821 (eBook)

Cover design by: Letitia Hasser, RBA Designs

Edited by: Megan Hand – Story Girl Editing & Julie Deaton – Deaton Author Services

DEDICATION

To my brother Denny,
I love you, miss you, and pray you are at peace.

Frankie

PROLOGUE

TEN YEARS AGO

My fingers dig into the brown dirt between the patches of dead grass that used to once be a lush front yard. A jagged stone cuts into the soft flesh of my knee as I try to get control of the involuntary lurching of my stomach, which has me crippled on all fours.

Tears fall in streams, and I gasp for air as I hear the sound of heavy footsteps near me.

"Frances—"

"Get away from me!" I scream at the soft voice.

"It's not—"

"I said get the hell away from me!" My stomach clenches against another wave of nausea as I hear her footprints begin to move away. "Goooooo!" I shout at her again.

I manage to look over my shoulder and see Whitney Carson's long blonde hair swaying as she walks quickly back across the cul-de-sac to her piss yellow, beat-to-hell Mustang. I barely make out the swell of her belly as she slides into the driver's seat and slams the door behind her. The roar of the engine tells me she's leaving.

One last heave and there is nothing left for my stomach to expel, leaving me with only my tears. My throat burns, my breaths coming in small gasps when I feel soft arms around my shoulders.

I hear the creak of the old screen door and my mama's worn shoes come into sight just before I feel her arms around me. "Baby girl, what's wrong? We weren't expecting you home from school until tomorrow..." Her voice is quiet, yet panicked as she kneels next to me, her white uniform dress getting dirty.

I finished my finals early so that I could come home early and surprise Cole and my mom, but the surprise was all mine. "Mama," I cry between ragged breaths. "I came home early to surprise you and—"

"Stop," she cuts me off, looking over my shoulder behind me. "Let's get you inside. If this has anything to do with that girl that's been coming around, he's not worth your tears. You're going to put your chin up and enjoy your summer." She tugs at my arm in hopes to get me to budge.

I shake my head back and forth violently. "No. I can't stay here," I manage through my tears. I can't stay and watch this happen. I can't stay and watch *them*.

"What do you mean? Where would you go?" Her voice grows with concern.

"I don't know, but I can't stay here." The hot summer air hangs heavy around us, and sweat beads along my forehead at my hairline. The thought of Cole touching Whitney Carson causes my stomach to flip again, and I dry heave as I pinch my eyes closed.

Mom rubs her hand over my arm as I try to gain my composure and move from all fours to sitting on the dirt. "Well, come inside until we figure this out." Her voice is soft and sad. "I've always told you he was—"

"Please stop—" I cut her off now, not wanting to talk about Cole with her.

I hear her deep sigh. "Come on. I'll run you a hot bath. We need to get you cleaned up."

The tears still fall in waves as my heart breaks with each step I take toward our house and away from Cole Ryan. As I think about it, the last few months begin to make sense. I sensed Cole pulling away from me. He'd become distant, not returning my calls or answering text messages. Mama called me and had told me about the rumors she'd heard, but we chose to chalk them up to small town gossip. Crescent Ridge is just that, a small town where no one has anything else to do but talk about other people and spread rumors.

Suddenly, realization hits me that the one person I trusted more than anyone in the world betrayed me. He's been my best friend since I was eleven, my first crush, my first love, my first *everything*. No other person will ever etch himself so boldly into my history as Cole Ryan did. No other person held the cards to destroy me like Cole Ryan did. And did he ever.

I bite my tongue, tasting the slightest hint of blood as Mama walks me up the raggedy old front porch of our house. "Keep walking, baby girl." She guides me through the front door. "Keep your chin held high," she says quietly, the screen door slamming hard behind us.

3

She looks at me with sympathetic eyes and her voice cracks as she speaks. "Now you can fall apart, Frances. Don't ever let him see you crumble; don't give him that control. He is not worth your tears."

And crumble is what I do as I sink to the faded wood floors of our living room, Mama rocking me in her lap, her fingers stroking my hair and wiping my tears. I cry and scream for the love I believed in, for the boy who owned my heart, and the loss of the one person I long for—the one person I had planned to spend my last breath with.

Mama holds me for hours as my tears come and go. At the first hints of the morning sunlight, I peel myself from Mama's lap, my head pounding from the hours of crying. I pull my cell phone from my back pocket and press the name of the only other friend I have.

"Ash." My voice breaks and I barely make out what she's saying, but one thing is certain. I'm getting the hell out of Crescent Ridge and never looking back. "I'm coming," I tell her.

Between my tears and gasping breaths, I disconnect my call and see Mama swipe at the tears on her aging cheeks. She sat here all night comforting me as I lay helpless in her lap. In the end, she's the one person who believes in me and has loved me unconditionally, and here I am about to leave her behind. Leave everything I know and love behind, without a second thought. For good.

I know that when I drive away from here today, I'll never be back—I can't come back. I'm leaving my broken heart behind, along with the only man I've ever loved.

I toss my bag and one small box of belongings from my childhood bedroom in the trunk of my car and slide into the driver's seat of my old Honda. Without a second thought, I put the car in drive and glance just once out my rearview mirror as I pull away. The last thing I see is Cole Ryan, hunched over the paint-chipped railing of his front porch as I drive away from Crescent Ridge, leaving him, my past, and my mama behind.

ONE

Frankie

PRESENT DAY

Standing in front of the floor length mirror, I glance at my reflection. My long brown hair falls in loose waves just above my shoulders. I pull my fingers through the waves, taming the ends to fall carefully into place before running my nervous hands down the length of my black dress, willfully brushing away any wrinkles.

Taking a deep breath, I close my eyes and try to will my erratic heart into settling down.

"Ready?" Ted calls to me from the bedroom.

"Almost," I answer him and open my eyes.

I reach for the diamond tennis bracelet on the vanity and fasten it around my wrist. One last look in the mirror and I meet Ted in the bedroom where he's been waiting for me.

Tall with dark hair just starting to gray at the temples, Ted is the epitome of striking. Wearing his custom charcoal gray suit, his blue eyes stand out against his tan skin. If he weren't a lawyer, he would be gracing the covers of a men's fashion magazine—he's that beautiful.

"You look stunning," he says with a soft smile. "The cameras are going to eat you up."

I shake my head and blush. "That's not what this is about. I want the guilty verdict. I want justice for those families—"

"And you'll get it," he cuts me off. "I'm so damn proud of you." He walks across the wood floor, wrapping himself around me. "You never cease to amaze me, Frances." He presses his lips to my temple. "I was disappointed when you left the firm, but now I understand why you did it. I think I get it—it just fits you."

I smile at his acceptance. "You know that the public sector was where I always wanted to end up."

He nods and runs his hands up and down my arms.

I lean into him and wrap my arms around his waist. His embrace is where I always find comfort. "I will always be grateful for my time at the firm. The experience I received there was immeasurable...and it led me to you." I pull back and stand on my tiptoes to press a kiss to his soft lips.

With his arms wrapped tightly around me in return, he releases a long sigh and mumbles against my lips. "As much as I could stand here and kiss you all morning, we need to get going or you're going to be late. You look great. Get your nerves in check and walk with your chin held high." He releases me.

I nod at him with a shaky smile. Ted always knows how to calm me. I grab my purse from the bench at the end of our bed and follow him to the car.

The morning is a blur as my stomach twists and turns in the hours leading up to the verdict. I busy myself by reading my closing argument over and over—even though I'd memorized it weeks ago and presented it to the jury three days ago.

We finally got word late yesterday afternoon that a verdict had been reached. The jury deliberated for two and half days...two and half of the longest days of my life. *How selfish,* I think to myself as I turn around and look at the Morrison and Longmire families sitting behind me. The loss of a child will truly destroy you.

I've waited two and half days for a verdict, and they've been waiting for two years. It took us two years to build the case we needed to bring Terry Nelson to trial for the sexual assault and murder of their two beautiful little girls, Sadie Morrison and Eva Longmire. Two six-year-old girls who were best friends and in the same kindergarten class. Two little girls who had their entire futures ahead of them, gone at the hands of a vicious predator. Two families that will never be the same again, ever.

Mr. Longmire nods once at me and offers a tight smile. I've seen him age significantly in these last two years, more than a man his age should. His hair is now graying and his skin is ashen. I've never seen a pair of eyes that hold as much sadness as his. He's worn, and tired, but hanging on for his baby girl. Losing a child in the most brutal of ways will do that to a man.

I turn back to my notes just as the defense team arrives. I have to tuck my hands underneath the table to hide the shaking. The defendant, Terry Nelson, is brought into the courtroom and placed at the defense table. I glance over my shoulder just in time to catch an encouraging smile from Ted as the bailiff enters with the jury. My heart pounds wildly as we all rise and Judge Vincent arrives and takes a seat.

When everyone sits, I inhale sharply, pulling the air deep

into my lungs, and scan the faces of each of the twelve jurors, looking for the slightest signs of what the verdict may be. Twelve jurors, men and women, young and old, who have spent the last five weeks of their lives listening to me present evidence, question witnesses, medical examiners, and detectives in hopes of bringing the Morrison and Longmire families the justice they deserve—for Sadie and Eva.

Judge Vincent addresses the jury before finally asking the foreman if the jury has reached a verdict. Blood rushes to my head, momentarily deafening me as the foreman speaks. A single piece of paper is passed between the foreman, bailiff, and onto the clerk. The clerk inhales and her eyes scan the paper in her hands. The very piece of paper that could send a murderer back onto the streets, or send him to prison for the rest of his life where he belongs.

My case was rock solid—or so I believed. The DNA and the evidence I presented told the story of the gruesome and violent murders of those two little girls; in my eyes, evidence doesn't lie...but the puzzle I had to weave together to convince the jury of those facts could say otherwise.

I hear the swooshing sound of my heart racing, but I'm unable to make out the words as the clerk begins to speak. I see her lips moving and her eyes dance between the defense team and myself. The piece of paper in her hand shakes slightly as she speaks.

It's only when my head clears that I'm finally able to register the words the clerk spoke.

"Guilty." On two counts of first-degree murder.

"Guilty." On handfuls of other charges, but the one that matters, first-degree murder is all I hear.

I bury my face in my hands, choking down the emotion

that has bubbled to the surface. Emotion I never show. Emotion I learned a long time ago how to bury.

The sounds of gasps and cries from the families behind me fill the small courtroom as the judge calls for order. Everything else happens quickly, and I'm honored to meet the jury and thank them for their verdict. I spend the next couple of hours meeting with the families of Eva and Sadie, walking them through the next steps and listening to them speak words of gratitude I don't deserve. Eva and Sadie should be here—that's all I can think about.

In the pressroom, I attend the press conference and speak to the media on behalf of the District Attorney's office, as well as the families of Eva and Sadie. I'm exhausted when I finally exit the courtroom after collecting my belongings. I find Ted in the hallway, waiting patiently for me, his phone pressed to his ear. When his eyes find mine, he hangs up quickly and saunters across the tile floor, pulling me into a tight hug.

"Proud of you, counselor."

For the first time in days, I feel like I can actually breathe. I take a deep breath, letting the stale air from the courthouse fill my lungs.

"Thank you." I'm finally able to muster. "Thank you for believing in me," I tell him, an exhausted smile pulling at my lips. "Now let's go get that drink you promised."

Pushing through the doors to Manny's, I see everyone assembled near the bar. Friends and colleagues that I have worked with throughout the years have been waiting on me to arrive to celebrate today's verdict.

"Congratulations!" Everyone cheers as Ted and I approach the bar. I toss my purse on a bar stool and reach for the glass of white wine that Eduardo, my co-counsel, is holding out for me. Pressing the cool glass to my lips, I let the smooth wine settle on my tongue before swallowing.

"I'm so damn proud of you." He leans in and whispers, wrapping one arm around my shoulders.

"I couldn't have done it without you. I mean that." I smile at him and squeeze his arm in a gesture of gratitude. Eduardo took me under his wing when I joined the county attorney's office a little over four years ago. I was an experienced trial lawyer, having learned the ins and outs of trial law with Ted's firm, but this is new. I'm on the prosecuting end now. This is where I always dreamed to be. Ted's firm helped me get here and Eduardo has been my mentor and basically my best friend since I arrived.

"I'd be surprised if they even try to appeal," he says, taking a sip of his vodka tonic. "You were *that* good. There were no holes in your closing arguments. You presented solid evidence and left nothing for them to come back at us with."

"She learned from the best," Ted says, leaning over my shoulder.

Eduardo's eyes glance away from mine and up to Ted's. "Mr. Winters," Eduardo says, reaching out to shake Ted's. "Nice to see you again." It's hard to miss Eduardo's visible disdain for Ted. His jaw ticks and he swallows hard, but as always, he is the epitome of professional and is always gracious.

"I've learned a great deal from both of you." I smile and wish for the pissing contest to end. "Let's enjoy *our* victory." I hold up my glass of wine to toast, raising my eyebrows, a silent plea to Ted to be nice and he obliges.

"To guilty verdicts," Eduardo cheers, raising his glass.

Ted gives his head a little shake but reiterates Eduardo's sentiments.

"To guilty verdicts," we all repeat and take a drink.

I notice Ted step away to take a phone call and I turn my attention back to Eduardo.

"First and only time I think I'll ever hear him say that," Eduardo jokes.

"I think that's the first and only time I'll ever hear him say that, too." I laugh.

My fiancé, Ted Winters, is partner in Winters and Seldon, one of the smallest yet most prestigious law firms in Los Angeles County. Ted is known for representing some of the most high profile, and even dangerous, criminals in California. What cases he doesn't win, he prides himself on reduced charges, jail time, and fines.

Not guilty—those two words drive him to be the greatest. He's the best of the best, and he hired me right out of law school. He taught me the way around a courtroom, the best oral arguments, and the tricks to dissect evidence and to look for what everyone else is missing. I took what I learned from Ted and am finally putting it to use as a Deputy District Attorney for Los Angeles County. I always wanted to be on *this* end of the law, finding justice and doing right by the law.

To avoid any conflict of interest, I avoid all cases where Winters and Seldon is concerned. There are plenty of other prosecutors to try those, and it's best, both professionally and personally, if I avoid any cases Ted or his firm are involved in.

As I look around the bar at my friends and colleagues, I

can't help but smile proudly at how far I've come—and for the people who've been with me on this journey.

As my smile fades, I feel the exhaustion hit me like a freight train and, with a few glasses of wine on top of that, I find the need for fresh air. I weave through a sea of bodies in the bar area and push through the large glass door, which leads out onto the rooftop patio. Los Angeles has far from quality air, but pulling the mild summer breeze into my lungs feels good. A sense of calm falls over me as the adrenaline from the day wears off. Carrying the stress of this trial on my shoulders for weeks has wreaked havoc on my sleep, my diet, and exercise, and I can feel the toll it's taken on my body.

I watch the cars below, crawling along the busy Los Angeles streets, and the hustle and bustle of the city just fifty stories below me. It's windy up here on the patio, and the soft afternoon breeze whips my hair around. I tilt my face to the sky and let the setting sun cast its warm rays on me when my phone buzzes in my hand. I hesitate, wanting to indulge in a few more moments of silence, but I think better of it.

Glancing down, I see my mom's home number flashing on the sleek screen of my oversized mobile phone.

"Hi, Mama." I take a deep breath, excited to hear her voice.

"Frankie?"

My heart sinks when I hear a man's voice. A voice I could never forget. A voice so familiar that it still haunts me to this day.

Cole. The only person to ever call me Frankie. My heart stills as I wait for him to say more.

"You need to come home," he says gruffly.

My stomach drops as his voice takes my breath away. The

pull it still has on me shakes me to my core. Before he says anything else, I close my eyes and find myself lost in time, back to when I was eleven years old, spending my afternoons down at the fault line, soaking up the last of the days sunlight with Cole by my side.

Crescent Ridge, Nevada resides right on top of a fault line, a town with less than eight hundred people, and sits on the California/Nevada border. A town I left ten years ago and haven't returned to—because of Cole.

I swallow hard against my dry throat. "Why?" I barely manage to ask.

"It's your mama, Frankie."

"Is she okay?" I ask frantically.

I hear bits and pieces of what he's saying, but nothing is really registering. Collapsed, stroke, scans, breathing...but before he has a chance to say anything else, I move into panic mode.

"I'm on my way," I tell him, disconnecting the call.

My hand shakes wildly as I grip my phone. This morning I was on top of the world. This afternoon, my world has done a one-eighty.

"I don't know, Faith, he called me first," I bark at my sister, who's frantically asking me questions. "He called and said something happened to Mom and I needed to come home. Where are you?" My voice peaks with annoyance.

"Disneyworld, Franny, remember?" she gripes at me, just as annoyed.

"Shit," I sigh.

Faith moved back to Crescent Ridge with her two kids three years ago after her divorce. The one weekend she finally gets a break, a vacation with her kids, something happens to Mom.

"I'll call the airlines and switch our return flights as soon as we hang up."

"Don't," I sigh. "Let me get home and see how bad it is. You've worked so hard to be able to give the kids this vacation. Enjoy the last couple of days there. The kids deserve it. *You* deserve it."

Faith is an amazing mom and is the sole provider for my niece and nephew. I send her money every now and then so she doesn't need to worry, but I know it's still hard on her. Faith and I were inseparable as little girls, and there isn't anything she wouldn't do for me, or me for her kids. If I can alleviate some of her financial stress, I'll always help.

Mama won't accept a dime of my money, telling me I've worked too damn hard to get where I am to give my money away. God knows she needs it though. Faith tells me the house is falling apart, but Mama won't hear of it when I offer a few dollars to fix things up.

"You call me as soon as you know something, and we'll still come home early if we need to." Her voice breaks.

"Okay. I need to go pack so I can get on the road," I tell her with an exaggerated sigh.

"Franny?" she says quietly.

"Yeah?"

"Thanks. I know home is the last place you want to go."

I swallow hard as I feel a lump form in my throat. "You're welcome." I'm barely able to speak. She's right. Crescent Ridge is the last place I want to be.

But it's where I have to go.

I begin to forge a trail in the floor between my dresser and closet, frantically pulling shirts off hangers and shoving pants haphazardly into my large suitcase while admonishing myself for not asking more questions about my mom.

Ted appears with an extra-large coffee from the chain coffee shop down the street, handing it to me before turning away to finish his phone conversation, his phone still pressed to his ear. Most nights are like this. He's hungry and tireless when it comes to his business and his clients. He instilled in me that work ethic, but where Ted is all business, I draw the line at my Mama and Faith. They are the only family I have and they will always trump business. Always.

Guilt settles in when I think of how I haven't seen my mom in five years. Five years ago, she got on a bus and rode to L.A. to see me. Five years since I've seen her face and felt the comforting hugs she always plied me with. I used to pay for Mama to come see me, but the last five years she's declined my offers. She tells me she's too tired to travel at her age. Now my heart aches that I've been so selfish and haven't gone to see her.

I slam my suitcase closed, zipping it up and pulling it off the bed. I drag the heavy case down the steps, letting it thump against each step as I descend the stairs. Ted doesn't notice as he stands, leaning his shoulder against the hallway wall, still on the phone.

"Bye," I whisper as I walk past him and drag the suitcase out the front door to my waiting Mercedes. I shove it in the trunk, while cursing at how heavy it is, then I settle into the driver's seat. I'm putting the ignition in reverse when I see Ted bounding down the concrete steps from our house, the top button of his shirt undone and his tie loosened. As I roll down the window, he leans in, pressing a chaste kiss to my cheek.

He sighs. "I really wish you'd leave in the morning."

"I can't, Ted. I haven't seen her in years and it sounds bad."

He nods in understanding. "Do not drive if you're tired. Pull over and stay at a motel."

"I'll be fine," I tell him, lifting the coffee he bought me. I press the cup to my lips and take a sip, feeling the warm liquid slide down my throat and settle into my belly. Truth is, I don't need the caffeine. The adrenaline running through my veins could keep me up for days.

"Then just call me when you get there." He looks over his shoulder and down the street.

"I will. Is everything okay?" I ask as his eyes scan the street.

His gaze returns to me, but it's hard not to notice the concern in his eyes. "Yes. Just want to make sure you make it okay, baby. Take care of your mom. Everything here can wait." He presses a quick kiss to my forehead before stepping away from the car.

I manage a tight smile as I reverse out of the driveway and toward the town I swore I'd never return to.

TWO

Frankie

Nearly eight hours later, I exit the interstate and onto the two-lane county road that will lead me into Crescent Ridge. More than forty miles with not a streetlight in sight is all that is left to travel. Stars light up the bright sky, guiding me home—to the one place I vowed I'd never return to. The evening sky was one of my favorite things growing up in Crescent Ridge. The stars provided hope that there was more than the small town I lived in. A town I was willing to stay in for Cole. I would've given up every dream I had—for him.

The sound of his voice on the phone echoes through my head, and my stomach clenches at the thought of seeing him. I swallow hard and push my anger to the side as I think about my mom and what I'm about to walk into.

As I ease my car down the long road that dead ends into the cul-de-sac where my childhood home sits, a flood of emotions overcomes me. Tears fill my eyes when I see how different everything looks since I fled ten years ago. The houses look smaller and the trees look bigger. Ahead of me lies a quiet street full of houses that have seen better days.

Gravel crunches beneath the tires as I pull into the small driveway. My fingers are wrapped tightly around the steering wheel and my eyes are glued to the front porch. Baskets of flowers once hung from the covered porch and flowerbeds used to hang from the porch railing, displaying beautiful arrangements of flowers.

It was the one splurge my mom indulged in. Our house was less than modest, but she claimed the flowers gave it an appearance that we cared about our home. Even in the dark, I can see that nothing is left but the hooks that the baskets used to hang on and the empty flowerbeds appear to have not seen a flower in years.

Where the porch was once painted white, it's now mostly gray from the weathered wood beneath where the paint has long since cracked and mostly disappeared. The three wood steps that lead up to the front porch lean to one side, and the dilapidated wood looks as if it could splinter and break apart.

I swallow hard against my dry throat when memories overcome me and take me back to a time where I spent summer nights sitting on those steps, shoulder to shoulder with Cole. My legs would be crisscrossed and tucked tightly underneath me while I talked to him, telling him stories and the plans I had for us. I planned our entire lives on those wooden steps, and I realize now that those plans were as dilapidated and weak as those steps had become.

Shaking off the thought, I remember Cole lying on his back, his long legs bent at the knee and propped on one of the steps. He'd lie there with a giant smile on his face as he listened to me talk. He rarely spoke when I'd tell him my dreams, instead he'd listen. He was a sponge, taking in every word. As we got older, he could recite every detail of my plans, and he'd whisper them to me as I'd fall asleep in his arms.

There were two things I believed in back then—Cole Ryan, and the plans I made for us. Sadly, both of those turned out to be nothing but a lie.

I navigate the delicate steps, carefully dragging my suitcase behind me. The front door is unlocked, just as it always was growing up. Crescent Ridge is small, and we never worried about anyone entering unannounced.

Stepping over the threshold and into the dark living room, I can see a dim light coming from the kitchen. I close the front door quietly and drop my suitcase and purse on the living room floor as carefully as I can without making too much noise. I rush quietly down the hall to check on my mom.

I twist the door handle and push open the door. I can hear the faint sounds of her heavy breathing, and my upset stomach instantly begins to settle. Tiptoeing across the wood floor, I lean in and press a gentle kiss to her forehead. She doesn't move, and the steady sounds of her breathing tell me she's still sound asleep.

I close the door quietly behind me and when I look up, there is a short lady in scrubs standing in the hallway drying her hands on a kitchen towel.

"You must be Frances," she whispers and pulls her glasses off her face, tucking them into the tight graying curls on top of her head. She rests the towel on her shoulder and smiles at me.

"I am." I walk over to her and hold out my hand.

She takes it graciously and shakes. "I've heard a lot about you. I'm Judy, the home nurse Mr. Ryan hired."

I nod and smile tightly. Cole's father, Stephen Ryan, was a considerate neighbor, always looking out for my mom, Faith, and me. He'd do odds and ends around the house without ever being asked, simply because he was a nice guy. We'd wake up on Saturday mornings and he'd be painting the porch or in the spring, Mom's garden would suddenly be tilled. He'd just show up and do things that he knew needed to get done. He'd make Cole mow the lawn, and he always took care of mom's car when something was wrong, never expecting anything in return. It doesn't surprise me that he arranged to have a nurse here for Mom, either.

"That was very kind of him," I tell Judy. As the "organizer" in me takes over, I start listing off what we need to do next. "I'd like to transfer payment over to me," I tell her as she stands, listening to me. "Mr. Ryan is very generous to have paid for your services up until now, and I'm sure they were costly—and probably more than he could afford." Judy raises her eyebrows and purses her lips in confusion, but I'm not about to tell her that Stephen Ryan isn't wealthy. "And I'm going to need to keep you around until I understand what I'm dealing with. I'm going to need your professional opinion on whether this is something she can recover from, or if I'm going to need to transfer her to a larger town where she can receive better medical care and placed in a care home if needed."

She shakes her head and reaches for my arm. "Slow down, Frances." She offers me a tight smile, and I exhale softly. "Let's go to the kitchen and sit down. Let me bring you up to speed on what's happening." She tugs at my arm and leads me toward the kitchen. The first thing I notice is the old linoleum floor that once was white has now yellowed and begun to wear in the high traffic areas.

The small round wood table I used to eat every meal at still has the burgundy fabric placemats in front of each of the four chairs, with a napkin holder and salt and pepper shakers sitting in the center of the table.

The appliances are old but still look to be in good condition, and the old Formica counter tops are faded and stained from years of use. Mom and I would use every square inch of countertop in this tiny kitchen as she taught me how to cook and bake. Those are some of my fondest memories with her.

"Sit down," Judy urges, pointing to the kitchen table as she pulls a mug from the kitchen cupboard and fills it with coffee. She sets it in front of me and pulls a sugar bowl from the other counter, placing it in the middle of the table before she sits down and picks up her own mug of coffee. With a quick sip, she wraps her hands around the mug, lacing her fingers together as if to keep her hands warm.

"Your mom has a long road ahead of her," she says quietly. "But I've seen so many people overcome this. A stroke can permanently debilitate her, but sometimes, many times actually, with the right medical care and therapy, I've seen people return to fully functioning adults. Only time will tell." She sits back in the wood chair and it creaks underneath her small frame.

"The doctors are extremely optimistic, Frances. You should be, too." She smiles at me.

I sip from my coffee as I feel a lump begin to form in my throat as I think about how scared my mom must have been having no one here.

"So, what we know," she says, taking a deep breath. "The

stroke was on the right side of her brain. The right side affects the left side of your body. She has some paralysis on the left side of her body, including her face. Her speech is impaired, but it's still very good all things considered. You'll notice a slur, but you'll still be able to understand everything she says. She also has some memory loss. How significant?" she shrugs, "we're not sure yet. That's why we're glad you're here. Once you can begin to speak with her, we'll be able to determine what she remembers and what she doesn't. We'll need you to help us gauge her memory loss so we can understand the severity of that."

I nod, knowingly, feeling slightly overwhelmed by what I've just been told.

With a deep sigh, Judy continues, "We're going to want her to rest for a few more days and not push anything. Next week we'll begin physical, occupational, and speech therapy. All of them have been arranged for in-home treatment. Mr. Ryan took care of all that."

I clear my throat in hopes that the agitation I feel growing doesn't come across. "Mr. Ryan, as wonderful of a neighbor that he's been, really shouldn't be making appointments and decisions on behalf of my mother. I'd like all medical decisions to be made by me." I rub my eyes in exhaustion. All of this is overwhelming and I just want to cry.

Judy reaches across the table and rests her hand on top of mine. "We tried," she says quietly. "Mr. Ryan said he left you multiple messages on your voice mail at work. That was the only number we could locate for you until he got someone to hack the password on your mother's cell phone and we were able to retrieve your mobile number." She looks at me sympathetically. "Her password was one of the things she couldn't remember." Her eyes fall to her mug of coffee. "Mr. Ryan insisted on not contacting Faith. He said something about her being through enough..." Her voice trails off, and I cringe as I think of that little red notification on my office phone that has been blinking for the past three days.

"I was at trial," I respond, lost in thought. "I assumed it was reporters and I ignored the voice messages." I shake my head as tears flood my tired eyes and I finally allow my emotions to get the better of me.

"Don't," Judy shushes me. "Don't beat yourself up. You're here now, and this is when we really need you."

I nod and wipe the tears from my cheeks with the back of my hand as I try to compose myself.

"Let's get you to bed so you can rest," she suggests. "I'll walk you through all the fine details in the morning when you get up."

I don't argue with Judy. Instead I quietly get up from the kitchen table and retrieve my suitcase. I pad lightly down the worn hard wood floors to my childhood bedroom at the end of the hallway. I pause before entering and stare at the old door's white paint, chipping off in little slivers. The glass doorknob feels smaller in my hand than it used to as I twist it and open the door. My hand searches the wall, flipping the light switch on when I find it. A dull yellow light casts a low glow in the small room, just enough to see that nothing has been touched since I left over ten years ago.

My heart stills at the sight of the posters on the wall and the pictures still propped perfectly in their frames on my dresser. The same bedspread is still spread across the mattress I slept on as far back as I can remember, and my bookshelf is still covered in books I'd read throughout my childhood.

I drop my suitcase on the floor at the foot of my bed and peel the covers back. The old white sheets are now yellowed, but they smell freshly washed. Mom always washed our bedding weekly, a habit, it appears, she continues to keep up even though I'm no longer here.

I don't bother to undress; I simply crawl into bed and lay my head on the old, flat pillows, letting sleep overtake me before I even have time to close my eyes.

I wake with a start when I hear my cell phone ringing. Scrambling to the end of the bed, I grab it from the top of the suitcase where I tossed it last night. Six twenty-seven shines brightly on the screen just under Ted's name. I tap the answer button, but before I even have a chance to speak, Ted is barking at me.

"Jesus Christ, Frances, I've been worried sick about you. You didn't even text me to let me know you made it." The agitation in his voice is palpable.

I close my eyes and toss myself back onto my pillow, holding the phone away from my ear as he chastises me for my lack of consideration.

"Sorry," I mumble and cover my eyes with my forearm to block the bright early morning light. "It was just so late, and..." I pause.

"You sound like shit. Get some rest and fill me in later— maybe actually call me this time," he snaps, disconnecting the call. I stare at the screen as his name disappears and wonder what the heck just happened. I've known Ted for six years, and he's barely raised his voice to me, ever.

I see Faith's text message from five hours ago, telling me

she's on the redeye flight home and will be here in the morning, which should be anytime now. Flipping the switch on the side of the phone to silence it, I roll over, covering my head with a throw pillow. I've only been asleep a few hours and I know I'll need a few more before I'm able to fully function.

Sleep doesn't come to me, though. I toss and turn in my lumpy old bed, wondering if my mom is awake, so I can see her and update Faith when she arrives. My stomach twists and I'm not sure if it's nervousness or hunger, but I finally push myself out of bed. The house is quiet as I make my way down the hall and through the living room where I find Judy sitting at the kitchen table where I left her just hours ago.

She looks twice at me before giving her head a little shake. "You really should get some more sleep," she says, turning back to her iPad and the book she's reading.

I ignore her remark at my appearance. "What are you reading?"

"Mary Higgins Clark. She's my favorite."

"Mysteries, huh? And do I really look that bad?" I shuffle over to the coffee pot that has freshly brewed coffee just waiting for me.

She glances at me out of the corner of her eyes. "Kind of," she murmurs.

I actually let out a loud laugh, and she begins to laugh along with me.

"Thank you for your honesty," I tell her, pouring myself a mug of piping hot coffee. "I'm used to getting mere hours of sleep, though. After I catch a shower, I actually clean up quite nicely." I join her at the kitchen table, in the same spot I sat a couple of hours ago. "So, Judy, shoot it straight with me. What can I expect when I see her?"

Judy sets her iPad down and looks up at me. "Like I mentioned before, her left side has paralysis. She moves slowly and struggles with her arm and leg. She also struggles to eat. We were cleared to bring her home from the hospital and to feed her, *but*," she emphasizes loudly, "we have to be very careful." She taps her pointer on the kitchen table. "She can choke very easily. We've been keeping her to softer types of foods to help with her ease of swallowing. There is a list on the counter." She gestures over her shoulder to a binder on the counter next to the refrigerator.

"I think where you're going to struggle the most, Frances, is with her speech," she continues. "She has, what we call, aphasia. She has trouble finding the correct words, or piecing together a sentence that makes sense. This is also extremely common after a stroke," she reminds me. "A speech therapist will be coming to help with this. Your mom's case is relatively mild, which is good," she sighs. "With on-going therapy, this is something she can hopefully recover from."

"Jesus," I mutter into my mug.

"Patience, Frances." She squeezes my hand. "You're going to need patience. She's trying so hard, and when she gets frustrated, you have to be there to calm her down. I see this with every stroke patient I've worked with. They want to return to everything they were doing before, only their body and their brain won't allow that."

I nod as I listen carefully.

Judy glances up at the small round clock on the kitchen wall. "She usually wakes up about eight, so you have an hour before she'll be up. At nine, Melinda, the day nurse, will be arriving. I'll be back this evening, but I wanted to be here with you to help you get settled in with her."

"How many nurses does she have?" I ask, wondering how many people have been helping mom.

"There are two of us. We normally don't work overnight as once she's in bed she really doesn't need us, but for the next few weeks one of us will be here. And eventually, she'll probably only need us here for a short time during the days as she becomes more independent."

I look over Judy's shoulder and into the living room. My eyes find the large framed picture of Faith and I that was taken when I was eleven and Faith was fifteen. My sad smile stares back at me, and I find myself momentarily lost in time, remembering that picture being taken not long after Mom moved us into this house.

I stand up and clutch the mug of hot coffee in my hands. "Will you excuse me, Judy? I'm going to step outside and catch some fresh air before cleaning up."

She seems a bit taken aback by my abrupt departure. "Of course. Take all the time you need. Your mom doesn't even know you're here. We didn't want to tell her in the event you couldn't make it."

I pause in my tracks and furrow my brows in confusion.

"I mean, Mr. Ryan said you're very busy," Judy adds quickly, as if it'll make me feel better.

"It's fine, Judy. I am busy, but never too busy for my mom." I smile tightly at her as guilt fills me. Everyone knows I haven't been around for the better part of ten years, and sadly, they weren't even sure I was going to come back now that my mom needs me. The front door opens with a loud creak as I step out onto the old wooden porch. Barefoot, I walk carefully as to not get any splinters. Taking a seat on the top step, as I did for so many years, I set my coffee mug next to me and wrap my arms around my knees, pulling them close to me.

Everything has changed so much with age, yet very little has changed at all. I turn my face to the sky and close my eyes, breathing in the morning air, pulling it deep into my lungs. Tears prick the back of my eyes as all my emotions bubble at the surface...my mom, the trial, Crescent Ridge, Cole Ryan, and everything I left behind.

I don't know if I'm strong enough to handle this—but right now, I don't have a choice.

THREE

Cole

I rub my eyes, sure that they're deceiving me...but they're not. My throat tightens as I look through the large picture window and across the street at beautiful Frankie sitting on those front porch steps. It's a sight I've seen a million times, yet this time is different—*she's* different.

She's older and more mature. Her body is the same, yet she's a woman now and not the girl I remember. I knew every inch of her back then, and my body trembles in remembrance as I watch her, longing for her like I did all those years ago. The longing never really went away; I just buried it behind my job, the bottle, and endless women who could never hold a candle to Frankie.

I lean against the wall and study her—taking her in. Her hair is longer now...she's ten years older, but she looks exactly like I envisioned her. She rocks back and forth slowly, her arms wrapped around her knees with her face tilted to the sky, just as she's always done, and my stomach twists at the sight. How

I've longed to reach out to her over the years—to apologize to her, to explain to her, but some things are better left in the past, including *us*.

The sound of her voice on the phone when I called was enough to send me on a bender. I spent the night at the garage, drowning my misery and regret in a fifth of Jim Beam, and even that didn't drown out the pain of my lies and how they hurt her—hurt me, and destroyed us.

She sits on those damn lop-sided steps that I've been meaning to fix for months, but never have. I couldn't. Those were the steps that Frankie had built her dreams on, planned her life—a life I was supposed to be a part of, a life that I let go of—for her.

I swallow hard against the lump in my throat as I remember her running her fingers through my hair as she'd tell me stories on those steps. There was nothing in the world I loved more than listening to her and having her run her fingers through my hair. To this day, no one is allowed to do that to me —touch me like that, that was Frankie's thing. It'll only ever be hers.

I close my eyes and push back the memories to the little place that's too painful to visit. I made a decision all those years ago and while I've regretted it every day since then, I still know it was for the best.

I push off the wall and walk down the hall to the bath-room, flipping on the shower and turning the water all the way to hot. I yank open the medicine cabinet and pull a bottle of ibuprofen off the shelf, shaking two pills into the palm of my hand. Tossing them in my mouth, I fight to swallow them against the back of my dry throat. I'm hoping the pills and hot water will lessen my headache and bring some relief to my aching body before I have to face Frankie.

Shoving my phone into my back pocket, I grab my car keys and jump into my aging Jeep Wrangler. I spent the better portion of two years after Frankie left restoring this thing. It was the perfect distraction and the only way to take out my frustration. I spent days and nights, for weeks and months, burying thoughts of Frankie while I restored it. She's now pristine.

I drive down to the old auto shop, Ryan Auto Works, the garage my dad opened when I was a little boy. It's no longer the shop we use, but I keep tools and personal vehicles I'm working on here. I couldn't bear selling this building after Pops died. This was the first building I ever held a wrench in and where I learned how to change a tire. This shop was part of me, just like Frankie.

The battered brick building has seen better days, the once vibrant red brick now faded from years of sun and weather. I lift the large metal garage door and it slides open, exposing the old Harley Davidson and the Ford Mustang I've recently purchased. When Pops died five years ago, I took over his auto shop business but also expanded to restoring vehicles—a hobby of mine.

Three guys run the auto maintenance side, and my buddy Carter and I do the custom refurbishing. It's a long and tedious process to restore a vehicle back to like-new condition, one that can take years. In fact, I have a wait list up to two years to take on new projects. In the last couple of years, I've made connections through recommendations with a couple A-list actors in Hollywood. Their projects will take us the better half of the next two years to complete, with the other guys taking on the bulk of the other auto repair work. A custom job can run upward of a quarter of a million dollars, and we have no shortage of people willing to pay. Our wait list is insane, and while the lure of big money sits on that list, I pride myself on quality, not rushing through a job.

We were fortunate enough to be able to build a new, modern garage on the other side of Main Street. In the last couple of years, Crescent Ridge has actually seen growth in development. We used to only have a diner, a local grocer, Pop's auto shop, a gas station, and small drug store. We've recently added a coffee shop, a dance studio, a bakery, and a library that serves as a community center. A small credit union is slated to open later this year, and I'm reinvesting in Crescent Ridge by building a small bar and grill that will cater to the evening crowd.

Progress is good, and it's been great for the economy here, but it's even better to finally see hard working people not struggle to find the jobs they so desperately need.

"Ryan!" I hear from behind me and I turn around to see Carter wiping his hands on a dirty towel.

"What's up, man?" I holler over my shoulder at him.

"How's Ms. Callaway?" He strides up next to me, using the towel to wipe grease off his fingernails.

I stare ahead at the motorcycle, making mental notes of everything I need to order to restore it. Distraction, it's what I'm good at.

"Fine," I mumble, walking closer to the bike.

"What's got you in a pissy mood? Shelley not putting out for you?" He laughs obnoxiously, following me into the garage.

I ignore his comment and him, kneeling down to twist a foot peg, hoping to loosen it. Damn thing is rusted on.

"Hello," he says, waving his arms around to get my attention. Attention that is focused only on the girl who still owns my heart. "Earth to—"

"Frankie's back," I tell him quietly, running my hand over the cracked leather seat of the Harley. Seeing the condition of this bike physically hurts me. I've always treated vehicles and motorcycles like small children—very carefully, delicately, and with utmost protection.

"Holy shit." I hear him mumble. "She came back?" He's as surprised as I was to see her back in Crescent Ridge.

I nod and use the handle bar to help pull myself back up. I prop my hands on my hips and turn to look at Carter. "She did."

His eyes widen as he waits for me to tell him more, only there's nothing else to tell. "And?" He tosses the dirty towel onto a pile of other dirty towels that need to be washed.

"And what?" I retort. "She's back. Her mom is sick. End of story."

"Have you talked to her?"

I puff air loudly through my nose and smirk. "I hardly think Frankie will be up for catching up. What happened in the past stays there. We've both moved on," I lie to him. I'll never move on from her, but he doesn't need to know that.

Carter has been my best friend since elementary school. Actually, Frankie was my best friend. Carter was next in line, but he fell right into first place when I hurt Frankie and she left.

"You haven't moved on, man." He slaps my shoulder and squints his dark brown eyes at me. "You're lying to yourself if that's what you believe. *She* may have moved on, but you, my friend...you have *not* moved on."

"Fuck off," I grumble, raking my hands over my face in frustration.

Clearing his throat, he toes a crack in the garage floor with his work boot. "Maybe you should come clean. Tell her the truth. Get that shit off your conscience." He raises his eyes at me, and I shoot him a dirty look.

Come clean? That's the last thing I'll be doing. I scoff, "Let it go, man. Some things are best left in the past."

He groans in frustration. "Why did you let her believe you were with Whitney?"

I see his feet retreat a few feet back, probably afraid of what my response will be. I take a deep breath and look up at him. "Because I needed her to go, Carter. She would've thrown her life, her career, her education away for me." My voice breaks, and I clear my throat to shove down my emotions.

"You could have just broken up with her ya' know. You didn't have to make her believe you were cheating on her, or that Whitney's baby was yours." He takes a deep breath, eyeing me carefully, knowing he's gone too far. He's wanted to call me on my shit for ten years and right now, I'm weak enough to let him.

I twist the throttle on the motorcycle, finding something to fidget with. "She would have come back here. She wasn't for a second going to just let me break up with her...that's not how Frankie and I were."

"You need to talk to her."

"No can do." I turn back to the rusty foot peg.

He shakes his head and strides over to the fridge we keep in the old shop, pulling out a cold bottle of water. "I'm just saying you may never see her again, Cole. Don't let this opportunity slip past you. It's rare in life that we get an opportunity to right our wrongs." He shoots me a disgusted look and leaves the garage. A look I wholeheartedly deserve.

I kick a wrench that's lying on the ground and feel the anger I've buried for so long bubble to the surface. "Let it go," I tell myself. "Let her go."

Hours later and feeling no better than I did when Carter left, I slam the large rolling garage door down. It makes a thunderous sound when it meets the concrete drive. I engage the lock and head back to my Jeep, starting it and revving the engine. I engage the clutch and push the gas a little too hard, causing the Jeep to lurch forward. Just as I near the street, I catch something in the corner of my eye. I slam on the brakes and the tires squeal.

What the hell!

"Would you look out!" I yell as Maggie Winthrop rolls by on her skateboard.

Maggie Winthrop is Frankie's niece, Faith's daughter, and a dead ringer for Frankie at nine years old. She narrows her blue eyes at me and hops off her skateboard before turning back to glare at me.

"Why don't you slow down!" she hollers back and adjusts the baseball cap that's turned backward on her head.

"You're a pain in the ass, Mags!" I holler at her before easing the Jeep onto the road.

"Back at you, Ryan!" She rolls her eyes at me and then hops back on her skateboard.

When Faith Winthrop moved back to town after her divorce, I was certain I'd hear from her. I've been waiting for the riot act—only it's never come. She was always Frankie's protector...but she's never spoken a word to me in the three years she's been back in Crescent Ridge. I catch her nasty glares and dirty looks in passing, but she's never once confronted me about what happened between Frankie and me.

Maggie, on the other hand, is never short on words. I often see her at her Grandma's house across the street, and she's always offering me the latest insult or jab—reminding me so fondly of Frankie from the past. Maggie is complex, much like Frankie was. She's a Tomboy, a ballet dancer, and a swimmer. She's talented and multi-dimensional, just like her aunt Frankie, and I find all of her qualities, including her smartass mouth, endearing—though I'd never admit that to her.

My stomach lurches as I roll into our cul-de-sac and park my Jeep in the driveway. I take a chance and peer through my rearview mirror at the house behind me, hoping to catch another glance of Frankie. When I don't see her, I hop down from the Jeep and walk toward the front porch of my house. A moment later, I hear the screen door across the street squeal before closing with a bang.

My feet feel like bricks as they come to an abrupt stop and I turn around. My lungs release the air I was holding and my stomach settles when I see the nurse I hired to care for Martha. She offers me a short wave as she walks down the driveway to her car parked on the street. I jog down to meet her, anxious for an update on Martha and anything she'll willingly tell me about Frankie.

I approach and she offers me a kind smile. "Mr. Ryan," she says, her voice soft and comforting. "Frances made it home late last night."

I nod and stand with my hands on my hips, one eye carefully trained on the house behind her in case Frankie appears.

"Martha is up and Melinda is preparing her breakfast," she continues. "She was so happy to see her daughter. Melinda will walk Faith and Frances through our afternoon care routine."

"Good," I tell her as she juggles her car keys in her hand.

"I'll be back again this evening and will make sure to update you immediately if anything changes with Ms. Callaway."

"That sounds great. Thank you again for your help." I smile at her as she opens her car door and tosses her purse on the passenger seat.

"Oh," Judy says, turning back to me and wringing her hands together nervously. "Ms. Callaway...I mean Frances," she corrects herself, "asked for billing to be transferred to her—"

I shake my head quickly, cutting her off. "Nope. Our agreement remains intact. I'll continue picking up the costs for her care until I determine that it should be transferred." I quickly add, "No need to argue with Frankie about it, just don't transfer it."

Judy sighs loudly but doesn't argue with me. "Yes, sir," she says quietly and slides into the driver's seat of her Nissan Sentra.

I wave to her as she drives off, and I cross back to my side of the street where I belong. Far away from Frankie.

There are very few things I can do to ever rectify what I did to Frankie. Even though she's moved on and is some big-time lawyer in Los Angeles, this is something I can do to help clear my guilty conscience.

FOUR

Frankie

I sit on the edge of the bed and hold Mama's hand. She's trying to smile at me through the tears glistening in her eyes. Only one side of her mouth is turned up; the other won't move, but I'm able to see through the tears at the sheer happiness in her bright blue eyes.

"Frankie," she mumbles, her speech slurred. It's hard to see my mom like this, but it's even harder to see how much she's aged in the last five years since I've seen her. I give her soft hand a gentle squeeze.

"I'm here. I'll be here to help Judy and Melinda as long as they need me." I offer her a reassuring smile. "And Faith and the kids are home now, too. We're all here."

She visibly relaxes and nods, closing her eyes and laying her head back against her pillow. I rub her hand softly as it sits in mine, but I swallow hard as I feel how frail her fingers have become.

There's a soft knock on the door and Melinda, the day

nurse, peeks inside. "I've got breakfast if she's ready." Mom opens her eyes at the sound of Melinda's voice.

"Yes, please come in." I raise the back of Mom's bed slowly so that she sits more upright, and Melinda sets a tray of food on the side table.

"Morning, Martha," Melinda greets Mom with a friendly smile. I'm so thankful to see the relationship between my mom and Melinda is so comfortable. "We've got oatmeal and blueberries for breakfast...and of course, your coffee." She laughs softly. Turning to me, she tells me how Mom demands coffee before any other food or beverage. That sounds exactly like my mom, and it brings me comfort that the stroke hasn't changed who she is.

For the next twenty minutes, Melinda feeds her and talks me through what to do and how to do it. The key is small bites and smashing the blueberries gently before feeding her. Mom struggles but manages to eat without choking, which is the goal.

"When Faith gets here, I'll show you how to help her clean up."

"I can do it," Mom mumbles and rolls her eyes. While difficult to understand, she still does pretty well.

"Martha, we know you can." Melinda smiles at her, but shoots me an unnerving look. "But your left side is still very weak and your balance is off. One of us has to be in the bathroom with you to help you wash up and also wash your hair."

Mom rolls her eyes again, and I can't help but giggle under my breath. She's still feisty and fighting for her independence.

"Where is everyone?" I hear Faith holler before the front porch door slams. Some things never change.

"I'll go get her," Melinda says kindly, patting me on the

shoulder. She takes the empty food tray with her, disappearing down the hallway.

"There you are," Faith huffs as she steps inside Mom's room, dropping her purse to the floor. "Oh, Mama!" Faith says, covering her mouth with both hands. "I'm so sorry I wasn't here." Mom shakes her head slowly and Faith leans over her, pulling her into a firm hug. "I'm so sorry, Mama," she whispers.

"Franny," Faith says quietly, letting go of Mom and walking over to me. "God, I've missed you." She hugs me tightly and rubs my back. Tears prick the back of my eyes as we embrace. Aside from Cole, Faith was my best friend growing up and still is even though she is older than me. We survived our fair share of sisterly fights and came out stronger than ever.

"Well, now that I have all three of you in one place, I hope we can go over care plans," Melinda says, cutting off my reunion with Faith as she comes back to the room carrying a large binder.

I pat my eyes with the sleeve of my shirt and Faith smiles at me.

"Judy and I have been doing this for years. This binder here," Melinda taps the top of the thick white binder with her pointer finger, "is your new bible. Study it. Learn it." She looks over the top of her glasses that are perched on the end of her nose. "I guarantee you, ninety-nine percent of what you'll need to know is in this binder."

For the next hour, Melinda schools us in Mom's care. She even has daily, weekly, and monthly schedules in the binder with the days and times of the various physical and occupational therapists that will be coming to help Mom. Faith looks at me from where she sits at the end of Mom's bed. Her wide eyes have a panicked look, and I can tell she's completely over-whelmed.

"Now let's get her cleaned up!" Melinda slams the binder shut, and Faith gets Mom's walker from the corner. We all follow her slowly but closely as Mom struggles to walk. Her left leg has extremely limited movement, so she kind of hops on her right leg and balances herself with her walker, which scares the hell out of me.

With four of us squeezed into a bathroom made to fit one, we help Mom get cleaned up, much to her frustration. Once she's settled back into bed to rest for the afternoon, Melinda shoos Faith and I out of the house. I assume she's had enough of me asking a million questions and Faith gasping and getting emotional every two minutes.

"I've got that neighbor girl, Jenny, watching the kids, do you want to go to the diner and get some coffee?" Faith asks, grabbing her purse. "I'm sure everyone there wants an update on Mom, anyway. We can kill two birds with one stone." She shrugs.

"Do they still make that apple pie?" I ask as my mouth begins to water, remembering the warm apples and perfectly sugared crust I used to eat as a young girl. Mom used to bring a slice home every now and then when her tips were good, and Faith and I would devour it.

"Damn right they do, but I'm not sharing a piece with you." She smirks. "You're the hot shot attorney who can afford to buy me a piece of pie now." She laughs and nudges me with her shoulder.

"I suppose you want me to drive, too?" I raise an eyebrow at her.

"You know it. Show me that fancy car of yours." She smiles at me. God, I've missed my sister.

We slide into my Mercedes and head into town—and by town, I mean the city block that holds every business in Crescent Ridge.

"How's Ted?" Faith asks as she fidgets with the seat belt. I almost laugh that she's buckling herself in. There's probably only five other people out and about in town right now, the chances of us being hit by lightning are probably greater than us getting into a car accident.

"He's good. Patient with me," I sigh.

"Are you still nervous about committing?"

I wince at that question. "It's not committing that makes me nervous, it's just—"

She puts up her hand to stop me. "You've had a shitty past, Franny. No need to explain. You've still managed to come out on top, though, so don't beat yourself up, and don't let Ted pressure you into something you're not ready for." She eyes me cautiously.

"I couldn't have done it without you, Faith." My voice breaks as I look at my sister.

She reaches out and squeezes my arm as we turn down Main Street. "Hey, turn here!" Faith yells suddenly, and I hit the brakes, cranking the steering wheel hard to the right. "You haven't seen this yet," she says, leaning forward. "Now turn left."

I ease the car down First Street, a street that used to be nothing but abandoned buildings from businesses that lost their way. This street looks like it's being revitalized, a handful of buildings having been updated.

"I never thought I'd see the day," I mumble under my

breath as I drive slowly down the street. Many of the exposed brick buildings have been modernized and updated.

"I know," she says with the same awe. "There's even a new little coffee shop with a bakery down there." She points straight ahead out the window. "Gus was pissed as all hell when they opened, and Mom was worried they'd take all the breakfast business from the café, but it hasn't affected the café at all."

"Interesting. I was sure this place would be a ghost town by now," I remark as we pass the coffee shop.

"I was certain, too, but that's not the case." She blows a puff of air from her mouth. "See that building on the end?" She nods her head toward the large red brick building with construction activity. "That's going to be a bar and grill. Only open late afternoons and weekends, catering more to the dinner and bar crowd. I heard a rumor that whoever was opening it was careful not to interfere with Gus and the diner."

I stare ahead in disbelief as I watch the little town that had all but died now rise from the ashes before me.

As we get settled into a booth, two cups of piping hot coffee appear, along with a bear hug from Gus. His arms are tight and his embrace so mighty he lifts me from my seat.

"How's your mom?" he asks, squeezing the air right out of my lungs.

Gus has to be approaching seventy, and he's owned this diner since I was a little girl. He hired Mama when Dad left, and he's been a constant source of support for her. When she had no money, he hired her. When we had no food, he fed us. When she needed extra hours, he let Faith and I do our home-work in the back corner booth while Mom picked up an extra shift.

"She's good, Gus. Getting better. It's so good to see you," I manage as I catch my breath.

He finally releases me, dropping me back in the booth. Shaking a finger at me, he scolds me, "Franny, we've missed you. Your mama was a wreck when you left." He shakes his head and tsks.

"Gus," Faith warns him with a stern look.

"Someone needs to tell her," he fires back grumpily.

"It's okay." I lay a hand on the table in front of Faith to shush her. "I know it was hard on Mama when I left, Gus. But sometimes we need to leave and not look back," I say quietly, feeling guilty for leaving a few people that I cared about behind without an explanation.

I look up at burly old Gus and shoot him a sympathetic smile while he just watches me, looking for an apology that I can't give him. Instead, I try to lighten the mood.

"Got any of that famous apple pie of yours?" I ask with a smile. "You know it was always my favorite."

He sighs and nods before walking away without another word.

"Is everyone going to be like this?" I ask Faith cautiously, leaning across the table.

She blows steam off her coffee and shrugs. "Don't know, but I sure as shit wouldn't worry about it. The only people that matter are Mom and me. Don't worry about anyone else. This town and Cole Ryan were nothing but a dead end for you. Look what you've made of yourself. Be proud." She smiles at me and sets her coffee cup down.

The sound of Cole's name falling off Faith's tongue brings up emotions I'm not ready to deal with. I swallow hard and take a sip of the black coffee, avoiding having to respond.

"How are Maggie and Matthew?" I ask, feeling guilty. It's hard to see my niece and nephew without seeing my past.

"They're so good. Thank you for always making sure they're taken care of." I wave a hand, dismissing Faith's comment.

"I love them so much. Anything I can do to help you—"

"Franny," Faith says softly. "It's okay to love them and still hurt for your own loss."

I nod quickly and choke back my emotions. This is the first time Faith and I have really talked about my niece and nephew and the pain seeing them causes me. I pinch my eyes closed, pushing back the sudden rush of tears. Our conversation is cut short when the little bell above the diner door chimes just as someone says loudly, "Well, well, well...look what the cat dragged in!"

Denim legs stop at the end of our booth, but I keep my eyes fixed across the table on Faith.

"What's up, Carter?" Faith asks with an annoyed tone, and I do my best to hide the smirk on my face as I hide it behind my coffee cup.

He's the same playful character he was ten years ago when I last saw him. "Aren't you going to say hi, Franny? Or are you too good for us now that you're some hot shot lawyer in L.A.?" He drags out the L.A. part.

My back stiffens and I sit up taller, squaring my shoulders and turning to face Carter. "Nice to see you, Carter. I see some things haven't changed."

Carter always hated that Cole and I were inseparable as kids. He was always second fiddle to me and it drove him nuts. He would find any reason to pick on me, mostly for me being a straight A student, a real nerd in his eyes. Cole finally knocked the shit out of him in eighth grade, and he resigned himself to the fact that Cole would always choose me over him and he finally backed off. However, with how things ended with me and Cole, I'm sure he's been waiting years to pick back up where he left off in eighth grade.

He feigns offense. "Haven't changed? Ah, Franny, you hurt me!" He smacks his chest right over his heart with his hand. "I was joking, but in all honesty, it's really good to see you," he says warmly, looking down on us. "You've made a good name for yourself, you should be proud of yourself, I know I'm proud of you. Someone from Crescent Ridge needed to make it big."

I'd almost believe his words if I didn't know him better, except I do know him and, in all honesty, he does seem sincere.

"Thanks." I manage to say without rolling my eyes.

"How's your mama?" he asks, leaning up against the table of our booth; he shows no sign of leaving anytime soon. I look over my shoulder at the glass door of the diner, wondering if Cole is with him.

"She's doing the best she can," Faith jumps in, answering for me. "Thanks for asking. Franny and I were just catching up, so if you don't mind..."

"Are you giving me the brush off?" he asks us both with a little laugh.

"Yes!" Faith says, rolling her eyes. "And you're terrible at picking up social cues, Carter. You really need to work on that."

I stifle a laugh, damn near choking on my coffee.

Carter narrows his eyes at Faith. "Just wanted to say hi to an old friend," he says, narrowing his eyes at Faith, then turns back to me. "How long you in town for, Franny? Maybe we can catch up another time."

"Highly doubtful," Faith pipes in again before I stop her with a look. Jesus, she's feisty today.

I clear my throat and tell him, "I'm not sure. I need to make sure everything is settled with my mom and that she's being taken care of before I make any decisions on when to leave. But, Carter, you and I both know catching up probably isn't a good idea." I deliver the blow kindly, and it actually hurts my heart to blow him off. We spent a lot of time together—a lot of good times—in high school. I'm glad he's still around for Cole. Not that I should give two shits about Cole, but I do. I always will, undoubtedly.

He nods in understanding, his hands propped on his hips. "Franny, I know shit was bad when you left, but—"

I stop him right there. "We're not talking about this, Carter, okay? I just came to get some coffee and pie with my sister. The past is done. There's nothing to discuss." My voice breaks, and I can feel tears stinging the back of my throat.

He sees my emotions and takes a deep breath, pulling his lips between his teeth as he watches me. His dark brown eyes narrow ever so slightly on me, not in anger but with something else. Understanding maybe? He leans forward and lowers his voice, "There's a lot of things you don't know, Franny. A lot of answers that you deserve—"

My hearts races and part of me wants to know what he has to say, but I'm not ready to unbury the past. "Carter," I stop him. "Please."

He raises his hands in surrender as he backs away. "I'm just saying there's a lot of shit that needs to be cleared up."

I shake my head softly. "What's done is done. We all need to move forward now. Goodbye, Carter," I say gently, offering him a sad smile as he throws an arm up in defeat and disappears through the doors he just came through minutes ago.

Gus stayed back, eyeing our little reunion. Now that Carter left, he finally drops off two plates of apple pie and tops off our coffee as Faith watches me quietly from across the table. When Gus leaves, she lets out a heavy sigh and pushes her plate to the side.

"What do you think he meant by 'things you don't know', Franny?"

I shrug. "I don't know, and honestly, I don't care. My focus is getting mom better so I can get the hell out of here and never look back." Again.

FIVE

Cole

There is no way in hell I can sit at home today knowing Frankie is just a hundred feet across the street from me. Just far enough way to not see her, but too damn close that it's driving me fucking mad.

I jump back in my Jeep and head down to the bar and grill to see what kind of progress is being made and bust some heads if I find anyone slacking off. I want this job done on time.

When I arrive, I hear the sounds of nail guns, drills, and saws as I push through the plywood makeshift doors. The sound of progress and the smell of sawdust hanging in the air hits me immediately—I like it. This old brick building was the perfect location for *The Fault Line*, the perfect name for my bar and grill.

The exposed brick walls fit with the industrial look I was going for. Large wrought iron lamps hang from the ceiling, and lanterns line the walls. Oversized booths will line the walls and tall pub tables will fill the center. Leather and wood accents on tables and chairs will really bring this place together.

"J.D.," I yell at the foreman standing with a stack of papers in his hand, scribbling away on the top sheet.

"What's up, my man?" He holds out his fist for me to bump.

"It's coming along," I comment as my eyes scan every surface, looking for something that isn't just perfect.

"It is. We're actually ahead of schedule, putting the finishing touches on the shelving in the kitchen today. Flooring goes in tomorrow, then clean up. Everything else will fall into place after that. Booths, the bar, and tables and chairs are scheduled to arrive in two weeks, along with all the kitchen equipment." He taps the stack of papers in his hand. "The electrician finished up this morning. What do you think?" He dips his head back and looks up to the oversized metal lights hanging from the ceiling.

"Looks fucking rad," I say, pleased at how the black wrought iron stands out against the red and white brick.

"It does. Good choices, man." He tosses the stack of papers onto a worktable.

"How are the restrooms coming along?"

"On track. Plumber comes after we finish up the tile work. I anticipate no problems."

"And the brick oven? Did the mason finish that up yet?"

He nods with a grin. "Yesterday. I want to be the first asshole to eat a pizza from that oven."

I chuckle. "You got it, man. I like everything you're telling me." I slap him on the back in appreciation. "Good work."

"So when do you think you'll actually open this place?"

I shrug. "As soon as possible. I've been working with a chef from Reno, who's helping me get the menu set up, and he knows industry people who are going to advise me on getting a logo, signage, coasters, and all that other shit that goes into marketing this place."

"Makes sense," he responds.

"My main concern is keeping the construction portion of this project on track. I'll worry about the other details, you just get the building done on time and on budget."

"You got it. On that note, I'm going to go check and see how the shelving is going." He walks off, leaving me standing in the middle of the large dining area.

"This place is fucking perfect," I tell myself with a proud smile, then I get to work, sweeping up dust and remnants of today's work before finally resigning to the fact that I'm going to eventually have to go home. I shoot Melinda, the nurse a quick text, checking in on Martha and asking her for some food recommendations. A few minutes later, I'm calling in a dinner order for Martha, the girls, and Melinda.

Gus has his cook preparing veggie potpies, mashed potatoes and gravy, and banana cream pudding for dessert. I'm also sending over a large salad for the girls, who will most likely balk at all the carbs and calories in the potpies and potatoes.

Gus finally comes waddling out of the kitchen, large paper bags hanging from his arms. "Everything is ready to go," he says, setting the bags on the long diner counter where I'm sitting on a stool, waiting.

Pulling sixty dollars from my wallet, I toss it on the counter. It's enough to cover the food and still leave a decent tip. "Thanks, Gus." I reach for the bags and stand up, making my way toward the door.

"You seen her yet?" Gus asks quietly, stopping me dead in my tracks. My heart jumps in my chest when he asks.

I turn slowly, squeezing the handles of the bags in my hand as he wipes down the counter with a dishrag. He keeps his eyes down and doesn't look up at me. I know exactly who he's referring to when he says "her".

"No. Not in person," I answer him, my voice clipped.

"She's still hurting, Cole," he answers sharply. "You can see it in her eyes. I don't know what went down with you two, Martha never told me the whole story. I only heard the rumors." He looks down at the counter, a disappointed look on his face. "The town gossip, but she left for a reason and never returned until now. The one thing I do know is that her entire world revolved around you." He looks up and shoots a pointed look at me, tossing the kitchen rag on the counter behind him. Crossing his arms over his chest, he lets out a deep, resigned sigh and points to the bags dangling from my hands. "Go easy on her. Carter was here today and already upset her."

I swallow hard and simply nod in response.

Fucking Carter saw her? Huh. *Well, isn't that fucking convenient.*

With three quick knocks, I wait for someone, anyone, to answer the door. Mixed emotions fill me. Excitement at possibly seeing Frankie, nervousness at what her response might be, but all of that evaporates when Faith answers the door. She looks over her shoulder quickly before stepping out onto the front porch to meet me, closing the door behind her.

"Cole," she says, her voice clipped.

"Faith," I respond to her, holding up the bags. "Wanted to

drop off some dinner for all of you. It's not much, but it's one less thing you need to worry about tonight."

With an exaggerated sigh, she asks, "Why're you doing this?"

I fight back a smile and rock back on my heels. "There's no ulterior motive here, Faith. Your mom was basically my mom. All those years she made sure I had everything I needed—" My voice breaks and I have to clear my throat. After a moment, I finish with, "I just want to do something nice for her...because I can."

She narrows her eyes at me, but reaches out for the bags. "Just leave Franny alone. Don't pull anything stupid. Please."

Franny. I hate that they call her that. She's Frankie. Always will be. I swallow hard and feel the muscles in my jaw tighten. "Enjoy your dinner. Please send my love to your mama." I clench my fists and turn around, jogging down the wooden front steps.

"Please, Cole." I hear Faith say from behind me.

With a shake of my head, I answer her over my shoulder. "You know me well enough to know that I don't make promises I can't keep, Faith."

With my feet propped up on the weathered porch railing, I twist a bottle of ice-cold beer around in my hand as I stare at the house across the street. Wanting, hoping for another glimpse of Frankie. I vow to sit here all damn night for one more look at her.

Stars fill the dark sky above so brightly that even the dull street lamp can't dim their brightness. Lights flicker on and off in various rooms at Martha's house, and as the hours pass so does my hope of seeing Frankie.

It's hard to miss the thunderous sounds of Carter's Harley as he makes his way down our quiet street. Killing the engine, he rolls to a stop in front of my house and hops off his newly refurbished bike.

Jogging up the center of the yard and right past me, he lets himself inside the front door. A minute later, he joins me on the front porch, a cold beer in his hand and another one for me. He sits in a chair opposite me, throwing his foot over his knee and taking a long pull of his beer.

"Beautiful night," he finally says, chancing a glance in my direction.

I nod in response, not saying anything.

"Saw your girl today," he says, shifting in his chair.

My girl. My stomach jumps when he says that. "So I heard." I twist the bottle cap off my beer and toss it onto the porch. Agitation rolls through me and my stomach twists with anxiety.

"Seems you two are on the exact same damn page." He blows a puff of air loudly through his nose. "Both of you seemingly wanting to leave the past in the past," he draws his fingers up and make air quotes, "but both of you are too damn stubborn to actually do it. You should've seen her eyes, Cole—"

I toss my beer bottle with an angry grunt, and it hits a post on the porch, shattering into a million little pieces. Standing up quickly, I turn and point a finger at my best friend. "You don't know shit," I hiss at him.

Quickly jumping to his feet, he drops his bottle of beer at my feet and grabs me by the t-shirt, yanking me to him. I'm about six inches taller and fifty pounds heavier, but he's not backing down. He never has when it comes to me—he's not afraid to put me in my place when needed, and that's what I appreciate about him. He pulls me even closer. The guy has some damn balls, that's for sure.

"Don't tell me I don't know shit," he spits at me. "I've watched you spiral down in a blur of trashy women and booze since you fucking drove Frankie out of town with your bullshit lies. I watched you lose the only family you ever really had because of those fucking lies. You lost the best damn thing that ever happened to you—for what, Cole? Explain it to me!" he yells in my face.

"I did it for her," I say, gritting my teeth. "I did it all for her."

His eyes narrow in disgust. "She left here thinking you knocked up Whitney Carson. She thinks you have a kid out there...that you cheated on her. Meanwhile, she was at college, busting her ass to make something of herself so you two could build a future together."

I shake my head...not sure who I'm more disgusted with—Carter for throwing the truth in my face or myself for all the fucking lies I've spun.

His voice hinges on desperation. "Just fucking tell her the truth, man. Then you can both move on—put this shit to rest." He releases his grip on my t-shirt and pushes me away from him. Then he jogs down the front porch and stops in the middle of the yard, turning around to say one more thing. "Before your dad died, he made you promise him you'd come clean and tell her the truth. If you're too big of a fucking dick to do it for yourself, or her—do it for him." He spins around on his boot and jumps on his Harley, disappearing down the long, dark street.

"Fuck," I grumble to myself, running both of my hands over

my face and through my hair. I grab another beer and head to the only place that I've ever really been able to think...the place where I'm the most connected to Frankie. The fault line.

It's pitch black out here with only the bright moon to guide my way. It's been almost ten years since I've visited the fault line—but I know the way like the back of my hand. The trees are taller and the trail Frankie and I forged so many years ago is overgrown, but I'd never forget my way here.

Rocks that we used to think were huge but are merely boulders still sit in position, marking the way to the cliff. I'm a few beers in and second guessing whether this is a good idea because the drop off the cliff would kill a person. It's more than a hundred feet of solid rock and straight down.

Just beyond the last tree, I come to the clearing I remember so well. I pause, allowing memories of this place to flash through my mind like a slide show. My chest constricts as my emotions bubble to the surface, and I let my feet carry me to the edge of the cliff. I sit down on the edge as I've done a million or more times before and let my feet dangle off the side. I sip my beer, barely able to swallow against the growing lump in my throat. The brain is a fickle little bitch, shoving memories to the forefront, the ones I've tried so hard to forget. I shake my head and close my eyes as I remember the very first time I showed Frankie this place.

"Where are you taking me?" she yells from behind me as I jog along the rocky trail. "Just come on! We're almost there," I yell back at her. I'm proud of how she keeps up. Being a couple of

years younger and a girl, I didn't expect for her to even be interested in seeing this.

Rounding the last boulder and passing the last pine tree, the clearing comes into sight. I come to a sudden stop and she damn near runs right into the back of me.

"What is this place?" she says in awe, stepping in front of me. She walks right over to the edge of the cliff and looks down. Not a fear in the world.

"Stay away from there!" I tell her. "That's the fault line and hundreds of people have fallen to their death right there. They never go after the bodies because it's too steep and dangerous. People are left to rot down there." I make my way right up next to her. What I said is actually a lie passed on down to me by my father, who didn't want me playing back here for fear I would fall down the cliff, and he promised to leave me there if I did. I don't want her to get hurt, so I retell the old wives' tale just as it was recited to me.

She sits down on the edge of the cliff and dangles her feet over the edge, tipping her head back to look at me. "You going to sit down or what?" she asks and I take a seat next to her.

"I thought you'd be afraid to see the edge," I tell her, dangling my feet next to hers.

"Why would I be afraid?" she asks, tipping her face to the sky.

I glance at her out of the corner of my eye, watching her squint into the sun. Her long dark hair almost touches the ground behind her.

"Because you're a girl, and girls are always afraid of everything."

"Well, that's a dumb thing to say." She pushes herself up and looks over at me. "*Girls can do anything boys can do,*" she snaps at me.

"*No they can't,*" I argue with her.

"*Wanna bet?*" Her eyes challenge me.

"*They can't get a hard on.*" I laugh as her face turns a bright shade of red.

"*Gross,*" she says. "*Are all thirteen-year-old boys as disgusting as you, or are you special?*" She scowls at me and narrows her eyes.

"*Oh, Frankie, I was just kidding.*" I nudge her with my shoulder.

She harrumphs and crosses her arms over her tiny breasts. Breasts that are just starting to fill out. Breasts I think about every night as I lay in bed thinking about her. "*Why do you call me Frankie? My name is Franny.*"

"*No, it's not,*" I correct her. "*Your name is Frances and Franny doesn't fit you. Frankie does.*"

"*Frankie is a boy's name,*" she says, pulling her legs up from the cliff and crossing them Indian style.

"*Well, you'll always be Frankie to me. I'm not calling you Franny or Frances.*" I pick up a rock and toss it into the canyon below. "*Frankie, that right there is the center of the fault line.*" I point to the canyon below. "*An earthquake split the land right down the center and created this.*"

Her eyes widen as I tell her the old wives' tale of how the canyon was created. She listens intently, her bright blue eyes studying me closely.

"*You can't tell anyone about this place, Frankie. This is our little secret,*" I whisper to her. "*You're the only person I've ever told about the fault line, okay?*"

She nods her head, agreeing to my deal. This was my place, now it's mine and Frankie's.

I've been sitting here for hours when the sound of branches snapping in the distance pulls me out of my trip down memory lane. I sit up quickly, trying to assess what animal is lurking in the distance. The sun is barely making its way to the sky so it's nearly impossible to see what's coming, but the fact that whatever is in the bushes is disrupting me from my thoughts is pissing me off. But it's the figure that suddenly appears that damn near stops my heart.

SIX

Frankie

With my feet tucked underneath me, I sit at one end of the couch in Mom's living room while Faith sits at the other end. We've spent most of the night catching up and talking about Mom, Ted, and wedding plans. Maggie and Matthew are fast asleep in sleeping bags on the living room floor, oblivious to our presence.

"I need to go thank Mr. Ryan," I whisper to Faith as I think of all the food that was delivered for dinner. "Melinda told me he sent dinner and Judy mentioned he has been covering Mom's medical bills. How can he afford that?"

Faith's eyes widen and her face twists in confusion. "That's what we're calling him now? Mr. Ryan?"

I frown at her. "That's what I've always called him. I've never called him Stephen."

She shakes her head back and forth. "Jesus Christ, Franny," she whispers loudly, leaning in closer to me. "You really are clueless, aren't you? Mr. Ryan died five years ago. The 'Mr. Ryan' that Judy and Melinda are so very fond of is Cole!"

My stomach drops and my heart races, a million thoughts swirling through my mind. "Cole?" I question, not sure if I heard her correctly.

She scoots closer to me. "Yes. Cole. He brought the food by this evening. You were in the shower cleaning up when he stopped by—"

"Judy said Mr. Ryan," I cut her off, "so I assumed it was *Mr. Ryan*. You know, Cole's dad." My pulse races as the pieces begin to fall together.

She shakes her head again. "He's dead, Franny. He had a massive heart attack one night and died in his sleep." Faith continues to tell me the story. "Mom said for a few weeks leading up to when he passed, he wasn't looking well. She said he'd stop by the diner and have dinner and speak to everyone in the past tense. It's like he knew he was dying. He told her he'd written a will, leaving the shop and house to Cole." She tilts her head toward the house across the street.

My eyes widen in shock when I think of Cole still living in that house. The house I spent so much time in growing up. The house I lost my virginity in. "I assumed Cole had his own place now," I whisper, taking it all in. Mr. Ryan is dead and Cole could be right across the street at this very moment.

"No." She shakes her head. "He still lives there. Mom said he fixed up the inside real nice, just hasn't gotten to the outside yet. Are you sure Mom didn't tell you any of this?" she asks, looking confused.

I pick at the blanket laid across my lap and shake my head. "No. I told her I didn't want to hear anything about anyone from Crescent Ridge, especially anything to do with Cole."

"Jesus, Franny." She shakes her head. "Cole's been taking care of Mom's yard for years. He still stops by and fixes things around the house for her. That garden out back," she points toward the backyard, "he still tills that up every year for her and helps her plant whatever it is she likes to plant in that garden. Maggie started helping them this year." She looks down at her daughter on the floor, her long dark hair splayed across her pillow.

A lump forms in my throat and I'm not sure if it's anger or sadness, or a combination of both. My mom did exactly what I asked her to do—and I'm shocked. The lady is a vault. Apparently a lot has happened around here these last ten years, and I'm oblivious to all of it.

I pull my legs out from underneath me. "I didn't know he died, Faith." Tears fill my eyes. "He was so good to us." Her eyes are filled with sadness. She reaches out and takes my hand in hers. Mom claims she and Stephen Ryan were nothing more than friends, but they relied on each other a lot over the years, and Stephen Ryan was a father figure to Faith and I growing up. I'm sick that I didn't know of his passing.

"God, Faith," I mumble, pushing myself to my feet and walking to the kitchen.

"It was a long time ago, Franny." She follows me into the kitchen. "Don't beat yourself up about it."

"I'm not beating myself up," I tell her, pulling a mug down from the cabinet. "Hot chocolate?" I ask her and she shakes her head no. Hot chocolate is my go to comfort drink. "It's just that I would've liked to have paid my respects. That's all."

She huffs, "Franny. Be real with yourself for a minute. You would not have come back for his funeral."

I look at my sister, who stands with her hands on her hips, and I give her a sad smile. She's right, and she knows it.

"You can go pay your respects while you're home," she reminds me. "He's as dead today as he was five years ago."

I bust out laughing. "Oh my god, Faith!" I throw a kitchen towel at her and she catches it. I mix my hot chocolate in the large mug and hand it to Faith. "Here, transfer this to that metal travel mug." I point to the mug with a lid on it.

She frowns at me. "You're not going to go pay your respects now, are you? It's almost five in the morning."

"No." I try to contain my laugh. "I need to go for a walk, get out of here for a bit. I just need some fresh air. All of this is so much to take in."

She looks at me in understanding. "Just be careful," she says, taking the travel mug off the kitchen counter. She begins transferring my hot chocolate from the coffee mug to the travel mug. "And don't wake me up when you come back."

The sun is barely beginning to rise in the east as my feet hit the old, cracked pavement. A ways down the street, I duck underneath the large but still low-hanging branches from the cedar tree that marks the entrance to the path that will take me to the fault line.

My heart races the closer I get. The trail is overgrown with brush, but I'd know how to find the fault line if I was blind.

The earliest hints of morning sun are hard to see under the shade of large trees. Birds singing fill the quiet, open space around me. Twigs and fallen branches line the trail that was once clear from the endless times Cole and I would visit the fault line.

Dried branches snap under my weight as I do my best to

not trip on the now hazardous trail. Another hundred yards and I'll be there—back to the ledge that overlooks the fault line. To the ledge where I'd sit for hours and plan my future. To the ledge where Cole and I would dangle our feet and share our dreams. This place holds so many of my childhood memories, even the memories that hurt. A place I should be avoiding—but it's also the one place in the world where I can find clarity.

At the fault line, I can close my eyes and forget. About my mom's stroke, about being back in the one place that hurts more than I ever imagined it would—this stupid little town where I left my heart and buried my dreams.

Ten years ago, I vowed to never come back here—yet here I am. As I approach the clearing, my heart, my dreams, and my future—everything I buried all those years ago—sits on the ledge of that cliff looking over his shoulder at me.

Cole Ryan.

"Hey, Frankie girl," his deep voice calls to me, and in the blink of an eye my entire world comes to a sudden stop. His bright blue eyes haunt me, still wreaking havoc on my heart.

Momentarily, everything stands frozen in time. Every memory of us at the fault line flashes before my eyes. I can recall the thousands of times I have walked into this clearing and found Cole, legs dangling over the ledge, waiting for me. But never in a million years did I expect to see him here...not today, not at five o'clock in the morning, not ever.

I squeeze the travel mug of warm hot chocolate in my right hand, debating whether to turn and run or chuck the sixteen-ounce mug of piping hot chocolate at his head. The broken-hearted girl says toss the mug, but the voice of reason in me, the lawyer, says turn and run.

My heart races and my knees shake. I'm paralyzed. The

sound of his voice plays over and over in my head. The hold Cole still has on me both frightens and upsets me.

Taking a deep breath, I turn on my heel and walk back to the path I just arrived on. I need to leave Cole and my past there...in the past. I'm too fragile to deal with these feelings and emotions, and I need them to stay buried where I left them.

Only sometimes feelings and emotions are a traitorous bitch.

Tears fill my eyes, and I hate that I'm getting emotional, especially with Cole so close by. I refuse to let him see me cry. I don't know if I'm crying because of him, crying for me, or crying because I'm exhausted. All I wanted was a place to think—alone. My feet do double time carrying me back to the brush-covered path.

"Frankie, stop," Cole demands, but I keep moving. The sooner I get back to the trail, the sooner I can get away from Cole. Tears soak my face and I struggle to see through the dusky morning light. I can hear him moving behind me, but I keep my eyes focused on the trail ahead of me.

"Stop!" he says, just as a hand grabs my elbow, halting me.

I keep my face turned down. My entire body shakes as his hand holds onto my elbow, keeping me in place. Those traitorous tears continue to roll down my cheeks, and I do my best to not let him see me cry—only my best isn't good enough. He sees it and he inhales sharply.

I yank my arm free from his grip and turn my back toward him, doing my best to catch my breath and not let him see anymore of my face or my emotions.

"You're always the one running. Stay. I was just leaving," he says, his voice quiet, yet concerned. I remember that voice, the way his tone would become softer when I was upset. I hear him backing away, the sound of his feet on the overgrown brush getting further away. After a few minutes, when I know he's gone, I swipe at my cheeks, drying them with my sleeve. I breathe deeply, trying to clear my lungs and my head.

Trudging back over to the clearing, I sit down in the very spot Cole just vacated, the spot where I've sat a thousand times before. I can almost smell his cologne and feel his arms around me from behind. Memories of all of the times I'd come here to clear my head, or look at the stars hit me like a freight train. The memories are too numerous here, almost overwhelming— to the point where I can still remember vivid details.

"Kiss me, Frankie." He grips my face with both of his hands, firm yet gentle. His blue eyes look into mine, waiting for me to kiss him, only I don't...I'm too afraid to make the first move. He smirks, running his tongue over his lips before he leans in and presses his soft lips to mine. I inhale sharply when I feel how warm they are, and I give in, kissing him back. This feeling is what I want to remember forever. Knees weak, heart racing, warm skin, and heavy breathing.

I meet his slow movements, allowing his lips to tug at mine as he kisses me gently. My hand grips his t-shirt for dear life, and my heart thrums wildly in my chest as he kisses me again and again. This is what love feels like, I tell myself. It's warm, and safe, and standing in front of me with his lips pressed to mine. There is never another kiss that I'll have in this lifetime that will ever beat this kiss. This is the kiss of all kisses.

Breaking our kiss, he pulls back, still holding onto me. "I've been wanting to do that for forever," he says quietly, his lips twisting into a shy smile. "And I'm going to do that a million more times." He chuckles.

And this is the moment I know I'm in love with Cole Ryan.

I shake my head, fighting off the memory. Tears form in my eyes again as I take in the beauty of the fault line that I've come to realize I've missed so very much, along with everything and everyone I've left behind. The tall trees and the beautiful canyon of rock wrap me in a sense of comfort I haven't felt since I left Crescent Ridge, albeit only temporary.

As the sun rises, calm finally settles in. The tears have stopped and my emotions are back in check, my head is clear. I breathe the cool morning air deep into my lungs and close my eyes. Pushing myself up, I decide to head back to the house to grab a couple of hours of sleep before the nurse arrives.

As I make my way back to the trail, I turn and look at the fault line one last time—leaving it and all the memories it holds behind me once again. The trail back seems longer than it did getting here, or maybe I'm moving slower. Either way, it's hard to ignore the pull that the fault line has on me. It was such an important part of my past, and it hurts to leave it behind—but leaving things behind is what we do to move forward.

At least, that's what I tell myself.

SEVEN

Cole

Seeing Frankie has me all wound up. In all the years I've known her, I've never seen her cry other than the night that she saw Whitney and me. The night that I pushed her away for good. A night I'll regret for the rest of my life. To know that I was the cause of those tears is eating me alive. To know that my lies, from more than ten years ago, still weigh on her so heavily is fucking killing me.

I pace the front porch, a cup of coffee in my hand as I wait for her to appear from the trail down the street. She's been there a long time, and I'm beginning to get worried. I should've fucking stayed to make sure she was okay, but feeling her body tremble under my touch—and not because I was pleasuring her—got to me. I bailed. Just like I've always done.

The sun is finally out and the morning air is beginning to get warmer. Leaning against the patio railing, I sip on my coffee...waiting. Waiting until she appears, walking slowly up the road. I watch her, much like I did yesterday, only this time

I'm doing nothing to hide it. Her dark hair whips around her face as a gust of wind catches her.

She pauses ever so quickly when she sees me watching her. Tilting her head down, she presses on, walking faster. She damn near jogs up her driveway, bounding up the dilapidated steps on her front porch, letting herself in through the front door. The door closes with a thud, and I finally breathe a little easier knowing she's home safely.

I kick the railing with the toe of my shoe, knocking off a piece of peeling paint and mentally add one more fucking thing to my to-do list, sand and repaint both front porches. It's time.

Hearing the thud of the door once again from across the street, I glance up to see Faith making a beeline in my direction. Her long hair is wild as if she just woke up, which it appears she has since she's still in her pajamas. I see the fire in her eyes as she draws nearer, and I'm doing my best to not openly laugh at her appearance.

"Morning, Faith," I say, my lips twisting into a smirk as she approaches. I take another quick sip of coffee and brace myself for what is about to come. "Run out of coffee grounds? I've got some in the house." I point over my shoulder with my thumb as she marches up my porch steps.

"Goddammit, Cole. What did I tell you yesterday?" she yells at me, stomping her feet on the old wood porch.

"What?" I look at her, amused as she props her hands on her hips.

"Franny—"

"Frankie," I correct her. Godammit, she's Frankie.

She rolls her eyes at me. "—wants nothing to do with you. Leave her alone, Cole."

"I was there first," I snap at her.

"What are you, thirteen?" she huffs at me.

I take a step toward her and lean down closer to her face. "No, Faith. I'm a thirty-two-year-old man, who went to the fault line to think. Frankie showed up, got upset, and I left. End of story. I'm sorry I was there when she arrived. I had no idea she'd go there. I'm sorry that I upset her." I hold one of my hands up in mock surrender. Faith is fucking pissing me off and I'm in no mood right now to deal with her bullshit.

She exhales loudly and her shoulders slump in defeat. "This is a small town, Cole. *Franny*," she emphasizes her name for me, "is going to be here for a while, at least until we get Mom back on her feet. I have never asked anything of you, but please, *please* don't make her being back in Crescent Ridge any harder on her than it already is." Her eyes are tired and she rubs her arms.

My eyes fall to my shoes and I exhale loudly. "That's going to be pretty hard unless I leave town, Faith." I look over across the street at the house where I know she's sitting right now. I set my coffee mug on the railing and lean against it with both hands. Dropping my head, I take in what it is Faith is asking of me. Make myself scarce.

Silence surrounds us as I take a deep breath.

"You destroyed her, Cole," Faith finally speaks, her voice breaking with emotion. "You were her future. She was working so hard to become successful to get you both out of here." Faith stops, clearing her throat to compose herself. "To come home and find out you cheated on her and got another girl pregnant...*that* destroyed her. That was supposed to be *her* future, Cole, *her* baby with you."

I look up from the rotted wood boards on the porch and gaze across the street. As I think about that day that changed everything, I bite at the inside of my lip and swallow my guilt. This is the first time Faith has spoken to me about the past. A past she knows nothing about—other than the lies I created.

Running out of steam, Faith adds, "As I'm sure you can imagine, it wasn't easy for her to come home."

I nod my head in silence, still looking at the little house across the street.

"If you have any respect for her, Cole, leave her alone."

I clear my throat and let Faith's words sink in. Maybe I should make myself scarce. But then the front door opens, and my heart leaps in anticipation of seeing her again, even just a glimpse. Damn, I'm pathetic.

My heart drops almost immediately when I see Maggie stepping out. "Mom!" she hollers from the open doorway.

"I'll be right there," Faith yells back, but makes no attempt to leave.

Changing the subject, I nod toward Maggie. "She reminds me so much of Frankie at that age." I can't help but say something.

Maggie stands on the porch across the street, her arms folded across her chest as she watches Faith's and my silent showdown.

Faith looks away at Maggie, then back to me. "Maggie told me about the little back and forth thing you two have going on."

I huff out a short laugh. "Is that right?"

"She doesn't know what happened with you and Franny, but Mom said something to her. So I know she's upset with you." Her anger seems to have subsided and she fights back a stiff smile.

"That's three Callaway women who have it out for me." I chuckle. "Seems like your mom is the only one who has, or may have, forgiven me." I turn to look at Faith, who is still watching Maggie across the street.

"Cole, just do what I asked of you, please?"

"She married?" I blurt out, catching Faith off guard.

She stands up straighter and cocks her head. I can see her debating whether to answer me, debating whether I even deserve that answer. "Not yet, but she's engaged. To a really great guy. Ted. He's a lawyer, too." Her mouth quirks up into an almost smug smirk, and I can tell she's happy to stick the knife in my back and twist it.

I feel a fire in my bones knowing she's engaged. "Ted," I snort. "Nobody great is named Ted."

"Cole..." she starts, getting annoyed with me.

"Was hard to miss that ring on her finger," I remark. "Looks like he treats her well." I grab the coffee mug off the railing and walk to the screen door.

Faith snorts. "If by 'well', you mean he doesn't cheat on her and knock up another woman, yep. He treats her really well."

I freeze, momentarily stunned by Faith's words. I deserve another knife in the back—as much as it fucking hurts.

With those parting comments, I let the door slam closed behind me and mutter a quiet, "fuck off," to Faith.

EIGHT

Frankie

I spent the day shadowing Judy, following her around and watching every intricate detail of her routine that's now seared into my brain. I helped her prepare food, get Mom up and walking, and listened to Mom struggle to read a simple page of words while Judy sat patiently and helped her. Basically, I did anything and everything to keep my mind busy and focused on Mom, not on my encounter with Cole this morning.

Today was exhausting, but encouraging at the same time. Faith insisted that we spend a couple of hours out of the house tonight, and I gladly agreed.

"You did *not* say that to him!" I scream at Faith, burying my head in my hands.

"Yes, I did." Faith strokes mascara on her eyelashes as I sit on the edge of the bathtub and watch her get ready for our night out. "I don't know what has me more mad, Franny—that Cole couldn't keep it in his pants, or that he was too fucking stupid to wrap it up and knocked up Whitney Carson."

I cringe at the sound of Whitney's name coming off of

Faith's tongue. Whitney was one of a handful of girls who was actually nice to me in school. Most were bitchy and wanted nothing to do with a poor tomboy from the wrong side of the tracks, so it hurt that she'd do that to me, especially with Cole.

"You know she still lives in the Ridge, right?" Faith asks, dropping her tube of mascara in her makeup bag.

I roll my eyes. "I didn't. But I honestly don't really care," I respond and stand up, trying to not get upset.

"You're not curious about her at all?" she asks and I narrow my eyes at her. "Like, you haven't gotten all FBI and stalked her social media?"

"No, Faith. Jesus. I have no desire to see photos of Whitney, Cole, or their baby." I huff and stand up, fixing the black top I paired with a pair of faded jeans and black low booties.

"Is that what you're going to wear?" She looks at my reflection.

I glower at her. "It's a shitty VFW, Faith. We're only going for one beer...because you're making me," I remind her. "I'm not clubbing it in West Hollywood."

She smiles at me. "I'm not making you. Melinda wants us gone for the evening. She said Mom needs her rest, and with both of us lurking around, she's all wound up. Plus, it looks cute. I was just giving you hell," she teases. "But throw on that pretty long gold necklace with the pendant. It'll dress it up just a bit."

I roll my eyes at her. Who made her fashion queen?

"I need to call Ted before we leave." I run my fingers through my hair and notice my tired reflection looking back at me.

"Go." She shoos me away. "Call Loverboy. I need about ten more minutes to fix my hair anyway."

I sigh as I leave her in the bathroom, and I check in on Momma, who is sitting in bed, propped up, and watching *I Love Lucy* reruns on a small television in her bedroom.

"Hey, Mom," I whisper as not to startle her. She tries to smile at me, but it's all lopsided. "You feeling okay?" I ask, sitting on the edge of her bed. I brush her hair off her forehead, tucking it behind her ear.

She speaks slowly and carefully, just barely above a whisper. "Yes."

"Good. Faith and I are going to run into town—Melinda wants us out of here for a little bit. Tomorrow, Judy said two of your therapists are coming. It's going to be a big day. You need to rest." I place my hand over hers. "I love you," I say, leaning in to kiss her cheek.

"Love you." She manages to say back slowly.

Guilt fills me for even considering going out tonight as I close her door behind me. I step into my room and pull my phone off the nightstand, scrolling through the text messages and missed phone calls, none of which are from Ted. He's pissed. When I find his name, I tap it and the phone immediately begins ringing. Four rings and I get sent to voice mail. He's so pissed.

I shoot him a quick text message to let him know I'm thinking of him and toss the phone back on my nightstand.

"Ready?" Faith pops her head in the room.

"Ready."

Faith arranged for a babysitter to watch the kids at her house which was a great idea. As nice as it has been having them here, with us going out it's best they're at home for tonight.

"I'll drive," I tell Faith and use the remote key fob to

unlock the car doors. I'm not a big drinker, and I know Faith likes to indulge once in a while, so I'll be the designated driver.

"Let me drive," she argues. "It's your night to relax."

"You're the drinker." I laugh at her. "And I'll drop you off at home later."

"What about my car?" she asks, glancing at her car that's parked on the street.

"Seriously?" I question her. "You live nine blocks away. I think I can manage to come pick you up in the morning."

Three minutes later, we turn into the small square, non-descript building sporting a large American flag. The local VFW has been the only bar in town for as long as I can remember. I suddenly recall the new bar slated to open and hope that it doesn't detract business from here. While it's great to see the economy and Crescent Ridge grow, I hate to see it at the expense of long time businesses, especially ones that support our local veterans.

Even though it's only eight o'clock, the VFW is busy. The bar is packed, and people crowd around tall pub tables, leaning in to talk to each other over the noise of the busy bar and music. Two pool tables take up space at the far end of the room and another wall is lined with dartboards. However, with how busy it is, those do not appear to be in use tonight. This place is such a far cry from the Los Angeles bar and club scene I've grown accustomed to.

Faith waves me over to a small table she found tucked away, closer to the pool tables. A waitress immediately greets us and Faith orders us each a vodka tonic. The noise level is quieter over here, which makes it easier to talk, and I become much more at ease after a few sips of vodka. The stress of this trip, and Mom, begins to suddenly unwind as the vodka hits my veins.

"Do they have Uber in Crescent Ridge?" I ask Faith over the table and she bursts out laughing.

"No." She shakes her head and sips her drink much slower than I'm doing. Maybe she should have driven. "Franny, we literally live five blocks from here. We can walk home if we need to. Sarah is eighteen. She can stay the night with the kids if needed."

Shit. Yep. I sometimes forget how small Crescent Ridge really is.

Faith and I catch up on life. The kids, her job, how she's doing—I keep the conversation focused on her. It feels good to relax and talk with my sister. I've missed her, and while we're close, our conversations are limited to emails and texts most of the time due to my busy schedule.

"Do you need more money?" I ask her, the vodka obviously loosening me up.

We never talk money, but I always help her. She never asks, nor would she, so monthly she gets a deposit and I sleep better knowing she doesn't need to worry about the kids or herself. She has helped me in more ways than anyone could imagine, and money is the last thing I need.

She shakes her head. "We're actually doing okay. I'm able to pay for Maggie's dance and swimming, and Matthew's t-ball is dirt cheap—so we're good." She winks at me.

"Well, you know if you need anything—"

"You do more than enough for us, Franny. You send money religiously. You do more for us than that lousy ex-husband of mine ever will." She squeezes the lime into her drink aggressively when she mentions her ex.

I frown, knowing how Rick took everything in their divorce. He pays close to nothing in child support, and he holds the ace of spades when it comes to secrets he can use against Faith. Well, actually me. So Faith lets him shirk off his responsibilities to protect me. We all want the past left in the past.

Another round of vodka tonics, and Faith and I are laughing, fondly detailing stories from our youth. "Remember that time you stole my bra and wore it to school? I think you were in fifth grade," Faith laughs, "and all the boys were making fun of you, because you didn't even have boobs!" she squeals.

"I didn't get boobs until eighth grade." I roll my eyes at her.

Faith squeals with laughter. "Well, remember that day, the boys were making fun of you and—"

Like a flashback from the past, his voice comes out of nowhere. My head snaps up quickly to find him with a pool stick held tightly in his hand, mere inches from me. His bright blue eyes radiate confidence and purpose. His lip curls slightly at the corner and he laughs before speaking.

"I kicked all of their asses," he chuckles, "and I'd do it again," he says, leaning in, his voice deep and commanding.

Our eyes lock, and I study every inch of his face. The small mole on his chin is barely noticeable through his five o'clock shadow. The corners of his eyes are beginning to show signs of crow's feet, and dammit if that doesn't turn me on. He's aged perfectly in ten years, better than I expected him to.

I couldn't see much of him this morning, and I was so upset that I wasn't really looking, but now...with him inches from me, I notice all of him.

Lean muscle and tan skin. Dark hair and blue eyes. The curve of his lips and his straight nose. The light scent of his cologne invades my space and he knows he's gotten to me. He grins and those perfectly straight white teeth of his peek out from those lips I was just admiring.

I can't look at him any longer. I shake my head and turn back to see Faith shooting daggers from her eyes directly at Cole. If looks could kill, Cole would fall dead right here at my feet.

My back stiffens and the hairs on my neck stand up when he begins speaking again. "Didn't mean to interrupt your conversation, ladies. Just happened to be within earshot—and that memory was a good one. We have a lot of good memories, don't we, Frankie?" I suddenly feel dizzy and I'm not sure if it's from the vodka or Cole.

I glance away and Faith snaps, "Cole."

I don't turn around to see him leave, but I feel his absence. I always knew when he was near—it was just that way with us, and I can tell he's gone.

The look on Faith's face tells me my senses were right, he's left.

"Why is he here?" I ask, annoyed and suddenly wanting to leave as I begin gathering my purse and jacket.

Faith reaches over and grabs my hands. "Because it's the only damn place in this town to get a drink," she reminds me. "He's gone. We're not letting him ruin our night, Franny. Sit down and relax." Faith calms me down, she always does.

I'm a few cocktails in, and the vodka is making me more agreeable than normal. And while the mood has shifted slightly, we continue on, pushing Cole Ryan to the back of our minds.

Except, there's no pushing Cole to the back of my mind. Not tonight. He's bold and makes his presence known. He's a force, tall and fierce. Still, I do my best to forget he's just over my shoulder, only a few feet away, and I order us another round of drinks to help assist in forgetting.

Faith continues down memory lane, and we giggle at her terrible memory of childhood events when two shots arrive at our table, courtesy of a different waitress. "From the gentleman over there." She points behind me and I refuse to look. I know exactly where those shots are coming from. The shot glasses are full of pink liquid and rimmed with sugar.

"Carter Richardson," Faith says, raising her glass. "Looks like he's here with Cole." Her eyes are fixed on the corner behind me. "No sense in wasting good alcohol." She shrugs, looking back to me.

Hesitantly, I reach for the shot glass in front of me. With a shaky hand, Faith and I toast. "To forgetting," I say, sparing a glance over my shoulder where I see Carter and Cole standing side-by-side, watching us.

"To forgetting," Faith says loudly enough for the entire bar to hear, raising her glass even higher. With a giant smile, she presses the shot glass to her lips and I follow suit.

The cold liquid burns nicely as it fills my belly. "To forgetting," I mumble again, puckering my lips as the sour aftertaste hits me. "If only it were that easy," I say, chancing another look at Cole.

And he smiles that fucking ridiculous smile that he always did—and my stupid heart skips a beat.

As the alcohol takes effect, my feet become numb and my lips begin to tingle. Faith has ordered us water in an effort to keep me upright. "Bathroom," I stammer as I push myself off the tall pub chair. "Have to pee, so bad."

Faith giggles as she holds a somewhat steady arm at my back. I square my shoulders and do my best to walk as straight as possible. It sucks that the bathrooms are in the opposite corner of where we're sitting. Neon lights flash Coors Light and Bud Light along the wall, in between giant television screens airing a baseball game.

Cleaning myself up in the sink, I splash some water on my cheeks, hoping to tame the pink flush that has inched up from my chest. The alcohol seems to be going down a little easier than usual.

With my pointer finger, I lean in close to the mirror and wipe eyeliner that's begun to run underneath my eye when an unfamiliar voice startles me.

"Franny?" The woman's voice is quiet but high-pitched. "Is that you?"

In the mirror behind me, I see a woman with long blonde hair exiting a bathroom stall. It takes a moment for recognition to hit me, but when it does, I whip around quickly, almost losing my balance.

"It is you," she says with a giant smile. "You look so good! I've heard all about your success," she continues talking and walking toward me. I see her lips moving, but don't hear a single word she's speaking.

My hand grips the edge of the bathroom counter as my eyes take in all five-foot-nine of Whitney Carson. *Whitney fucking Carson.*

I close my eyes, drawing in a deep breath, willing myself not to lose my shit in front of her. Her face, the curve of her belly...the vision of Cole pressed to her has been imbedded in my mind for the last ten years, and here she stands—being as friendly as ever.

She ties a little black apron around her waist and continues talking to me with this giant smile—a genuine, warm smile. The kind of smile that you'd offer a friend you haven't spoken to in a while, not the kind of smile you offer the ex-girlfriend of the man you cheated with.

"Whitney," I barely muster out before cutting her off and turning back around to lean over the sink. My hand trembles and fumbles recklessly with the knob to turn on the cold water. I feel like I'm going to be sick. Stars dance in front of my eyes, and my throat closes up as I pray for her to leave. "You work here?" I'm instantly pissed that Faith would bring me here knowing I could run into Whitney.

"Just started...are you okay?" she asks when I suddenly feel her hand on my back.

I shrug her off and splash cold water on my face again, doing my best to keep my composure. Anger courses through my veins and my knees shake uncontrollably.

Whitney takes a cautious step back. "I knew you'd still be upset with me, but I assumed—" she starts before I cut her off sharply.

"Don't *assume* you know anything about me or my feelings," I snap at her. "Don't *assume* that, because something happened ten goddamn years ago, that I'm okay with it today!" I yell at her.

Emotions that have been bottled up all this time finally rise to the surface, rearing their ugly head. Standing up, water drips from my chin and I reach for the paper towels, pulling a handful of them from the wall dispenser to pat my face dry.

My hands still tremble as Whitney continues to distance herself, seeing the full extent of my anger.

"It's just that Cole—" Whitney starts again, but I don't pay attention to her words.

It's hard not to hate everything about Whitney. She's tall, beautiful, and rich. She was everything I never was. I understand why Cole would be attracted to her. Her long blonde hair was stick straight and soft, whereas mine was dark, drab, thick, and wavy. She had the most striking eyes and petite yet long frame. She was stunning and popular.

I was just...*me*. Smart. Crazy smart, a real book nerd. I got good grades and never cared about what I wore, mostly because I couldn't afford to care. It never dawned on me to care about what I looked like until I went to college and Ashley, my roommate, insisted I care. I always believed Cole liked me for *me*, not for the clothes I wore, or the color of my hair.

"Don't breathe his name around me," I seethe. "Don't talk to me. Don't look at me. Do you understand?" I point a finger at her, daring her to touch me. I'm not a fighter by any means, but she'd better not test me tonight. "Don't pretend I'm okay with whatever it was you two—"

"Stop! Just stop!" she yells at me, cutting me off. "I know you're angry, and I didn't want to do it, but Cole asked me to."

"Asked you to what?" I bark, rolling my eyes at her as I crumble the paper towels in my hands into a perfect little ball. "Spit it out," I sneer at her.

She looks me in the eye and pulls her bottom lip into her teeth Her eyes dance with regret. "You have to talk to Cole, Franny. He needs to tell you. He promised me he'd tell you. I thought he already did..." She frowns as if she's thinking back.

It doesn't matter. Whatever he needs to tell me doesn't matter.

"Never going to happen," I declare and toss the paper towels into the open wastebasket, shoving past Whitney toward the door. "Cole and I haven't spoken, nor will we."

"For what it's worth, I'm really sorry, Franny. I never meant to hurt you," she says when I pass her, tears dancing on her eyelids.

I don't care about her damn tears. I don't blame her fully, but she was the catalyst that fucked up my plans.

"Screw you, Whitney." I manage to say as I yank the bathroom door open so hard it bounces off the wall behind me. Laughter and music greet me back in the bar as I make my way back to our table. A cocktail waitress drops another round of shots on the table just as I throw myself back into my seat.

"Everything okay?" Faith asks, squeezing a lemon into her shot.

I eye it, reaching for a glass. "Does it look like I'm okay?"

"Well, obviously not, but Cole hasn't left that corner so I don't know what has you worked up now," she says, picking up the shot glass. "Lemon drop." She smiles at me until she sees how really upset I am and her smile turns to a frown. "What's wrong?"

"Just ran into Whitney Carson in the bathroom," I spit out and pick up the shot that's on the table, tossing it back. The vodka burns as it travels down to my stomach. "Or is it Whitney Ryan now?" I slur bitterly, slamming my shot glass down on the table.

"Oh, shit, Franny," Faith stops me. "Just so you know, they're not together. I don't know the whole story, because honestly, I don't want to know the details. But I know for a fact they're not together. Whitney married Jackson McDermott about seven years ago. He graduated with me and works for the sheriff's department."

"How sweet." I roll my eyes and wave over the waitress. "Another round. Make it two." I tell her and she nods and walks away, her cowboy boots thumping along the wood floor as she leaves.

Faith swallows hard. "I tried telling you about Whitney before we left, but you cut me off."

"Yeah, not a real big fan of talking about Whitney, or Cole for that matter."

Faith sighs and takes a sip of her shot. "I don't expect you to forgive them, Fran," she says, "but you have to let go of the hatred. It's not healthy."

I slowly raise my middle finger to her and she busts out laughing. "God, I've missed you." She giggles, suddenly pausing. "And if I didn't know for a fact she was married, I would think there was a lover's quarrel happening right now," Faith says, nodding over my shoulder toward the corner behind me.

I chance a glance over my shoulder and see Whitney speaking very animatedly with Cole. Her arms flinging and foot stomping tell me she's really giving it to him. He doesn't speak, but he shakes his head at her, all while drinking from a bottle of beer with his eyes fixed on me.

"Ugghhhh," I mutter and Faith laughs again.

"Whatever happened with you two in the bathroom obviously got to her as well," Faith says.

Our shots arrive and, without a second thought, I pick one up, licking the sugar off the rim before tipping it back and finishing it—to forget. Tonight is about forgetting. Right now, my entire body is buzzing and I want to forget everything.

Cole. Whitney. My own damn name. I just want to disappear.

"Faith," I slur and hiccup. "I'm drunk. Certifiably drunk." I point my finger at her and giggle.

"Good. You needed to let loose," she says, her eyes sympathetic.

"So did you," I remind her, the mood shifting. "I don't know how you do it all alone, Faith," I tell her, speaking about the kids.

"Mom helps." She shrugs. "And they're good kids, Franny. You help me financially and that's the hardest part, honestly."

I look at my gorgeous sister through blurry eyes and think about everything she's sacrificed. "Don't underestimate yourself," I tell her.

Faith was always good at letting others shine at her expense. She never wanted the spotlight or the attention. She was fine carrying the load and letting someone else accept the recognition. Selfless. Caring. I don't know what I'd do without her.

She slides another lemon drop shot across the table toward me. "Last one," she says, holding up her glass. "What should we toast to?"

I tip my head back and glance over my shoulder. "To letting go of the past," I say quietly.

"I like that," Faith whispers and squeezes my hand.

"Me, too."

NINE

Cole

"The target is moving," Carter says, jabbing me in the back with a pool cue.

I've been lost in my thoughts after Whitney told me about running into Frankie in the restroom and their subsequent exchange. I snap my head around to see Frankie fumbling with her purse and Faith laughing as they walk arm in arm toward the door. When Carter and I arrived at the bar tonight, we were both shocked as hell to find Frankie and Faith here. Carter took it upon himself to give me the play-by-play every time Frankie took a breath, and while I shouldn't care about what Frankie's doing, I do. And Carter knows it. So much for leaving the past in the past.

"I'm out." I toss my pool cue onto the center of the pool table, abandoning my game and taking one last swallow of beer before slamming the bottle down on the table. By the time I get to the parking lot, Frankie and Faith are nowhere to be found. I instantly relax when I see Frankie's car parked out at the edge of the parking lot, glad that she didn't get behind the wheel after drinking as much as she did tonight. I scan the area in hopes of seeing them, but I come up empty handed.

With a booming thud, the door of the VFW slams shut behind Carter as he exits and meets me in the parking lot. His eyes find Frankie's car with her California license plates and he looks at me. "Only two ways they could've went. Toward home or toward Faith's." He points with each of his hands in opposite directions. "They're about equal distance. Let's divide and conquer. You head toward home and I'll head toward Faith's. One of us is bound to find them."

"And what exactly are we going to do when we find them?" I ask with a laugh and a shake of my head.

"I don't know, dumbass, maybe just make sure they get home okay? Unless you wanted to kidnap them and hold them hostage, and if that's where this is going I'm going to have to gracefully bow out." Carter rolls his eyes at me and twirls his keys in his hand.

"You've never been graceful about a damn thing." I punch his shoulder. "Go. You head toward Faith's. If you find them, make sure they get there and call me so I know they're okay."

"You got it." He nods before jumping into his old pickup truck.

I scan the area one last time before getting into my Jeep and heading toward home. It takes me all of two minutes to get there and not a sight of Frankie or Faith along the way. I don't know what the fuck I was thinking staying at the VFW when I saw them walk in. She's my addiction, always has been. I told Carter I wanted to leave her in the past, yet I'm drawn to her like a junkie looking to get his next fix. My mind says no, yet my body—my heart—says yes.

"Fuck," I mutter to myself, angry at how conflicted I am now that she's back.

Just as I get inside and kick my shoes off, my cell phone rings, Carter's name flashing on the screen. Before I even say hello, he's speaking, "I found them," he says and it sounds like he's out of breath.

"Where were they?"

"Couple of blocks from Faith's house. I got Faith home just in time for her to get sick, but, uh...Frankie..." He hesitates.

"What about her?"

"She's passed out cold...here in my truck. I left her in the truck when I got Faith in her house and when I came back out, she was passed out."

I groan and run my hand over my face. "Just bring her back here. I'll help get her in her house."

"We'll be there in two minutes," he says before hanging up.

I slide back into my shoes and wait for them out front. Carter's truck rolls up slowly and he parks in front of Frankie's house. I jog down the driveway to meet them when he steps down from the pickup truck, his eyebrows raised in amusement. I glance in the driver's door window and there lies Frankie on the bench seat, her knees pulled to her chest and her head lying on the seat.

"Go get the front door," I tell Carter as I walk around to the passenger door and pull it open.

I nudge Frankie gently to see if she'll move, but as Carter already assessed, she's passed out cold, nothing but dead weight. I wedge my arm under her legs and pull her gently across the seat toward me. With my other arm, I lift her into my arms, her head falling against my chest. Her dark hair falls in piles around her shoulders and her pink lips are parted slightly as she breathes softly. She smells like heaven, a combination of coconut and vodka. She stirs slightly in my arms as I carry her up the driveway and to her front porch.

I hear Carter mumbling before he turns around. "Door's locked," he states matter of factly, jiggling the doorknob again just to make sure.

I sigh in frustration. "They never lock the door. It must've been the night nurse. Where are her keys?"

"Keys?" He looks between Frankie in my arms and his car. "I left a purse with Faith, but Frankie has nothing with her."

"Nothing?" I ask, wondering if I heard him correctly. "She drove her car to the bar. She had to have keys with her."

He shrugs and I sigh again. We look at each other for a brief moment before I turn around.

"Where are you going?" he asks and jogs down the front porch steps after me.

"Home," I answer him.

"With Frankie?" He catches up to me and shoots me a curious look.

"Well, I can't very well leave her outside on the porch all night, can I?"

My feet carry us across the street and up the middle of my front yard to the porch. "Get the door for me, will ya?"

Carter scrambles up the steps in front of me to open the front door, only he pauses first. "Cole, maybe she should stay with—"

"Not a fucking chance," I snap at him. "Open the door."

And he does, stepping aside to let us in. "Maybe I should stay—" he begins before I cut him off again.

"Nope, we're all good here. Just shut the door behind you."

"She's going to be pissed, you know." He looks at me with

Frankie wrapped in my arms. "But I'd pay a thousand dollars to be here in the morning when she wakes up in your house." He chuckles.

"Get out of here, Carter," I yell at him.

"Two thousand!" He steps over the threshold and back out onto the front porch.

"Goodnight," I say through gritted teeth.

"Fine. But call me tomorrow. I can't wait to hear about this."

With his parting comments, the front door slams shut. I shuffle carefully down the dark hallway to my room. It's the only room in the house where there's a bed. Frankie can stay here, and I'll take the couch. My knees hit the edge of the bed and I carefully lay her down. I flip on the bedside lamp so that I can see enough to get her shoes and jacket off.

She's dead weight as I shift her from side to side, pulling her jacket off her thin arms. I brush the hair from her face, tucking it behind her ear. Memories flash before my eyes of all the times I touched her hair. I pause, taking in her beauty. She's exactly the Frankie I remember. Her small nose is sprinkled with light freckles, so light that you wouldn't notice unless you were looking for them. Her pink lips are full, and a small dark mole sits right on the edge of her lower lip. Again, you wouldn't know it was there—but I've studied, memorized every millimeter of Frankie's body. I know every mole, every mark, every curve, and the feel of her soft skin.

She suddenly moves, curling into a ball in the middle of my bed. She pulls her hands up, resting them on the pillow next to her face. It's there; the large diamond ring hangs from her left ring finger, slapping me back to reality—a reality where Frankie isn't mine and never will be.

My heart aches at how I've hurt her—how I changed the course of our lives with one simple lie. She's happy, I tell myself, as I've done every night since she left. Trying to convince myself again that what I did was the right decision. That what I did was best for her—for us. But I know I'm full of shit as I swallow back my disgust and choke on my own lies. This was what I wanted, wasn't it?

If it was, then why does it still hurt so fucking bad?

I sit on the edge of the bed for hours, watching her, studying each steady breath, and every movement she makes. She hums lightly every so often and exhales loudly when she tosses and turns, her sleep unsettled. Only when the sun begins to rise do I leave her. I close the bedroom door and head to the kitchen to make a pot of coffee.

Hours pass and exhaustion rips through me, but I refuse to close my eyes before Frankie wakes up. I stand at my front window, eyes glued to the house across the street as they were for years after she left. Years of regret I've kept buried deep inside me begins to rise, gnawing at me. When Frankie walks out of my door this morning, it may be the last time I ever speak with her.

What do you say to the one person who owned you—every little fucked up piece of you...that you tossed away so she could live her dreams? What do you say when you have fifteen seconds to explain that it was the biggest mistake of your life?

'I'm sorry' seems so weak. 'I fucked up' sounds so insincere. I struggle to find the words buried deep inside me as I squeeze my coffee mug in one hand and run my other hand across my face.

I pinch my eyes closed and breathe deeply when I suddenly hear the soft sounds of shuffling behind me. I turn, frozen in place by bright blue eyes that I'd never forget in a million years. She looks away quickly and nervously twists her jacket in both hands.

Stepping toward the door, she pauses. "I'm not sure how I ended up here—" she starts then stops, pulling her lips between her teeth.

My heart thrums wildly in my chest and my stomach drops as the words I was previously looking for are nowhere to be found. "Frankie." Her name rolls off my tongue, barely a whisper.

Her entire body stills, clearly affected by me. Her eyes remain turned down on her feet.

"Carter found you and Faith walking last night," I start, breaking the unbearable tension filling the space between us.

She nods and takes a step toward the front door. I mimic her movement and step carefully in front of her, blocking her, trying to pause her escape. She stops and finally lifts her head. Her blue eyes meet mine and she pulls a deep breath into her lungs.

"I don't remember—" she starts before I cut her off.

"You had a good time last night." I smirk. "The drinks," I add just to make sure she knows what I'm talking about. "You deserve it."

She sighs and nods her head slightly. "I need to go," she says softly, shuffling from foot to foot, waiting for me to move out of her way. Only I can't. Something inside me keeps me rooted in place, prolonging this moment.

"Can we talk?" My plea sounds desperate. Hell, I *am* desperate. Everything I wanted to leave in the past is standing in front of me, and this is my chance to right my wrongs, speak the truth...apologize.

She shakes her head from side to side. "Not today," she says quietly, yet I can hear her voice waver...the emotion in her voice is clear.

"Please," I beg. "Just five minutes."

"Why?" she asks, squaring her shoulders, trying to come across as confident—only I know her better. She's crumbling... just like I am at the thought of losing this opportunity.

"Because I need to tell you some things." I take a small step toward her and she immediately takes a step back, retreating from me.

Running.

Fleeing.

The once strong Frankie, who would always stand up to me, always fight me, stands defeated in front of me...This is my doing and I need to rectify it.

"God, I'm sorry," I say, barely above a whisper, and she instantly begins to shake.

"I can't," she says, holding out her hand to stop me. "I can't do this right now." Tears fill her sea blue eyes.

"Frankie." I reach out my hand to steady her as she shakes her head, stopping me from touching her. Her dismissal stings, but isn't unexpected.

"Don't," she says firmly, clearing her throat.

I hold up both of my hands in a show of surrender. "When you're ready." I step aside so she's free to leave.

She takes a deep breath and bolts for the front door. I watch every movement as she fumbles with the doorknob, suddenly pausing. Turning around slowly her eyes find mine and my heart skips a beat.

"I don't think I'll ever be ready, Cole." Her voice shakes and I see her bite the inside of her cheek before she turns back around quickly and disappears through the front door, taking with her every ounce of hope I had in speaking with her ever again.

~

I tip my beer back, downing the last swallow before tossing the bottle onto the pile of empty ones that have collected since I started drinking three hours ago. I couldn't stand to sit on the porch and look at Frankie's house across the street, couldn't bear a chance at seeing her again after she fled this morning. So I sit in the backyard, under the pergola drowning my misery in shitty beer.

I study the Aspen trees that have begun to sway out along the fence line, not sure if they're swaying from the alcohol in my system or from the light breeze that's moved in. I hear the door from my house open then close, and I recognize Carter's heavy footsteps approaching from behind me. From the corner of my eye, I see a black purse fall to the ground next to me as I balance myself on a patio chair, my feet perched on the table in front of me.

"What's that?" I ask, not chancing a look at the purse. I know damn well what it is.

"That is your ticket at one more shot with Frankie." He smiles as he slides into the seat opposite of me. Carter called early this morning and I filled him in with the Cliff Notes version of what happened. He pulls a beer from the bucket on the center of the table and twists off the cap, flicking it onto my brick patio. Asshole.

I huff loudly and close my eyes, my face tilted to the sky. I can almost feel the edge of fall beginning to creep in as the afternoons are just starting to deliver the slightest hint of cooler weather.

Beneath my eyelids I see Frankie trembling, a vision that haunts me. Just like the vision of her driving away ten years ago and never coming back. I shake my head, trying to forget, except when you hurt the one person who means the world to you, there is no forgetting. I fucking hate myself for the pain and destruction I've caused.

"There are no more tickets and no more chances," I tell Carter, my voice hard.

"It's like I don't even know who the fuck you are anymore," he barks at me as the legs of his chair grate against the brick patio.

I lean forward quickly, my chair dropping onto all four legs as I glare at him. "What the fuck is that supposed to mean?"

"I watched you destroy everything, Cole. I watched you sacrifice the one thing that meant everything to you. And now it's pretty fucking hard to miss the trail of destruction that sacrifice left behind. I was there after every fucking bender you went on and every whore you fucked as you tried to forget about Frankie. I was also there when you finally got your shit together and started building something pretty fucking amazing in this town." His eyes soften when they meet mine. "This is about Frankie. You have one last opportunity to talk to her and I just handed it to you on a silver fucking platter. You owe this to yourself." He walks to the middle of the yard where a large fountain sits. "Actually, you owe this to Frankie," he says without turning around. "She deserves the truth."

My blood simmers, my temper flaring. "You don't think I already know that!" I push myself up from my chair and rest my hands on the patio table.

"Do whatever you want, man," he sighs and walks back toward me. "When she leaves this time, I'm not going to be the one to pick up all your shitty pieces." His shoulder bumps mine hard, knocking me off balance as he moves past me.

"Take the fucking purse with you when you leave," I snap at him.

"Fuck you, Cole," he says as the patio door slams shut behind him, leaving Frankie's black purse sitting at my feet.

"And fuck you, too," I mumble, as if he can hear me.

TEN

Frankie

The massive pounding in my head and the nausea rolling through my body have kept me in bed all day. I keep my eyes closed as I reach for the nightstand to get my phone but remember that it's in my purse—wherever my purse is. I try to recall the last time I saw it.

At the bar last night.

"Shit," I mumble to myself and roll over, pulling my comforter over my head. There's a light rap on the door, and I groan as I pull the covers back down and roll over to see who it is.

"Looks like someone else could use a little nursing today," Judy snickers and steps inside the room. She's carrying a glass of water and a small packet. "Alka-Seltzer," she says, setting it on my nightstand. "You can thank me later."

"How's my mom?" I ask guiltily, my voice raspy and dry.

"She's good. She'll be better once I update her on your condition," she says, raising an eyebrow at me. "She's been asking about you and Faith."

"Shit," I mumble again under my breath. "What time is it?"

"Six-thirty. You've slept all day. Faith called for you earlier as well. She's home with the kids, Matthew isn't feeling well, but she was more concerned about you and your," she taps her chin, "over-indulgence last night."

I try to roll my eyes, but it hurts too badly. "Matthew? Is he okay?"

She nods. "Said something about allergies and just being stuffy. But she didn't want to come over in case it was something more. Didn't want to spread the germs to your mom." She gestures toward Mom's room down the hall. "I'll be back in a little bit with some soup for you. In the meantime, take that Alka-Seltzer." She shoots me a pointed look and closes the door behind her.

I push myself upright and take a deep breath as my stomach rolls. I grab a robe and slowly make my way to the bathroom for a hot shower. My entire body aches, my muscles thrumming in tune to my pulse as I step into the scalding water. My body twists, conflicted by the combination of pain and pleasure. Pain at the heat from the water, and pleasure from the relief it's providing to my sore body.

I keep my eyes pinched closed, fighting back the memory of Cole's blue eyes that held me paralyzed this morning. Waking up to a room that was so eerily unfamiliar as it was familiar was not expected. Never in a million years did I think I'd be waking up in his bed, wrapped in sheets that smell exactly as I remember him—masculine yet sweet. A scent I'll never forget. A scent that I can't shake, my skin breaks into goose bumps as I think about him—Cole.

The hold he still has on me rattles me to the core. Feelings I'd long since buried have risen to the surface. This morning, the urge to run was as strong as the urge to stay and listen to what he had to say. But I ran—to protect myself, to not allow him to see the hold he'll always have over me.

"Shit!" I grumble and pull the hot, steamy air deep into my lungs.

I wash and condition my hair, and scrub my face and body before plugging the drain on the tub. Filling it up with hot water and bubble bath, I pile my long hair on top of my head before sliding into the water and letting my muscles finally relax.

By the time the water in the bathtub cools, my body doesn't hurt as much. After draining the tub and drying myself off, I pull on my long silk robe. The soft fabric feels light and comfortable against my tender skin. With my arms full of my dirty clothes from last night, I open the bathroom door and a blast of cool air hits my face. Only it's not the cool air that catches me off guard, it's the smell of *him*. Cole. His masculine cologne fills the small hallway that surrounds us.

With his left hand fisted and his right hand raised to knock on my bedroom door, he hesitates, a deep sigh resonating from him. His gray t-shirt pulls tightly across the back of his broad shoulders as he once again raises his hand and lightly taps on my bedroom door. He taps his foot anxiously as I study every inch of him from behind.

Memories from the past come rushing in and I stand frozen in place, staring at Cole's back.

"What's wrong?" Cole asks as I lean against the doorframe of his

bedroom. My heart races in my chest as he stands with his hands propped on his hips and a devious smile on his face.

"Nothing," I tell him, stepping into the bedroom on wobbly knees.

His lips stretch into a smile. "C'mere." He reaches a hand out for me. My shaking hand reaches out in return, and he captures it, pulling me tightly into him. As I lean my head against his hard chest, he rests his chin on top of my head. I've always fit perfectly in his strong arms, and as they engulf me in his embrace I finally begin to calm down.

"We don't have to do this," he whispers into my hair.

"I know." I manage to say, taking a deep breath, "but I want to."

His arms squeeze me tighter. Safe. Comforting. Cole is my safe place in this world.

"I love you, Frankie. Always have, always will."

I tip my head back and press up onto my tiptoes, capturing his soft lips in mine. "Then make love to me," I mumble against his lips and begin walking us toward his bed. Lacing our fingers, he lets our hands fall against my hips. "Look at me," he says quietly and I raise my eyes to his. Blue eyes look down on me with concern. "You can say no, Frankie. At any time. Tell me to stop, and I will."

"I know." I nod my head nervously.

"I'm going to touch you...and dammit, Frankie," he mumbles, unwinding his hands from mine. "If you don't want to do this, you need to tell me now." My seventeen-year-old heart beats wildly in my chest as his fingers skim the edge of my shirt and brush against the soft skin of my stomach. He inches them higher, pulling my t-shirt up with his hands.

Instinctively, my arms raise and he pulls the shirt off, tossing it to the floor.

"I want this...I want you," I whisper to him, my voice shaking nervously. Cole has been patient and caring as he's waited for me to be ready for this night. I've always wondered what my first time would be like—and while I never imagined I'd be seventeen, I always knew it would be Cole.

His rough fingers trace my collarbone where he hooks them in the straps of my bra, sliding them over my thin shoulders. I take a deep breath and chew on my lip as Cole's eyes devour me." I've never wanted anyone like I want you, Frankie."

Pressing his lips to mine, he breathes life into me—he's always been the drug I needed, the drug I could never get enough of. My fingers fumble with the button on his jeans, and I feel him smile against my lips at my sudden bout of courage. We both let out a nervous laugh as I finally wrestle the metal button from its hole and I slide the zipper down, allowing his jeans to hang open, his erection on full display.

Cole wastes no time ridding me of my jeans in return until both pairs are left in a pile at our feet. We stand in nothing but our underwear, our chests rising and falling with each rapid breath. Cole's hard erection presses against my stomach and I can see the want in his eyes.

"I hope you're not in a hurry, Frankie girl." He walks me back toward the bed until the mattress hits the back of my knees. "Because I plan to touch every part of you...twice, and I plan on this taking all night long." He smirks at me.

"Your dad—" I manage to say before he cuts me off.

"Is out of town picking up parts for the shop. Won't be back until tomorrow afternoon." My stomach jumps at the thought of *spending all night with Cole. He lowers his head and his tongue traces small circles on my neck while his fingers unfasten my bra. My fingers dip inside the waistband of his boxer briefs, finding his erection waiting for me. While I've touched Cole here before, even tasted him, something feels different about him today. He feels harder and wider today, causing the butterflies to dance in my stomach again.*

He gasps and hooks his fingers in my panties, mimicking what I'm doing to him, only his fingers dip lower, touching me where I'm most sensitive and my body shudders.

"You're wet." He dips his finger lower as his other hand removes my panties altogether. His fingers separate my lips and my head falls back at the feel of him working me. My breath quickens as he moves faster, and I remember the last time he touched me like this. It was like fireworks and a lightning storm all collided when I climaxed.

"On the bed," he orders, pulling me from my memory. He helps me down to the center of the soft bed. Removing his boxer briefs, I can't help but take in the sight of Cole naked. Tall and dark, his lean muscles twist and flex with every movement. Every muscle in his abdomen stretches as he reaches out and positions my legs where he wants them. A trail of dark hair runs from his belly button down to the patch of hair between his legs where his cock stands waiting.

Cole drops to his knees at the edge of the bed and pulls me closer to him. His fingers pressing into the soft flesh of my hips as he positions me.

"I'm going to make sure you're ready," he tells me, touching me again.

His finger trails slowly through my soft folds, spreading my wetness. The tip of his finger barely penetrates my opening as he tests my readiness. If this were anyone else, I'd be mortified, but with Cole, he's always owned me. We've been way more intimate with each other, sharing our lives, our dreams, our fears... this is just intimacy in the physical sense—the final bond between us.

My hips jerk when his lips suddenly press against my aching core, his tongue working slow circles around my sensitive center. My body shakes as he takes his time, teasing and tempting me. My hands alternate between pulling his hair and grabbing the comforter as I try to keep my body from losing control. A low moan escapes my lips and Cole looks up to me with a smirk on his face.

Cole finally slows and crawls up my body carefully. "You sure?" He looks me in the eyes. His blue eyes dance, speaking a million unspoken words. They speak of truth, of honesty, of everything good in my life. He may only be nineteen, but they speak of love and comfort, and safety. They tell me I'm his and he's mine. He is my compass when I am lost. He is my strength when I am weak. Everything I am is because of him and I'm about to give him the only thing I have to offer—me.

I nod and take a deep breath, grabbing his biceps. "This is the only thing I've ever really been sure of," I whisper.

He leans down and presses a light kiss to my lips. I can taste myself on him, the slightest hints of saltiness left on his lips. I should be grossed out, but there's something oddly intimate about it.

He aligns himself at my center and gently presses forward. "Look at me, Frankie. Don't close your eyes."

I bite my lower lip as the pressure builds and with a quick thrust, he makes his way inside me. Closing my eyes, I push back the pain as my body slowly accepts him. I pinch my eyes closed harder and pull my lips between my teeth as he fills me as the pain subsides slowly. While it's far from comfortable, it's not nearly as bad as Faith told me it would be. Cole is careful to move slowly and every movement he makes is tender and full of concern.

His arms shake as he balances the weight of his body against the mattress. He presses a sweet kiss to my forehead as he makes one last push to fill me completely. "I love you, Frankie girl. Always have, always will."

I'll never forget the sound of his voice calling me Frankie girl, or this feeling that I know is love. Pure, genuine love. This is what it feels like to be loved by Cole Ryan.

Tears sting my eyes at the memory, and a lump begins to form in my throat. I clear my throat and shake my head, pulling myself out of the past. Cole snaps his head around, his eyes widening in surprise as I stand mere feet away from him.

"Frankie," he says quietly as I shuffle nervously from foot to foot. "Judy said you were back here and to knock." He points his thumb over his shoulder at my bedroom door.

"Why are you here, Cole?" I push past him, opening my bedroom door. I toss the pile of clothes in my hands into a laundry basket that has been sitting in my room since I left all those years ago. My hands shake as I tighten the belt on my robe.

And just like he always did, Cole follows me into my room,

closing the door behind him and leaning against it just like he used to.

"Because I have something you want....and to get it back, you're going to give me something I want." He raises his eyebrows and narrows his eyes slightly. His perfect lips twist into a little smirk.

"Ooooooh, really." I chuckle nervously and roll my eyes.

"Yeah, really." He steps away from the door and takes a step toward me. Our eyes are locked on one another as he invades my space.

"What do you want so badly from me, Cole? Seems like you've taken everything possible from me already." My voice shakes with emotion that has snuck up on me and I clear my throat to shove it down.

He stops mid-step and blows out a long puff of air. I watch him close his baby blue eyes for a moment. "I deserved that," he says softly, resuming his advance toward me. I can smell him and my knees shake. Musky and clean. "I want thirty minutes of your time. That's it." His presence is even more intimidating as he moves closer. He was always tall, but now he towers over me. His blue eyes lock on mine and I inhale sharply.

"And what do I get in return?" I take a small step backward, making myself just out of his reach. His eyes drop to my chest as my robe falls off one of my shoulders. He licks his bottom lip slowly as his eyes find their way back up to mine.

"Two things. Your purse." He takes another step toward me, trapping me into the corner of my room, and with one more step he closes in on me. His hands grip my upper arms and his thumb strokes the thin, soft fabric of my robe. I gasp at his touch, my arms trembling under his grasp. "And the truth," he says, pinching his eyes closed before opening them again. "You deserve the truth."

"What if I don't want the truth?" I try to shrug him off of me, but he inches even closer, pinning me firmly up against the wall. I can feel every one of his rigid muscles through the thin fabric of my robe, and my entire traitorous body reacts to his closeness. My nipples tighten against his chest and my heart races along with his. The air between us is wrapped in the slightest hints of beer and the same cologne that enveloped me in his bed last night. Heat pools between my legs as Cole brushes the knuckles of one hand over my cheek before pulling his hand away while his other hand grips my other arm firmly.

"Would you rather live the rest of your life believing a lie?" He releases my arm and I can feel the warmth of his breath against my face he's so close. His blue eyes penetrate mine, looking for my answer. An answer I can't give because I want nothing more than the truth, but I don't know that I'm strong enough to handle his truth.

I close my eyes, my entire body trembling—with fear and with need...of the truth and for Cole Ryan.

Both of his hands drop to his sides as he takes a step back, and I immediately miss his closeness. "You know where to find me," he says, his voice is full of despair. "When you're ready."

I swallow hard against my dry throat as Cole disappears out of my bedroom, the door slamming closed behind him.

I spend the next couple of hours curled up next to mama, hoping that being near her will calm me down. The walls are thin in this house, and from the look on her face when I came into her room, I know she heard everything.

Not a word is spoken about Cole, but he is the elephant in the room. Mama looks at me with sad eyes, knowing he's my one true love—but also the person who broke me.

She squeezes my arm with her good hand and tucks my head under her chin while we watch a movie in her room, her silent way of comforting me. I finally give in and kiss her good-night, so I can put myself to bed in hopes of sleeping all thoughts of Cole away.

But for the next few hours, I toss and turn wildly in my bed as the realization settles in...there is no getting over Cole. I can still smell him in my room. I can still feel his hard body pressed against mine. Sweat beads along my hairline as I wrestle between wanting to know the truth and leaving the past behind me.

Seconds, minutes, and hours tick by when I finally give in and push myself out of bed. I slip into a pair of flip-flop sandals and pull a sweater on over my silk camisole and pajama shorts. Twisting my doorknob slowly, I pray the hinges don't squeak as I pull the door open and sneak quietly down the hallway.

Once I'm safely outside, I haul ass across the street and right up the front steps of his porch. I ball my fist and beat on his door—hard. It might be three-thirty in the morning, but I'll be damned if he's going to sleep when I can't.

I wiggle my toes as I wait a few seconds before banging again. The turn of the lock jolts me as the door flies open.

Cole is stepping into a pair of jeans. "What the fuuu—" he mumbles before suddenly stopping when he sees me standing in front of him. His jeans never made it the entire way up, and I can't help but stare at the familiar way they hang open, resting on his hips. His boxer briefs are on full display, along with his toned abs and that trail of fine hair that leads from his navel down into the waistband of those briefs. I pinch my eyes closed for a moment, drowning out the memory of what's underneath those briefs.

I meet his wary gaze and, square my shoulders and lift my chin, taking in a deep breath and clearing my throat. "I'm ready."

He blows a puff of air from his mouth and shakes his head. Running a hand through his mussed-up hair, he opens the door wider with his other hand. "It's three-thirty in the morning, Frankie, but by all means come on in."

I step over the threshold, my shoulder brushing against his bare chest. I pull my sweater tighter and wrap my arms around my waist as Cole closes and locks the door behind us. I notice my bare legs poking out from under the sweater as I catch a glimpse of myself in a mirror. Maybe it was a mistake to come straight here in my pajamas, but it's too late as I follow Cole through the main living room and into the kitchen.

"Want something to drink?" he asks over his shoulder as he pulls a coffee filter out of a cupboard and drops it into the coffee pot. It's impossible to miss how his body has changed from the lean young man he was ten years ago into the solid man he is today. The curve of every muscle is on full display with every movement he makes.

"No, thanks." I drop my eyes from him and rub my arms briskly to fight off the shiver that just rippled through my body.

He glances at me quickly before he dumps coffee grounds directly into the filter without measuring and presses start on the display. The coffee maker purrs to life and the smell of fresh brewed coffee begins to fill the kitchen.

"Suit yourself, but this isn't going to be a quick conversation, so—" He stops himself and looks at me, pinning me with his blue eyes. Pulling his bottom lip in between his teeth, he leans against the kitchen counter, his hip resting against the stone countertop as he clears his throat. "What I'm asking you, Frankie, is that you please hear me out. That you promise not to leave or walk away until I'm finished." His tired blue eyes plead with me to stay—to not run like I always do.

I begrudgingly nod in response and his shoulders fall as he visibly relaxes, a deep sigh escaping his perfect lips.

He whispers, "Thank you," before turning and pulling two coffee mugs out of his cupboard. He empties the coffee pot into the two mugs, handing me one, clearly ignoring my earlier response declining a drink.

"Trust me. You're going to want coffee." He looks at the clock on the wall, reminding me that this is the middle of the night and not exactly a convenient time for this conversation—not that there ever would be a good time. "Follow me." He nods his head and I follow behind him down the hallway toward his bedroom. Only we don't turn left into his bedroom, we turn right into what I remember was his father's room. He flips on the lights and what used to be his father's room has been transformed into a huge office with a library and sitting area. French doors were added that lead to an outdoor patio, but Cole gestures me over to the sitting area. A plush couch and two oversized chairs are positioned in front of a stone fireplace, creating a comfortable ambience.

My eyes take in the room, blinking in awe at how beautifully the space was transformed and just how remarkably different it looks. I would've never guessed this was once a bedroom. The closet doors have been removed and replaced with built-in bookshelves.

Cole notices me looking and entertains my curiosity. "After Pops died, I had a hard time coming in this room. Everything reminded me of him and how sick he got. Carter suggested I make the space something usable instead of leaving the door closed and shutting my memories inside here. So we made it my office and sitting room." His face looks pained as he speaks of his father's memory and the space that was once his.

"It's beautiful," I remark quietly. "You've done a lot to the house. You'd never guess that from seeing the outside—" I stop myself, realizing how bitchy that sounds. But the front porch is basically a dilapidated mess, however once you walk through the front door you're moved into an entirely different world.

He nods, taking a seat on the couch. "There are some memories I wasn't ready to touch just yet." He swallows hard and sips his coffee, my heart sinking because I know his meaning—the front porch. We'd spend hours on each other's porches talking, sharing...planning our futures. Our last night together we sat on his front porch and I told him of my plans to get us out of Crescent Ridge...to get married and start a family. I should have sensed something was different about him that night, but I didn't realize then that he was already so far gone from me at that time.

He pins me with his gaze and I take a seat opposite him on one of the oversized chairs. I tuck my feet up under my bottom and hold the large mug of coffee in both hands. For not wanting a drink, I'm thankful for something to hold as it steadies my shaking hands.

"Frankie," he pauses, "before I start, I have to ask you...are you happy?" His eyes fall to my left hand, particularly my ring finger where Ted's ring sits.

Anger bubbles just below the surface, because that's not why I'm here. I'm not here to talk about whether I'm happy. I'm not here to talk about Ted. I'm here for the truth about what happened all those years ago.

I sigh loudly, showing my annoyance. "Cole—"

His eyes are full of pain as he cuts me off. "Answer me, Frankie."

"I am," I reply. "I'm happy." I lie. I don't even know what I feel anymore. I'm comfortable with Ted. He provides some level of stability to my life, but I can't say he's the love of my life.

He nods again, and leans forward, resting his elbows on his knees. His head falls forward and he shakes it back and forth as if shrugging off unwanted thoughts. Silence fills the space between us as I wait for him to begin, and I squeeze the ceramic mug again to calm my fraying nerves.

Clearing his throat, he lifts his head and looks directly into my eyes. His fingers are laced together and he bobs his knees nervously. I've never seen Cole so out of sorts. Ever. Cole was always the epitome of collected and put together, never letting his nerves or anxiety get the better of him.

"Ten years ago," he starts, his voice steady but low, "you believed a lie I put into place." I inhale sharply and my back stiffens. "I was never *with* Whitney Carson. Ever."

He wasn't...?

My heart pounds in my chest and I rub my stomach that hurts so much it feels like I might vomit. But...I'll never forget seeing them kiss on his front porch or the swell of her stomach when she ran over to me that night after I saw them. What does he mean he wasn't with her?

"I saw you—"

He shakes his head. "You saw me kiss her. That's all, Frankie. Let me finish, please."

Kiss her. He makes it sound so trivial. He kissed her when he was with me. He kissed her when he was *my* boyfriend. Anger courses through my veins and I feel heat flush my face as he continues.

"That was the first and only kiss...despite the rumors you may have heard. I begged her to play along with my lie and she hated it." He rubs his forehead and his eyes are full of shame.

I chew on my bottom lip, drawing blood as I bite back the wrath I want to unleash from inside me.

"The last time you came home...prior to that," he clears his throat. "I saw how much you'd changed. In a good way, Frankie. You were blossoming into the woman you were always meant to be. Your face brightened when you'd talk about your classes, your friends, and preparing for law school. You were living your dreams, and I was holding you back." His voice breaks and he pauses to clear his throat. I scoff but don't say anything, and I can feel my blood pressure rise as he recalls that visit home. I remember it as clearly as he does. "Frankie, I was never leaving Crescent Ridge. I didn't have the ambition you did. I was always meant to take over Pop's auto shop and live here." He points his finger toward the floor as if all of Crescent Ridge is here in this house. "You were bound for bigger things, and as much as I loved you...still love you," his eyes hold mine at that confession, "you were bound for bigger things than Crescent Ridge, and me, so I used Whitney to push you away."

My eyes blur with tears and I can feel my chin trembling. I

know this is his story to tell, but goddammit it's my story, too. It was my future he decided to change without a discussion. One single lie he let me believe changed our lives forever. My head spins as my lungs tighten and I can barely breathe. I feel like I might hyperventilate, but manage to speak.

"So you thought you'd make a decision that impacted me? Us? Without talking to me first?" I snap at him. The mug of coffee shakes in my hand, threatening to spill because of how angry I am and how hard my hands are shaking. "So you made up a story about Whitney Carson and let me believe that story for ten fucking years, Cole?" I scream at him, no longer holding back.

Tears flood my eyes and my chin trembles. "You could've just broken up with me. You could've told me you didn't love me anymore!" I scream.

He shakes his head and rakes his hand over his face. The tears I've been holding back break free from my eyes as a sob escapes my throat. I feel Cole's hand brush against mine as he pulls the coffee mug from my hand and kneels down in front of me. He pulls my hands into his and holds on for dear life. "God, Frankie, I'm so sorry." His voice breaks.

"The baby?" I ask in between sobs, pulling my hands out of his grasp. I don't want him touching me.

"Wasn't mine." His voice is firm, and I believe him. "Branson Miller was the father. She gave the baby up for adoption."

"But you let me believe—" I choke out. My entire world just came crashing down around me with Cole's confession.

He nods and swallows hard. "Biggest mistake of my life. Behind letting you go. I used her to push you away, Frankie."

All the anger I've been holding onto, the bitterness, the

rage breaks free and I raise my hand and slap him across his face as hard as I can. The slap echoes in the room, such a satisfying sound that I'm able to ignore the intense sting in my hand. I hate violence. Despise it. But something inside me snaps. He closes his eyes and pulls his lips into his mouth as I lose control. I kick my feet out from underneath me and begin kicking toward him, pushing him away from me. "I hate you!" I cry, the tears coming in buckets. So many decisions were made on Cole's lie and I hate him for that. "I fucking hate you!"

His large hands grab my upper arms, pressing them to my sides as he tries to calm me, but my mouth has a mind of its own now. "Fuck you, Cole. Fuck. You." The tears come harder as my fury grows. Ten years of pent up anger I release. The prison I've been living in just opened its doors.

He stops my assault by pulling me up from the chair and wrapping me in his arms tightly, engulfing me in his embrace. "I'm so sorry, Frankie. Please forgive me," he begs.

But there aren't enough apologies to forgive what he's done —what he's destroyed. I shake in his arms, but I'm too tired to fight anymore. I fall into his chest, letting him hold me and I simply cry as I release ten years of hurt and anger. I cry for his lies and for mine. I cry for the pain he's caused and how those lies changed the course of our lives forever. The days we'll never get back, and the sacrifices I made based on those lies. Everything inside my body hurts.

Cole felt he was doing something good by letting me go, when in reality he destroyed everything I ever wanted and everything we had planned together. His lies destroyed everything I believed in.

ELEVEN

My face still stings from her slap. She got me good, and fuck, I deserved so much more than a slap across the face. Her entire body trembles under my embrace, but I refuse to let her go. She'll run and I'm so fucking tired of her running. I've been holding her for nearly an hour, and I'll hold her for twelve more if that's what it takes for her to stay and talk to me. I need her forgiveness...hell, I need *her*.

Her crying has finally subsided, and I press my lips to the top of her head, praying she can feel the kisses I'm pouring into her, feel the love for her I never let die. I believed I was doing the right thing in letting her go—letting her live a life she deserved outside of this shitty small town, and me.

To see the damage I've caused to her is unbearable. The pain on her face when I told her about my lie damn near destroyed me. The hurt she's been holding onto all this time is something I'll never forgive myself for.

Frankie finally wrestles herself out of my arms, and I gently guide her down to the couch. She eases herself onto one end and looks up at me. "Why, Cole? Why couldn't you talk to me?" Her voice trembles and I shake my head.

Because you deserved better than what I could give.

I swallow against the growing lump in my throat and sit down next to her. Her hands sit on her lap, and I want so badly to lace my fingers through hers, but I won't try to touch her like that.

I simply answer her honestly. "Because I loved you too much to let you sacrifice your dreams for me." I choke back the tears I feel forming in my eyes. It's the most honest I've been with Frankie, and also myself.

She nods her head slowly and sniffles. "And I loved you so much that I would have sacrificed everything—for you." She turns her head and looks at me. "You were the only thing I ever wanted, Cole. I fell in love with you the first day I met you. I was eleven years old—" Her voice shakes with emotion, and I remember that day like it was yesterday, because that was the day I fell in love with her, too. "What's that saying? The truth shall set you free?" She takes a sharp breath. "Bullshit, sometimes the truth hurts worse than the fucking lie."

She pushes herself up from the couch and turns toward me. "So fuck you and fuck your truth, Cole." Her eyes hold the pain of the world and I hate myself for that. Tears pool in her pain filled eyes when she turns on her heel and walks away, grabbing her purse that's been sitting on top of my desk on her way out. As her footsteps lead her away from me, I hear the faint sound of her sobs begin again as she disappears down the hallway, the front door slamming behind her as she leaves.

～

"So, you told her everything?" Carter asks me again while pouring himself a cup of coffee. I don't have it in me to retell the entire conversation, or discuss the pain in her eyes or the disgusted look on her face...or the one that displayed pure hatred toward me.

I nod my head as it's about all I can muster up the strength to do right now.

"And from the looks of you, I assume it didn't go well?" He stands, his hip leaning against my kitchen counter.

I rake my hands up my face and through my hair, stopping to rub my eyes that burn from lack of sleep and frustration. "What the hell kind of question is that, Carter?" I bark at him as I push myself up from the kitchen table, the legs of my chair scraping against the hardwood floor. "Of course it didn't fucking go well." How the hell did he think that conversation would go? That I'd tell her the truth and she'd fall in my arms and forgive me?

"So what now?" he asks.

I sigh in frustration. "What the fuck do you think? We move on. She knows the truth now. It didn't change anything. She still hates me. End of story."

Carter furrows his brows at me and slams his mug of coffee on the kitchen counter. "So you're just gonna let her walk away again? Because, if you do, you're a bigger fucking idiot than I already thought you were."

My anger intensifies and I clench my fists. "What choice do I fucking have, Carter? I told her the truth. I cleared my conscience. She slapped me. I apologized. She left. Seems pretty fucking clear to me—"

I'm cut off by the loud bang of his empty ceramic mug being tossed into the stainless steel sink. "You're a bigger pussy now than you were ten years ago, you know that?" He moves across the kitchen and positions himself right in my face. He may be shorter and smaller, but Carter is the only person who's ever had the balls to stand up to me. Disappointment crawls across his face. "I watched you self-destruct for ten fucking years because of a lie you told Frankie. I watched what it did to both of my friends and the pain it caused. Now that you've confessed to Frankie, you're just going to let her go—"

I cut him off. "How many times are you going to have this conversation with me? She's engaged, Carter." I pound my pointer finger into his chest, causing him to take a step backward. "She's marrying another man. She told me she was happy." I feel my anger turn to sadness, and I pause, trying to swallow back my emotions.

My heart races and my stomach flips as I think about that diamond ring on her finger, and her saying the words 'I do' to someone else. It should be *me* she's saying those words to. It should be *my* ring on her finger. But I have to come to terms with the fact that I pushed her away and she's moved on. Rightfully so.

My voice lowers to just above a whisper. "She's happy," I repeat.

Carter stands there watching me with cautious eyes, allowing the words I can't say to speak for themselves. She's happy, and I'm not going to ruin that again. I need to let her go. Those words sting, which is why I can't say them—or maybe because I don't want to believe them.

Carter takes a deep breath and swallows hard, his cautious eyes turning dark. "She's as big a fucking liar as you are," he hisses at me, bumping his shoulder into mine as he passes me, nearly knocking me over on his way out.

~

"Hello?" I answer my cell phone from a number I don't recognize with a Los Angeles area code. A familiar sounding voice fills the line, but I'm having a hard time placing who it is.

"Is this Cole Ryan?"

"Speaking."

"This is Jack Vanderbilt. A good friend gave me your information, said you're the best of the best when it comes to auto restoration."

I'm momentarily taken aback by the fact that Jack fucking Vanderbilt is calling me. He's a television morning show co-host, he has his own production company, and he's also a radio host. He's one of America's most popular celebrities and has his hand in every aspect of the entertainment industry.

"I appreciate the referral," I respond, grabbing a notebook from my desk.

For the next several minutes, he rattles off the details of the car he has and would like me to refurbish from bumper to bumper. He doesn't blink an eye when I tell him it'll cost upward of two hundred thousand dollars, and that's a blind estimate. It could go higher once I get my eyes on the car and see its condition and what I'm going to be working with.

As I do with all my clients before I accept a vehicle, I do a thorough inspection. But Mr. Vanderbilt also doesn't blink an eye about flying me to Los Angeles to do the inspection, or the cost I've asked to do it. He takes my information and tells me his assistant will be in contact within the hour to schedule travel arrangements. Hell, I'm surprised his assistant wasn't the one who called me. He wants this done as soon as possible and is willing to pay a premium to get it done.

For the last eight years, I've had non-stop restoration business and it's helped me invest back into Crescent Ridge. I'm not only thankful for the income it has brought in but for the distraction that I know I'm going to need now more than ever.

I prop my feet up on the corner of my desk and lean back in my desk chair. My head drops back as I rub my temples where they've been pounding since Frankie left. Last night's beerfest, the lack of sleep, and all my emotions simmering at the surface are all taking its toll on me. Maybe a short getaway will do me some good and allow me to clear my head.

I push myself upright, glancing out the window and across the street. I must've sat in this chair for nine thousand nights looking out this window, waiting to see if Frankie would come home, and here she is fifty yards away, only it still feels like seven hundred miles. Headlights catch my attention and I recognize Faith's car rolling to a stop outside just as Frankie bounds down the front porch, dragging a suitcase behind her. Faith meets her in the driveway where they both embrace.

Faith holds Frankie's head and kisses her forehead before they both wipe tears from their cheeks. My heart sinks when I realize she's leaving me—again.

Faith helps Frankie load her suitcase into the trunk of the Mercedes and my heart beats wildly, adrenaline coursing through my veins. I push myself up from the desk and hurry to the front door. My gut says to let her go, but my heart won't let me.

It takes me less than five seconds to cross my front lawn where I pause at the edge of the street. The pain on Frankie's face takes my breath away as she cries into Faith's shoulder. Faith rubs circles on Frankie's back, comforting her as she looks over Frankie's shoulder and sees me approach. A quick shake of her head warns me to stay where I'm at, but everything inside me is calling me across that street.

"Frankie," I call to her, her head snapping up.

"Don't," Faith warns me as my feet carry me across the broken asphalt. I ignore her warning but proceed cautiously.

"Frankie, please—"

"Please what, Cole?" she barks, rubbing her eyes with the back of her hand. Her pale face is splotchy and red from crying.

"Please, don't go."

She lets out a low guttural laugh and slowly puts one foot in front of the other, descending down her driveway toward me, stopping just out of my reach.

"What right do you think you have asking me to stay?" she asks, her chest heaving as if she's just run a marathon. Her wavy hair is piled on top of her head and her lips are pursed. Her bloodshot eyes highlight just how beautiful the blue irises are, and her dark lashes are coated in tears as she licks her lips and waits for me to answer.

"I don't want you to go," I tell her, reaching out my hand as if she'll reach out in return and take it. Instead she takes a step backward as if I'm dangerous. My heart plummets as she retreats.

"You ruined everything!" she screams at me, stumbling backward. Faith jogs down and wraps her arm around Frankie's shoulder and guides her back up the driveway. "You ruined my life," she cries and buries her face into her hands.

"Stop it," Faith says, hushing her and whispering into her

ear before turning back to me, disappointment in her eyes. "Leave, Cole."

I ignore Faith's request. "I didn't ruin your life, Frankie—"

"Stop!" Faith yells over her shoulder at me and if looks could kill I'd be a dead man. "Leave."

I raise my hands in surrender and walk backward across the street, my eyes never leaving Frankie.

Only my gut tells me this is it. This is the last time I'm going to see her. "I'm sorry, Frankie. I'm so goddamn sorry. Please listen to me." My voice breaks and I let it. She's hurting and it's literally eating me alive.

The taillights on her Mercedes blink as the driver's door opens and she slides into the front seat. Déjà vu hits me as the car roars to life and she puts the car in reverse, backing out of her driveway. There's something more real about her leaving this time, something so final. Just like before, she drives away leaving me here in Crescent Ridge, and there's not a damn thing I can do but let her go.

TWELVE

Frankie

I don't even know how I manage to focus on the road in front of me. Between bouts of crying and internal rationalization, I know leaving Crescent Ridge, again, is for the best. Mom is doing better than I anticipated, and now that Faith is home, and with the help of the nurses, I know Mom is in good hands. There's no need for me in Crescent Ridge.

The further I get away from that little town and my past, the more I realize how I never really got over Cole. I buried us, but never dealt with us. Cole is a scab covering my broken heart that never fully healed. The kind that pulls up at the edges when bumped slightly and begins to bleed all over again. Seeing him again, listening to his apology ripped that scab off and reopened that gaping wound.

All of the pain we endure over the course of our lives leaves us full of battle scars. In time, the pain eventually heals, but the scars always remain, reminding us of where we've been, and the battles we've endured. Except Cole will never be a scar—he'll always be a gaping wound on my heart that never heals.

The clock on my car display tells me it's just past nine-thirty in the evening. I still have three hours ahead of me until I make it back to Los Angeles. I've tried calling Ted numerous times, only his phone goes straight to voice mail, so I call the only other person who knows about my history with Cole—Ashley, my college roommate and best friend.

As the phone rings and rings, it's hard not to remember all that Ashley and I have been through, and memories of freshman year come racing back.

A light sweat sprinkles my forehead as I jog across campus to get back to my dorm room as quickly as possible. I finished my last final of my freshman year and my mind is on one thing—getting home to Cole.

"Ash," I holler as I push open our dorm room door, pulling the key from the lock.

"In here," she answers me with her soft voice. I find Ashley, my roommate, with her head stuck in the built-in wardrobe, pulling shirts off of hangers and folding them neatly before placing them in moving boxes.

"I'm done. I'm headed out," I muster as I try to catch my breath.

She lifts her head and twists her lips into a pout. "You said you weren't leaving until tomorrow."

"I know, but I just want to get home. There's no sense in delaying—"

She interrupts me. "So you're going to tell him?"

"I can't not tell him, Ash." I take a deep breath and wipe the small beads of sweat from my forehead with the back of my hand.

She cocks an eyebrow and glances at me out of the side of her eye. "You sure you don't want to spend the summer with me in Malibu? Take the summer off to decide what you're going to do? Relax with me at my parents' country club?" She grins at me and bites her lip.

I release a loud sigh. "Ash, you know I can't afford to spend one night in Malibu, let alone the summer. And I know what I'm going to do." I pull my last duffle bag off the twin-size bed that was mine for the last nine months and steady the strap over my shoulder.

Ashley steps over the box of clothes she was just packing and places both of her hands on my shoulders. "It's my parents' house, silly. You wouldn't have to pay a thing, you know that. And I'm going to be home alone most of the summer while my parents are in Europe. I need someone to keep me company. My parents would consider that payment enough," she pouts.

I offer her a tight smile. "I can't. I need to get back to Crescent Ridge—"

"No," she interrupts me. "You need to get back to Cole Ryan." Her eyes lift knowingly.

"Cole..." I smile. "I miss him—"

"I know you do, but Frances, Crescent Ridge is in the middle of the desert. Literally in the middle of nowhere. You should be where it's civilized and—"

"It's not in the middle of nowhere," I correct her.

"Close enough. The nearest town is thirty some miles away. You don't even have a Starbucks for Christsake."

I tap her nose jokingly. "We have the Ridge Diner and their coffee is better than any one of those sugary Starbucks drinks."

She sighs loudly and blinks her green eyes rapidly. "It's just that I'm really going to miss you, and next year won't be the same—"

"That's your fault." I laugh at her. "You were the one who wanted to rush a sorority and move into the house."

She rolls her eyes at me and tosses her long blonde hair over her shoulder. "It's a legacy thing. My mother did it, my grandmother did it...they'd kill me if I didn't. They almost killed me for not doing it this year." She sighs.

I reach out and touch her forearm. "Hey, I'm happy for you, Ash. You're going to be living with a great group of girls. I'll be fine. And I'll be fine in the Ridge." I pull the strap of the duffle bag up a little higher on my shoulder to balance the weight since it's so heavy.

She gives me a longing look before returning to her packing. "You tell Cole he better take care of you."

Ashley and I are polar opposites on pretty much everything, but we became the best of friends the day I moved into the dorms at the University of Southern California. We're the unlikely duo. She's blonde, I'm brunette. She's rich, I'm not. She's destined to be a trophy wife and I'm studying my ass off to be a lawyer. She's all about having fun, and I'm all about trying to graduate as soon as possible so I can start my career and life with Cole Ryan. She's everything I'm not, and I'm everything she's not.

"Give me that piece of shit phone of yours," she grumbles, swiping away a stray tear. She begins pounding on the screen

before handing the phone back to me, and I notice that she's changed her name from Ash to Best Friend.

I smile at her warmly. "You are my best friend, Ashley."

She lets out a little laugh. "I'm your only friend." Sadly, she's right.

"You're such a bitch." I swat at her and begin moving toward the door.

"You love me," she calls after me.

Turning around, my lips pull into a giant smile. "I do." I'm so lucky to have Ashley for a friend. I'm not sure I would have survived my freshman year away from Cole without her. She's the kind of friend who'd help you bury a body and take that secret to the grave with her.

"Frances? Please call me if you need anything." She raises her eyebrows and pulls her lips between her teeth. "And maybe call me, just to talk, ya know." Her voice breaks.

I glance over my shoulder and see her choking back her emotions. I turn around and walk over to her, pulling her into a tight hug. "You know I will."

"And when you come back in the fall, check your shitty attitude at the door. You've been a real piece of work the last few weeks." She squeezes me back hard.

I smile and tilt my head at her. "I'm just tired. You know I haven't been feeling well."

"You're love sick," she sighs with a chuckle.

I roll my eyes, but she knows the truth. My heart swells at the thought of seeing Cole in only seven short hours. "Maybe just a little bit."

The sound of her voice pulls me from the past. "I was wondering if you'd ever call me again now that you're some famous lawyer," she says, answering the phone with a small laugh. Normally I'd joke around with her, only I'm not in the right frame of mind.

"Ash?" I respond, my voice breaking.

I hear her inhale sharply at the sound of my voice. The tone of her voice changes from joking to serious. "Frances, what's wrong?" I can hear shuffling on her end of the line before she speaks again. "Talk to me. Are you okay?"

I can feel the lump in my throat growing as it sits heavily at the base of my neck. I swallow hard, trying to choke it down. "There's so much I need to tell you." My voice cracks again. Emotion is not something I show freely. I've been trained to bury it. Stick to facts. Articulate issues and derive solutions. It's the lawyer in me. Only Cole isn't an issue I can derive a solution to. "Cole—" I manage to get his name out as the tears start to fall.

"Jesus, Mary, and Joseph," she says under her breath. "Start from the beginning. I've got all night so don't spare any details."

This is what I love about Ashley. She'll drop what she's doing at the drop of a dime for me and I couldn't love her more for it. She knows my deepest secrets and has held my hand through the hardest events of my life. She is a true friend, and I'll be indebted to her and her family forever. After college, Ashley moved to Washington D.C. to work as a lobbyist on Capitol Hill. We may have lived across the country from each other, but our friendship and support never wavered.

As I get myself together, I take a deep breath and start at the beginning, telling her how out of the blue Cole called to tell me about my mom. As the sky gets darker and lights of Los

Angeles become nearer, Ashley listens intently for the next hour and a half and I spare her no details on what happened back in Crescent Ridge.

"He still loves you." I hear her pop the cork on a bottle of wine. Oh, how I wish I was sitting with her on a couch, sipping on a glass of wine. "He fucked up so bad, Frances, but he still loves you." She pauses. "And I know you love him. He was the kind of love you never get over."

I hold my breath for a moment as I think about what Ashley's just said. "I'm getting married, Ash. To Ted. I moved on from Cole a long, long time ago."

"But have you really? What if there was no Ted?" Her voice echoes in what I assume is her wine glass.

"Well, there *is* a Ted. So we're not playing what-ifs, all right?"

"I'm just saying, if the circumstances were right—"

"Ashley!" I bark at her and she instantly quiets. "Besides, there's no coming back from where we've been." My heart aches as I say that.

"Did you tell him about—"

"No!" I cut her off. "That's my secret," I start before she interrupts me this time.

"No, Frances. It's not. He deserves to know the truth." I hear her sigh loudly as she waits for me to respond. Only I can't. Because she's right. "Look, Frances," her voice is quiet and calm, "just think about it. He deserves to know the truth about this as much as you deserved to know the truth about what happened between you two ten years ago. And the truth fucking hurts, but maybe it's time everything is out in the open."

I nod, swallowing the lump in my throat. I know she can't

see me, but I know my best friend and I know she knows I agree with her.

"Call me when you get home," she says. "It's getting late, but I'll be up and I need to know you made it back safely."

"Okay," I whisper and bite my bottom lip.

"I love you, Frances, and you're going to get through this and come out stronger on the other end—just as you've always done."

"Love you, too, Ash." I disconnect the call just as the tears begin to fall...again.

It's nearly one in the morning when I finally pull into my neighborhood. A few more blocks and I'll be home—leaving Crescent Ridge and all of that stress behind me. I remember that Ashley wanted me to call, so I quickly press the dial button from my steering wheel, allowing the Bluetooth in my car to call her back. Ringing fills the quiet car until she answers.

"You made it?" she asks, her voice just above a whisper.

"Yeah. Just turning down my street right now."

"Good. I was getting worried. I figured you should've been home by now."

"Yeah, you know L.A. traffic," I begin just as a white BMW that I don't recognize comes into view...parked in my driveway. "Ash?"

"Yeah?"

"There's a car in the driveway..." My voice hitches. "I've been trying to call him for the last two days and he hasn't answered or returned any of my calls which is so unlike him."

Ted never has people over, and he doesn't really have any friends—this has to be another attorney from the firm and they're working on their case here instead of the office this late at night.

"Don't panic," she instructs.

"I'm not panicked," I lie, because something just doesn't seem right.

"I'll stay on the line with you until you're inside."

My heart races as my gut is twisting into knots. I step out of the car, leaving everything behind except my phone and car keys. My hands shake as I fumble with the key in the lock of the front door, finally pushing it open. There on the floor of the foyer sits a Louis Vuitton purse and a pair of black pumps.

"Oh, Jesus," I mumble as I choke down the wave of nausea rushing through me.

"Talk to me, Frances," Ashley says, but I can't form any words.

The house is mostly dark as my feet carry me up the stairs to the master bedroom. "Please, no," I whisper to myself over and over as panic washes over me.

"Frances," Ashley calls to me, her voice growing more urgent. "Tell me what's happening."

I reach the master bedroom doors, pausing as my fingers wrap around the lever handle. I can hear the soft sounds of laughter coming from behind the double doors. Bile rises up into my throat as I turn the handle and push open the door.

My eyes find a trail of clothes across the bedroom floor and over to the bed where Ted has a woman pinned beneath him. He doesn't even bother to stop fucking her when his head jerks around to find me standing in the doorway, watching him. The woman squeals in delight, not knowing that I'm watching my fiancé fuck her in my bed. I hang up on Ashley as my entire body shakes from the sight of Ted with another woman.

In one swift motion, I reach for my left hand, yanking the obnoxious diamond ring off my ring finger before throwing it at Ted. It lands with a thud on the bed next to him.

"Frances!" Ted calls to me in surprise as I turn on my heel and run down the steps and out the front door to my car.

"Fuck you!" I scream as the door slams closed behind me. I sit momentarily in the driver's seat, stunned and shocked at what I just walked in on. In a million years, I never would have expected this from Ted. My cell phone rings and rings as Ashley tries to get in touch with me, but I'm too in shock to even form words at the moment.

Without another thought, I push the start button and back out of the driveway, destination unknown. Funny how life can be a fickle little bitch. In a matter of seven hours, I left my past in Crescent Ridge and lost my future in Los Angeles.

THIRTEEN

Twelve hours ago, I watched Frankie drive away from me for the final time. And for twelve hours I've sat on this front porch and stared at the empty driveway across the street, hoping I'll see her pull back in.

I rub my eyes with the heels of my palms, hoping to relieve some of the burning, but nothing will take away the sting of watching her flee. Twice I've watched the woman I love leave —and the second time wasn't any easier than the first.

The first time, I was too big of a coward to cross the street and let her go the way she deserved. This time, I begged her to stay and the reality of the pain I caused slapped me in the face.

Frankie's face twisted in pain at the lies I put in place hurt more than watching her leave. For me, I'll rightfully live my miserable life in the prison of my lies.

The front door slams across the street and Faith bounds down the rickety steps, twisting a sweater tight around her waist. Her hair is wild and her flip-flops smack the bottom of her feet as she crosses the street. Dammit, she's headed right for me, and I'm in no fucking mood to deal with her attitude right now.

"What the fuck do you want, Faith?" I bark from my chair.

"Why did you pull that shit yesterday, Cole?"

"What shit are you speaking of? The one where I asked Frankie not to go—because that's not shit, Faith. That was me laying it on the line." Maybe a decade too late, but at least I did it.

She snorts and moves closer, narrowing her eyes at me. "Laying it on the line? By telling her about your twisted, fucked up lies, and then hoping she'd forgive you at the drop of a dime and stay?"

I push back out of my chair, the legs screeching on the worn wood as I stand up. "Do you have any idea how long I wanted to come clean and tell her the truth? Any idea how much I fucking love that woman? Do you, Faith?" I can feel my blood pressure rising as I move in on her. Rage fills me and my voice booms as I stand over her. "Any fucking idea how much it kills me knowing that she's engaged to someone else?" My voice breaks and I turn around so Faith can't see the tears stinging the back of my eyes. "Fuck," I mutter under my breath.

"*Was* engaged—" Faith says, snapping her mouth shut as I quickly turn back to face her.

"What do mean 'was'?"

She looks away from me and snaps her mouth shut.

"What do you mean, Faith?" I ask again.

She turns and looks at me, narrowing her eyes. "It doesn't matter, Cole. She's gone. You chased her away...again."

The truth in her words hurt, but I'm not letting it go this

time. "No, back up. What the fuck do you mean *was* engaged, Faith? I'm not asking again. Answer the goddamn question."

"It's none of your business," she snaps at me.

"Oh, it's my business all right. Frankie will always be my business."

"Oh, fuck off, Cole."

I stand on the porch, my hands clenched in anger. "No, you fuck off. I am so tired of you barking orders at me. What happened was between Frankie and me. And yes, I fucked up. For the rest of my life, I'll live with the regret of my lies. I apologized. I told her the truth—and if I never see her again, all I want is her forgiveness—" Fuck, my voice breaks and I can barely speak against the lump in my throat, but I swallow hard and try. "I love her, Faith. For the rest of my life, until my last breath, I will always love her."

Tears float in Faith's eyes and she steps away from me. "Just leave her alone, Cole. That's all I ask. She's hurting so much right now. Your admission, Mom, Ted—she's fraying at the seams and I'm so afraid she's going—"

I stop her and ask with a plea in my voice. "Tell me what happened with Ted."

She sighs and runs her hand through her hair, tucking it behind her ear. "He cheated on her. She found him in bed with another woman when she got home last night."

My jaw ticks wildly and my knuckles hurt from clenching my fists. The rage I felt earlier was nothing compared to what I'm feeling now. "She saw them?" I ask for clarification and Faith simply nods.

"She's not in a good place right now, Cole. I beg you to please leave her be. She needs time."

I rake my hand over my face, trying to calm my anger. "I

143

don't make promises I can't keep, Faith. But I'll tell you this much. I made the mistake of hurting her once. I'll never make that mistake again."

Faith purses her lips. "What does that mean?"

"That means you can hold me to my word."

She throws her arms up in the air and hisses, "Jesus, Cole. I said leave her alone."

"Goodbye, Faith!" I bark over my shoulder as I head into the house to pack. If I'm going to Los Angeles for work, I'm going to make this trip worth my while.

"If you do anything stupid, I'll kill—" The sound of Faith's voice disappears as I slam the door closed behind me.

I startle awake as the airplane glides to a smooth landing in Burbank. The flight was just over an hour and I must've slept the entire way because I barely remember putting my seat belt on. That's the most sleep I've had in the past two days, and while I'm exhausted, adrenaline still courses through my veins. I exit the airport to find a driver and town car waiting for me.

"Mr. Cole, I'm William." The driver reaches out his hand to shake mine before taking my small carry-on.

I take in the sights as William weaves through the Hollywood Hills like an expert before we pull up to a gated driveway.

"This is us," he announces as he pushes a button and the large gate rolls open. It amazes me how spacious these home sites are for how many seem to be built next to each other.

The car rolls slowly down the long drive, surrounded by a

large, lush front yard, perfectly manicured with a giant fountain right in the center. The house we pull up to is not what I expected. It's historical, most likely built in the late 1930s. A large garage with six garage doors sits just off and behind the house. William pulls up and parks outside the one open garage stall.

"Mr. Ryan, I'll inform Mr. Vanderbilt that you're here." He looks at me through the rearview mirror. I nod and open my door as he continues. "I believe the vehicle you'll be looking at is just inside. Feel free to get started."

"Thank you," I tell him, stepping out onto the driveway. I take in the large house and the enormous yard, impressed but not overwhelmed. It's not until I step into the garage that I catch my breath. Sitting before me is a 1971 Corvette LS6. It's in shitty condition, but these are a rare find. Literally. Only one hundred and eighty-eight were ever produced. I've never worked on one and only ever seen one at a luxury car auction. That particular car sold for over two hundred thousand dollars.

I run my fingers over the faded body and stick my head inside the open window, salivating at the sight of it. It needs everything. A complete overhaul inside and out. I pull out my phone and take a couple of pictures while jotting some notes about the specs.

"Mr. Ryan!" I hear my name before I hear the footsteps approaching. I whip around to find Jack Vanderbilt strolling across the drive, headed directly toward me. He's shorter than I expected, but his inviting smile makes him approachable, likable. "Jack Vanderbilt. Pleasure to meet you." He reaches out and shakes my hand.

"Cole Ryan. Please, just call me Cole." He nods, placing his hands on his hips before he stands back and admires the car.

"How in the hell did you get your hands on one of these?" I shake my head, still in awe of the beauty.

He huffs out a laugh. "Money."

"Well, no shit," I respond and let out a small laugh in return. "Sure makes it easier, huh?"

"It sure does." He steps forward and kicks the tire. "I got into cars as a teenager. Used to putz around on them with my grandpa. I never took a liking for fixing them up, but I sure like to drive them." He chuckles. "Your name came up several times when I was looking to purchase this car. Everyone says you're the best in the country. Low profile, good work, honest."

I swallow as he talks about me. It's weird to hear my name gets tossed around in circles that Jack Vanderbilt runs in.

I turn to look at him and a sense of pride washes over me. If I've done anything right in my life, it was starting this business. "I appreciate that," I tell him. "And this car here is a dream. I'd be honored if you'd let me restore it."

He circles the car, inspecting it alongside me. "So what do you think it will cost to restore it?"

"Depends on what it looks like under the hood. My guess, from the condition on the outside, is that everything will need to be replaced. Engine, motor, the whole nine yards. You're easily looking at one seventy-five, maybe closer to two."

He doesn't bat an eye at the numbers I've just thrown at him. "Let's do it," he says, clapping me on the shoulder.

"Sounds good. I'll draw up a contract and have it sent over. Fifty percent down, and remaining balance is due at delivery. I'll have my guys come and load the car and transport it to my shop once we've both signed the contract. Timing will be difficult to nail down because getting these parts will be the trickiest part of the job."

Jack stands with his hands on his hips and a giant smile on his face. "Understood. I don't care if it takes two years, I want this baby back in pristine condition."

"And that you will." I reach out my hand to shake his. My dad always taught me that a handshake was the way to seal a business deal. He never dealt with contracts, but when I'm working on vehicles that will cost upward of a quarter of a million dollars when I'm done, a contract is what we do.

"I look forward to working with you, man." He looks at his watch and points to the house. "I have to run, but I'll tell my assistant to be expecting the contract."

"Yes, sir."

"Jack," he corrects me. "And William will take you wherever you need to go."

"Thank you. I'll be in touch." And just like that, Jack Vanderbilt disappears.

Glancing back at the car, I grin. A month ago, I'd be damn near giddy at the idea of a project like this to bury myself in. But now, I don't need to bury myself. I need to find Frankie.

"Sir, we're here." William's voice pulls me from my daydream. William steers the car into the drive of The Hollywood Roosevelt Hotel. I should've known Jack Vanderbilt would put me up in some swanky Hollywood hotel. I'd have been fine at the Holiday Inn out in the suburbs.

I reach for the door handle, but not before William gets to

it and opens it for me. "Sir, I'll get your bag to the bellman. You can check in inside. The room is already taken care of, charged to Mr. Vanderbilt's account."

Account? Why in the hell would anyone need an account at a hotel? And I have one small suitcase. I don't need a goddamn bellman to deliver my bag. I nod, grateful for his help. "Thank you, William. I appreciate all of your help today." I reach for my wallet to pull out some cash to tip him, but he holds out his hand to stop me.

"No thanks needed. It was my pleasure." He nods at me and slides back into the driver's seat and slowly drives away. I reach for my suitcase just as the bellman does, but I win, not turning over my small carry-on to a man when I'm more than capable of handling it.

I check in and decide to call it a night, placing a room service order. The suite I'm booked in is reminiscent of some sleek modern new hotel, not a hotel built in the 1920s. Everything in this room is crisp lines, modern design, and vibrant colors with a canopy draping the king-size bed. Not exactly my style, but it's definitely quintessential Hollywood.

A giant cheeseburger, a double order of French fries, and two beers are delivered just as I finish showering and changing into clean clothes. A million thoughts run through my head and my body is tired from the multitude of emotions I'm feeling. Excitement at booking this new car deal with Jack Vanderbilt, devastation over losing Frankie, but also a small sense of determination in finding her and making her mine...again.

Over dinner I text Carter, telling him about the Vanderbilt deal, then I write up the business proposal, terms and conditions, cost estimate, transportation agreement and timeline, packaging it all together and sending it off to Jack Vanderbilt's assistant for his signature. After checking on the progress at The Fault Line, I turn my focus to Frankie...and plotting how I'm going to get her back.

FOURTEEN

Frankie

"Jesus Christ," Eduardo hisses as he sits on the edge of my desk. "In your bed?"

I nod and swallow hard. "In our bed." I'm numb as I tell Eduardo the details of finding Ted with another woman in our bed. The irony is that I should be devastated, broken apart by Ted's infidelity, but I'm not, I'm just...numb. This feeling is so unexpected and the first sign that maybe I didn't really love Ted as I thought I did.

"How long do you think it's been going on?" He grips the edge of my desk and lowers his voice so others in the office can't hear.

I spin from side to side in my desk chair as I think about Eduardo's question. "Not sure. He's been distant for a while, but that happens when he's working on a case. He throws his attention, every ounce of his energy into his cases, and I just assumed that's what was going on." I rub my temples, hoping the growing headache that's come on eases soon. "And I was so busy with my own case..." My voice trails off and I rub my tired eyes. I haven't been sleeping well and I'm not sure if it's because of everything that's happened with Ted or the unsettled feeling I have from leaving Crescent Ridge after Cole spilled the truth about our past.

"Do not blame yourself," Eduardo says, snapping to get my attention. "This is about Ted and his issues. This is not about you and what you were or were not contributing to the relationship. Good men don't cheat on their fiancée, Frances." He raises his eyebrows at me and I nod my head like a robot, just numbly going through the motions of life. "Honestly, you dodged a major bullet finding this out now. Can you imagine if you found out after the wedding?" He picks up a pen off my desk and taps it on his leg.

"I don't want to think about it." I shake my head and shove files of case notes into my bag to study when I get back to the hotel later.

"So where have you been staying?"

"The Loews in Santa Monica," I sigh.

He whistles and pushes himself off my desk. "Damn girl. That's going to get expensive, quick. You know, I have a spare room you can stay in. Jeremy and I would be glad to have you." I smile at him, grateful. Not only is he an excellent attorney, a great mentor, but he's an even better friend.

"You're too sweet." I reach out and squeeze his arm, thankful for his friendship. "I don't want to be an inconvenience, though."

He places his hands on my shoulders. "Stop it. You'd never be an inconvenience. We'd love to have you. Seriously. Stay as long as you want." He smiles at me.

Eduardo is the epitome of perfection in his Tom Ford suit. He's smart, has a great sense of humor and strikingly handsome, he belongs on the runway in Milan, not prosecuting cases for Los Angeles County.

"Thank you," I whisper and pull my laptop bag up on my shoulder.

He reiterates, "I mean it. We'd love to have you."

I run a tired hand through my hair, my fingers getting stuck in the messy waves. "Let me think about it. My mind is in a million places right now and I just need some time to think about my next steps." Like what I'm going to do with my life. Do I stay in Los Angeles? Do I take this new freedom to look for new opportunities elsewhere? I lean into Eduardo and he pulls me into a gentle hug.

"Go. Sleep. We'll talk tomorrow," he says, releasing me. "And look over those notes. I'm dying to pick your brain about this case." It's only three in the afternoon but I feel like I could sleep for days as the exhaustion begins to hit me.

"Deal." I do my best to smile at him, but he sees through my façade. It takes me over an hour to get back to Santa Monica in this traffic, but the time in my car actually allows me to decompress. I let the valet park my car and as I breeze through the entrance, the concierge startles me.

"Ms. Callaway!" he calls from his granite perch. I stop and turn to him as he hustles over to me. "You have a delivery. Shall I send it up immediately?"

I smile at the older gentleman who's wearing a nametag that says 'Roger'.

"Yes, please. That'd be wonderful."

"Very well." He nods and heads back to his desk where he lifts the receiver of his phone and begins speaking.

When I finally make it back to my room, I kick off my shoes and slide down onto the love seat. This morning, after I knew Ted would be at his office, I went back to the house to grab a suitcase full of things I knew I'd need for a few days while I figure out my next steps.

I grabbed a handful of work clothes, athletic clothes, a few casual outfits, my make up, and my accessories, carefully ignoring the engagement ring that sat on the sink in the bathroom where Ted conveniently put it after I threw it at him.

I plan to sneak back tomorrow during the day to grab a few more important things and send a delivery service to pick up the rest of my belongings. It's amazing that everything important to me will fit in a few small boxes. Last night I cried—mostly because I felt ashamed that Ted had cheated on me, that I had failed in yet another relationship. When I finally stopped and was thinking more clearly, I realized I wasn't sad about the absence of not having him in my life—it was that he humiliated me.

I allowed myself to be deceived by another man and that's what pained me more than the fact that I'd just caught my fiancé with another woman—in our bed. I stare numbly at the wall, a sad realization at the lack of emotion I'm showing over losing a fiancé. A firm knock on the door pulls me away from these thoughts and I push myself off the love seat.

"Delivery," the male voice calls from the hallway.

"Coming," I answer just as I twist the knob and pull the door open.

In the hallway is a cart with a huge bouquet of flowers, a bottle of wine, a bag of what I presume is food from the amazing aroma I'm smelling, and a giant basket full of fruits, nuts, and granola bars.

"Ms. Callaway?" the gentleman from room service asks as I admire the display in front of me.

My stomach begins rumbling as I draw in the scent of the food on the table. "Yes, that's me."

"May I enter your room?" he asks as his hands grip the sides of the rolling cart.

"Please," I tell him, stepping aside and holding the door open for him. He carefully guides the rolling table into the room and begins removing the contents, setting them on the small glass dining table and centering the bouquet in the middle. Lastly, he sets the basket of fruit on the sideboard.

He sets up a place setting and leaves the bag of food next to it on the table. As he's wheeling the now empty cart out, I fish some cash from my wallet to tip him. I don't even need to read the card stuck in the middle of the flowers to know they're from Eduardo and Jeremy. No one else would think to feed me —all of me, my stomach, my heart, and my soul. These two men are the absolute best.

I open the boxes of food to find an array of choices: chicken Caesar salad, angel hair pasta tossed with grilled veggies, grilled beef tenderloin, and even a cupcake for dessert. They left nothing out.

I lean in and smell the vibrant flowers and slide the small greeting card from the envelope. "We love you. Eat. Drink. Cry. Come stay with us. E and J." I giggle at the card, touched by their sweetness and generosity, then slide down into the dining room chair, taking a bite of the beef tenderloin. It's moist and cooked medium just as it should be and my stomach growls again as I swallow the tender beef. There is enough food here to feed a small army, however I'm thankful for the variety to choose from. It's been almost a day and a half since I've eaten and all of it looks and smells amazing.

I reach for the bottle of wine, a Pinot Grigio, and uncork it, pouring myself a glass. I toss back a large swig of the chilled liquid, allowing the burn to settle on the back of my tongue before swallowing. The food and the wine temporarily take my mind off of my circumstances and I decide a hot bubble bath will help even more.

Carrying a fresh glass of wine to the bathroom, I set it on the edge of the tub and start the water. I dump in some bubble bath and twist my long hair up into a messy knot on the top of my head. Discarding my clothes, I slink into the silky, warm bath water and let the bubbles consume me. My tense muscles instantly begin to relax as I sip from my glass of wine.

I close my eyes and shut off my mind, allowing myself to just be. I learned a long time ago that life isn't easy. I've weathered storms more brutal than Ted and his betrayal. My phone rings from the other room and I ignore it. Nothing will pull me from the cocoon of warm water right now.

My mind is slightly fuzzy from the glass of wine as the water finally cools to the point where I decide to get out. Carefully, I pull the plug, the water swirling at my feet. Patting myself dry, I wrap the towel around myself, lotioning my arms and legs when a loud knock at the door startles me.

"Shit," I hiss, whipping around, looking for a robe. It's probably room service back to collect the dirty dishes. "Just a minute!" I decide I'll poke my head outside the door and make a mad dash back to the safety of the bathroom while they collect what they need from the room.

I open the door carefully, using it to hide my towel-sheathed body behind it. "Give me one second," I say, peeking around the door, but my breath catches when I see haunting blue eyes staring back at me.

Cole instantly puts his foot between the door and the jamb

so I can't close it. He doesn't speak. He doesn't move. He just stares at me. His face is a pool of hurt, of forgiveness, of longing, yet he says nothing.

"What are you doing here?" I finally ask. My heart beats erratically, bounding off the walls of my ribcage.

He pulls his lips into his mouth and closes his eyes for a brief moment before shaking his head and pulling his foot from the door. "I'm sorry," he mumbles and retreats backward, shoving his hands in the pockets of his worn blue jeans. He's wearing a black leather jacket that matches his dark hair. He's beautifully handsome—even with the hurt he carries on his face.

"How did you know I was here?" I grip the door with one hand and my towel with the other.

He shakes his head again, looks away from me and down the hallway. Swallowing hard, he turns to look back at me. His voice is soft, almost strained. "I went to your office. You weren't there, but there was a man asking a secretary to order flowers and food for you. I heard where he was having it sent." Eduardo. He heard Eduardo.

"So you just came here?" My tone is harsh, and I instantly regret it.

He nods slowly and clears his throat. "I shouldn't have." He takes another step backward as his eyes fall from mine, down my body. I realize now I'm standing in the doorway, the solid door no longer protecting me.

"Then why are you here?" I snap, tightening the towel around me as if it can protect me from the sudden rush of emotions that has been noticeably absent the last few days.

"Because I love you." He doesn't hesitate and his voice doesn't waver. He means what he's saying, his voice may be defeated but it still displays his conviction. He stares at me as his breathing becomes more ragged. "Faith told me what happened—your fiancé...I'm not sorry about that, Frankie. Because I love you. I've always loved you."

My stomach lurches and my heart drops. Faith told him about Ted. Something inside me snaps. Tears fill my eyes and my lips tremble. "So you thought you could just show up in Los Angeles and find me?"

"Forgive me, Frankie." His voice and eyes are so full of emotion. "I came here to ask you to forgive me. I'll get on my fucking knees and beg if that's what it takes." He takes a step forward, closing in on me.

My chest rises and falls with each rapid breath I take. I raise my chin and close my eyes. "If I forgive you, will you leave?"

He exhales loudly in defeat and takes a step back. He shakes his head then pulls his bottom lip into his mouth, holding back whatever it is he's wanting to say. "Never mind," he mumbles. With sad eyes, he studies my face the way he used to so long ago. With a quiet exhale, he closes his eyes, holding them closed for a few moments before he turns and slowly walks away.

His shoulders are slumped forward and his hands are still tucked deep in his front pockets. His large frame suddenly seems smaller as I watch him walk away, the distance between us growing with each step he takes.

"Cole," I call to him and he slows to a stop. He doesn't turn around, instead he simply stands in the middle of the hallway, defeated and broken. "For what it's worth, I forgave you a long time ago." My words echo in the hallway and his head falls back for a moment before I see him nod. In acceptance or in defeat, I'm not sure. However, without a word, without turning around to look at me, he continues walking away from me. This time, he's the one that leaves.

It's been nearly two hours since Cole knocked on my hotel room door, told me he still loves me, and then walked away. After he left, I promptly finished the bottle of wine Eduardo and Jeremy sent over. As much as I didn't want him here, my heart ached to see him walk away, just like I've done to him. More than once.

I've damn near worn a hole in the carpet as I paced my hotel room and retraced every word I said to Cole in my mind. Hanging onto the words, "I love you." He told me he loves me and asked me to forgive him, and then he left. Something felt so final about his leaving; the look in his eyes was sheer defeat, and my heart hurts.

Another knock on the door, quickly followed up with a man announcing, "room service," stops me in my tracks. I open the door and invite the gentleman from room service back in to clean up what's left from dinner. He works quickly and quietly, placing the dishes and empty bottle of wine on his cart.

As he's leaving, he turns back to me. "Ma'am? Do I need to have security remove the man from outside your door?" He looks embarrassed as he nods toward the door.

"Man?" I question him.

"The gentleman sitting outside your door."

Cole.

He didn't leave.

I sigh, with relief or stress I'm not sure. "No. Thank you. I'll take care of it."

"You sure, miss?"

"I'm sure. Thank you for asking." I smile at him politely and walk to the door, opening it so he can leave with the tray of dishes.

He offers me a concerned smile. "Have a good evening, ma'am."

I follow him through the open door, careful to keep it propped open with my foot. Sure enough, Cole is sitting on the floor, just outside the door, with his knees pulled to his chest and his head resting back against the wall.

"Cole?" I call his name softly.

He makes no effort to move, just opens his eyes and looks at me. Pain, grief, and regret stare back at me. Emotions I'm all too familiar with myself.

"You came back?" I ask, and he swallows hard, nodding his head once.

This beautiful man looks beaten and worn, a shell of himself. A thousand storms dance in his blue eyes and my heart thunders inside my chest. It thunders with hope, or maybe it thunders with relief. Either way, it beats only like this for Cole.

"Can we talk, Frankie? Please." His voice is strained and hoarse, and my resolve breaks as his eyes beg me to let him in.

"Yeah," I finally muster.

For a brief moment, hope flashes across his face as he pushes himself up and walks past me through the open door, into the sitting area of the hotel room. He stands wringing his hands together nervously as I follow him inside and invite him to join me on the love seat.

His square jaw ticks as he pulls his hands to his face and rubs his eyes. I fight the urge to reach out and pull his hand into mine as he wrestles with what he's going to say.

Pulling my feet up, I tuck them under my bent legs, Cole watching every move I make. We both study each other carefully as we settle in.

"Cole," I start, breaking the silence and pause for a moment. "Why are you here? In Los Angeles?"

He clears his throat and sits up straighter. "Work...and you." His eyes soften when he mentions me.

"Work?"

He nods. "I had to come inspect a car and decide whether or not I was going to take the job." I scrunch my forehead in confusion and he sits up straighter as he begins to explain. "In addition to the garage, Carter and I restore cars. We did one, just for ourselves, about eight years ago and sold it at one of those luxury car auctions. We made a killing." He chuckles. "Anyway, we decided to turn it into a business. We've been very lucky to pick up several high-profile clients along the way—"

"That's why you're in L.A.?" I'm shocked, but not surprised to hear of Cole's accomplishments.

He nods again and rubs his cheek. "Yeah. I needed to see if this was a car we could restore. And when the client just happened to be in Los Angeles, my gut told me it was for a reason, Frankie...and I needed to seize this opportunity."

"With the car?" I ask, my voice barely above a whisper.

He grins smugly. "And you."

"Cole—"

"Frankie, just hear me out." He slides over closer to me on the love seat. "I've never been a believer of fate and all that bullshit. But when you left the other day, I was convinced I'd never see you again. A few hours later, my phone rings and it's fucking Jack Vanderbilt wanting me to restore his car."

I audibly gasp when I hear him say Jack Vanderbilt. *The* Jack Vanderbilt—the guy who essentially owns Hollywood.

His gaze holds mine as he continues. "So there I sit...a plane ticket in my hand for Los Angeles and I know it's now or never, Frankie. You left an engaged woman, and I respected that...but now—" He takes a breath, gathering his courage I assume. "Now you're single, Frankie." He shifts closer to me, and I can smell the lingering scent of his cologne mixed with the whiskey from his breath. "I wanted you to live your dreams —and your dreams were bigger than me. But the one thing I never admitted to you...hell, to myself, was that you were *my* dream. There wasn't a day in the last ten years I haven't fucking missed you—haven't regretted what I did."

He reaches for my hand and I let him take it. His hands are just like him, a complete contradiction. Rough and soft. Old and new. He places his other hand over mine and the warmth of it seeps into me. God, I've missed his touch.

"Come back to me." The whites of his eyes are tinged pink and his lip quivers as he waits for me to respond.

A lump grows in my throat as our entire past flashes before me. Running hand in hand with him to the fault line. Our first kiss. Our first fight. Every first I had was with Cole.

He rushes on, as if he's afraid I'll say no right away. "I don't know how it would work, Frankie. You're here, I'm back in the Ridge...but if you'd give me a chance, I'll do anything—if you'll just let me try. I love you, Frankie." His voice cracks and a tear falls from his eye, down his perfectly tan cheek, disappearing into the light scruff that lines his jaw.

"I love you, too," I respond. It's the truth. I'll always love him. Hearing myself say the words, though, reaffirms it. Cole inhales sharply and waits for me to retract what I said. But I won't. I can't. "I love you, Cole. I never got over you—or what you did, but I forgave you a long time ago. I had to, for my sanity...I just don't know that—"

He stops me, such intensity and desperation in his eyes. "Try. Fucking try, Frankie. You've never given up on anything in your life—*try*."

I exhale loudly, a million thoughts running through my mind. He moves even closer, cupping my cheek with his hand. I close my eyes and allow myself to sink into his touch, to just feel him.

"Try," he whispers, gently sliding his hand over my ear.

A soft sigh escapes me. I am weak to him. I will always be weak when it comes to Cole.

"We'll take it slow, Frankie," he promises me. "We'll figure it out one day at a time. Just give us another chance." His lips press against the corner of my mouth and I let him kiss me. "Please," he pleads against my lips. "I've never needed anything in my life. But you, Frankie...I need you."

FIFTEEN

I would beg, plead, and sell my soul to the devil for one more chance with Frankie. When I kissed her, I could feel her entire body tremble under my touch, like it did all those years ago. She still feels the connection we have—just like I do.

Now she sits wrapped in my arms that are locked like a vise grip, and I ignore the growing cramp in my forearm. I won't let her out of my embrace. Her head rests against my shoulder, turned just slightly so I can feel her soft breath against the side of my neck with each exhale.

We talked until she couldn't keep her eyes open any longer and she slid right into my arms. I'll hold her just like this all night if I have to, but I want her to be well-rested, and propped against me as she is isn't going to achieve that.

So I carefully release my grasp and slide an arm under her knees, shifting her carefully. She weighs next to nothing and it's easy for me to carry her to the bed. As I get her tucked in, her hand reaches out and wraps gently around my wrist.

"Stay," she mumbles, settling into the pillow. Everything inside me screams to climb into this bed with her and hold her —love her, but I promised her a million times over the course of the night that we'd take this slow.

I press a kiss to her forehead. "I'm going to let myself out," I whisper, not wanting to fully wake her up.

"Please...stay." Her voice is hoarse and sexy.

"Probably not a good idea, Frankie."

"Just lay with me. Hold me like you were." She shifts in the bed and pulls the comforter back further, making space for me right next to her.

My heart races and my cock stirs, knowing I'll be close to her in bed.

"Please," she begs one more time, and I nod, kicking off my shoes as she rolls to her side and tucks her hands under her cheek, falling back into an easy sleep. I stand and watch her for a minute. She's angelic—the pink curve of her lips, her long eyelashes and her wavy hair all tucked perfectly into the white sheets.

Taking off my jeans and t-shirt, I fold them neatly, placing them in a pile on the dresser. I slide into the bed, careful not to wake her. Once I'm settled, I pull her into my arms and hold her tight against my chest. She feels exactly like I remember. Running my hands over her soft skin, I inhale the scent of her coconut lotion. This is what I envision heaven to feel like... Frankie and me together.

I finally drift off to sleep to the soft sound of her breathing, knowing there is nowhere else in the world I'd rather be than in this hotel room, in Los Angeles, with Frankie in my arms. While uncertainty still looms all around us, for the first time in ten years, I finally feel whole.

Soft fingers brush over the curve of my chin and up my cheek, and for a brief moment I'm utterly confused at who's touching me. I haven't had a woman in my bed in months, but the light hint of coconut brings it all back to me.

Frankie.

"Morning." Her voice is gravelly and utter perfection as she rests her arm across my chest. If I could wake up to her skin on mine every morning for the rest of my life, I'd die a happy man.

"Morning," I manage in return as her finger draws circles on my chest.

"You stayed," she remarks and I turn from my back to face her. We lie face to face, like we've done so many times, but this time I study every detail of her face. Every freckle that peppers her nose, and that tiny mole that rests on the edge of her bottom lip that is almost always covered by lipstick. I reach out and run my thumb over it.

"You asked me to," I answer her, and her fingers continue their exploration, tracing my lips. Her touch is gentle, almost ticklish, but I savor it.

"I'm glad you did." She moves closer to me and rests her hand on my abdomen.

I close my eyes, fighting the growing erection just south of her hand. But the silk strap of her camisole hangs off her shoulder, exposing her delicate shoulder and the swell of her breast, making it fucking impossible to think of anything else.

"Frankie," I moan, letting her know she's edging into dangerous territory.

"Cole..." Her voice trails off as she leans in and presses a kiss to my lips.

My dick is rock hard now and it's going to be hard to hide it under this thin sheet. She snakes her leg between mine and I roll to my back, bringing Frankie with me. Straddling me, she presses her center against me and rolls her hips. I clench my teeth, amazed at how this girl can unravel me in a split second.

Grabbing her hips, I hold her still as she tries to move on top of me. She pulls her bottom lip into her mouth and my adrenaline is pumping so hard, because I know that if we go here, I'll never be able to let her go. I'll never be able to walk away from her. But fuck it, I want nothing more than to be inside her. I clench my fists and groan as she continues to roll her hips over my rock hard dick.

"Touch me," she says, lifting my hand from her hip and sliding it under the hem of her camisole. She guides it over the soft skin of her stomach, inching higher until her heavy breast sits inside my palm. I squeeze gently, accepting her invitation as she closes her eyes. My other hand naturally makes its way to her other breast. Her nipples are rock hard and I give each one a firm squeeze, causing her to gasp.

"Cole," she mumbles my name as her head drops back. I pinch each nipple even harder, causing her hips to rock against mine. I push myself up, wrapping my arms around her waist as I press my lips to her neck, tasting her. Her arms dangle over my shoulders and play with my hair at the base of my neck as my tongue explores the soft skin behind her ear.

Lifting the hem of her camisole up and over her head, I toss it to the floor beside the bed. I kiss my way to her full breasts, pulling a nipple into my mouth and biting gently. My tongue lavishes each puckered bud and my cock hardens further as her body reacts to my touch. Her body has changed since the last time I touched her. She's more woman and less girl now. The curve of her hips and the heaviness of her breasts are all new territory for me, territory that I plan to explore for the rest of my life.

Reaching behind her, she palms my dick through my boxer briefs and I groan, almost losing control. "Wait, sweetheart, wait." I roll her off me and pin her beneath me. Pushing myself back, I drag her silk pajama shorts down her legs, discarding them at the foot of the bed.

Frankie lies completely naked underneath me, a sight that, twelve hours ago, I never thought I'd see again. My breath catches at how beautiful she is just as my self-control wanes. I swallow hard as I slide my hands up her calves, over her thighs, and up to the apex of her legs—to the very juncture that calls to me.

"I don't have any protection," I tell her as my finger brushes the soft lips that no longer bear the soft curls she had as a teenager.

"I'm on birth control," she gasps as my thumb finds and begins circling her clit. "And I'm clean. It's only ever been you and Ted." I snap my eyes shut when she says Ted's name. I want to put my fist through that man's face when I think of him touching Frankie like this. I push those thoughts aside and bring attention back to the woman I have writhing beneath me.

"I'm clean, too," I tell her, leaving it at that. I couldn't even come up with the names of the faceless women I've fucked trying to get Frankie out of my system. Women who were nothing more than a means to an end. A quick fuck.

I pull my boxer briefs down, kicking them off my ankles and onto the floor next to her pajama bottoms. As much as I want to dive into Frankie, I want to savor this moment and her. I want this to last more than the ten minutes I'm afraid it won't if I dive into her.

I lower my face to her stomach, kissing the silky skin of her belly and leaving a trail of kisses behind as I move lower, finding the spot I've been dying to taste. My tongue slides easily through her soft lips, finding that hidden and throbbing little bud. Frankie gasps and bucks her hips as my tongue works her into a frenzy.

My body's reaction to hers is about to send me over the edge. Her hands grip my hair as her breathing quickens and her thighs try to clamp closed around me.

"Cole!" she yells between ragged breaths. "Jesus, Cole!" Her entire body shudders underneath me as she comes undone. Then her hands fall from my head to my shoulders, where her nails dig into my flesh as her body begins to come down from its high. I want to savor this woman for hours, but I know that we don't have that much time.

I sit back and position myself at her wet entrance, her knees falling open wide as her body continues to shake from the intensity of her orgasm. Nothing makes me happier than seeing her pleasure, and her chest rises and falls quickly with each rapid breath she takes.

Her blue eyes open and find mine as I hover over her, taking in this moment. Her dark hair is wild against the stark white sheets of the bed. As if every star in the sky is aligned, I press myself into her. For the rest of my life, I'll never forget this moment.

I lower myself down and press a kiss to her lips and she returns it with as much intensity. A kiss that tells her I love her without ever saying the words. A kiss that seals our fate, whether she knows it yet or not. I will never let her go again— or lose her ever again. This moment bonds us, seals us together as we should've always been.

She gasps, wrapping her legs around my waist as I sink further into her. This is home for me. Frankie is my home. She owns every good memory I have—she is what I live my life for. Her.

As much as I'd love to fuck her fast and wild, that can wait. This is us reconnecting. This is us apologizing, forgiving, and forging a new beginning. This is what making love feels like. It's safe and comforting, pleasure and peace, intensity and passion all in one act. It's letting go of the past and forging ahead with one simple connection.

I slide in and out of her while she peppers my lips with gentle kisses. The act of sex has never been more intimate for me—this is me pouring my love into Frankie and her accepting and returning it back to me. Her soft moans tell me all I need to know and I finally lose myself in her.

"I love you," I whisper against her lips as I feel my release spill into her. "God, I love you."

She wraps her arms around my neck and pulls me down on top of her. Her arms hold me against her tightly as we both catch our breath. We lie like this for minutes until I finally slide out of her and roll onto my back, immediately missing our connection.

Frankie pulls the bed sheet over her, tucking it under her arms before she rolls to her side and watches me. Awkward silence fills the space between us as I roll to my side to look at her, wondering what she's thinking.

"So now what?" she asks. I can see the fear in her eyes, and it just about kills me. She just gave herself to me, and we solved nothing last night. There are no answers to our situation, only pleas to start over.

My heart stammers as her eyes mist over. I don't have the answers, but I'll do whatever it takes to make her happy. "I don't know, Frankie. I just know that I love you—and I want you with me, I want us together...but I won't ask you to leave Los Angeles for me. I can't do that."

She reaches out and places her hand over my heart as her lips tremble. She closes her eyes and I see a tear slip out and roll down her cheek. My heart breaks for how she must be feeling. I imagine she thinks I'll abandon her again. She has to know I'd never do that again, never.

"My business is back in Crescent Ridge..." I pause. "So I think we just need to take some time to figure this out. We can try this long distance while we figure it all out." She gives a shaky nod, and I add, "I want you to know, Frankie, that whatever you decide about us, I love you more than anything in the world. I always have."

She opens her eyes, the whites tinged pink.

"More than anything," I whisper.

I lean in and press a long kiss to her lips before sitting up. "I have to go. My flight leaves in a little over two hours and I still have to get back to my hotel and get my things." I dress quickly as Frankie stays tucked in bed, doing her best to hide her concern and sadness.

"Cole," she says my name softly. "Thank you for the best night ever."

I swallow hard and my heart drops, as if she's saying a final goodbye. She offers me a crooked smile, a smile that holds fear of the unknown...a smile that wants to trust, but is still hurt.

Holding back my own fear, fear of losing her again, I wink. "This was nothing." Then I bend over, pressing one more kiss to her lips. "This was just the beginning."

SIXTEEN

Frankie

"Girl, you better tell me who that handsome lumberjack of a man was that was standing in this office yesterday afternoon looking for you," Eduardo says under his breath as he follows me into my office. He's on my heels and pressing for answers. Eduardo knows how to charm answers out of anyone. It's what makes him an amazing attorney. He knows when to smile, knows when to focus and be serious, but it's his charm that seals the deal every time.

"I don't know what you're talking about," I throw over my shoulder, walking as fast as I can in these damn heels. The safety of my office is still out of sight. I juggle my briefcase and purse in my arms as I lift my arm to glance at my watch, hoping Eduardo takes a hint that I'm busy, when in fact I'm just late. I don't have any current cases and my calendar is still clear from my extended absence from when I went back to Crescent Ridge.

My office door closes with a bang behind us and I spin around to find Eduardo with a smirk on his face. "Details.

Now." He saunters over as I throw myself down into my office chair.

I let my purse and briefcase fall to my feet as I sink into the oversized leather chair. "I don't even know what you're talking about," I lie to him and roll my eyes. Except my entire body shivers when I think of Cole's hands all over me just a few hours ago.

I cross my legs to drown out the throbbing between my legs and fall lazily into a daydream...Waking up next to Cole this morning...His touch, his body, everything was exactly as I remembered. He still knows my body like no other, every tender spot, every curve. He still owns me.

"Hello, earth to Frances." Eduardo snaps his fingers, pulling me out of my daze. "Oooh, he's got you good." He purses his lips and rubs his hands together, leaning against the edge of my desk. "Tell me. Who is he?"

I sigh and look at Eduardo hesitantly. "An old friend."

He briskly shakes his head from side to side, not buying a word of what I'm telling him. "Not buying that bullshit, sweetheart. Try again." His lips pull into a wide smile exposing his perfectly straight, white teeth.

"My ex," I finally blurt out in defeat and sink further into my desk chair.

"Good God, woman...this is going to be a good story. Spill it."

I shake my head, fighting back the tears that sting behind my eyes. I'm not ready to share this yet. The way Cole can open me up scares the living hell out of me. He made promises and begged for new beginnings, and I'm honestly scared out of my mind. There is no one who can destroy me like he can—and I'm not sure I'd survive another break-up with him.

Eduardo reaches for my chin and tilts my head to the side. "Is that a love bite?" he gasps, brushing my hair over my shoulder.

I snap my head away from him and pull my hair back over the front of my shoulders, concealing my neck.

"Stop it!" I push Eduardo away, smacking his chest.

"I'm kidding!" He busts out laughing, and I swat at him childishly with both of my hands. He leans away as I smack his arm. "Please tell me you did not sleep with him...or did you?" Eduardo grasps my forearm, his tone turning more serious.

I look at him guiltily and pull my lips into my mouth. Clearly, I suck at lying.

"Oh, girl, you did. What the hell were you thinking?"

"Shush." I pull him closer. "This is not the place to talk about this." I look over his shoulder to see if anyone is watching us. I narrow my eyes at him and pick up my purse, shoving it into my desk drawer. A sign that I need him to leave so I can get my day started, but he shakes his head.

"Nope. Nuh-uh. You're not going to dive into work before giving me every gory little detail. I saw that hunk of a man walk in here yesterday—"

I throw my hand up to stop him, and he grabs my wrist, forcing me to smile at him. I'm a mess of emotions. Happy...sad...scared.

"He is gorgeous, isn't he?" I smirk. "Dark hair, rippling muscles, those blue eyes...his big..."

"Stop it. You're making me feel things about a straight man," he jokes with me. "But seriously. Can we go get coffee and talk?"

I power up my laptop and turn back around in my desk chair to face him.

"Fine. But you need to go with me to Ted's house at lunch and box up a few things."

He winks. "Deal."

"Jesus Christ, Frances," Eduardo hisses as he takes a sip of coffee. "Your life just came full circle."

I nod and let out a soft sigh, running my finger around the rim of my cardboard coffee cup.

"So what are you going to do?"

I look at my friend sitting across the table from me and all that fear comes racing back. I barely manage a whisper, "I don't know."

He reaches out and pulls my hand into his. "Don't make any decisions right now. Take your time to think about it."

I swallow hard, choking down the lump in my throat. "There's just so much to think about," I start. "I love working as an attorney and there isn't really an opportunity for that in Crescent Ridge...but I don't know that I want to lose him again—"

Eduardo shakes his head animatedly. "Do not make this about him, Frances. This is about you. You get to do what *you* want to do. Go where *you* want to go. If he cares about you, that's what he'll want as well."

"He does," I admit, remembering Cole telling me that very thing last night, that I was *his* dream. "He told me we'd make it work regardless of where I am."

"Good." He squeezes my hand and offers me a tight smile. "But just so you know, there are a million things you can still do in the legal field from Crescent Ridge. You can teach classes online, you can volunteer with numerous non-profits, and don't fool yourself, Frances, people need legal assistance even in Crescent Ridge. You could start your own law office."

My heart leaps in my chest as Eduardo encourages me with all the opportunities I have.

He adds, "You may not make ass loads of money...but, Frances, you're not making ass loads now. That's not why you practice law. I see your passion—that's what it's about."

"It was never about money for me." I stare at the steam coming off my cup of coffee and hope suddenly fills me. "That's not why I do this."

Eduardo nods approvingly. "I also saw what the Morrison-Longmire case did to you. Yeah, you brought justice to those families, but I also saw how it ate you up." He pats my hand. "That's not healthy. Maybe a slower pace will be better for you."

I look at Eduardo and smile...a true smile. One that pulls at my lips and no matter how hard I fight it I can't make it go away. "Thank you, Eduardo. I don't know what I'd do without a friend like you."

He smirks. "I don't either...because no one else is going to help you pack up your shit at Ted's house." He shudders at the sound of Ted's name, but I can't help but laugh. For the first time in a long time, I feel the beginning of happiness.

"Your life literally fits into six boxes," Eduardo remarks, hanging the last of my clothes in the hanging garment box.

I close a box of important documents and jewelry that I'm

taking with me. "When I moved in with Ted, I sold everything I had. I didn't need to bring anything here. And for anything we've acquired together...he can have it, I don't want it." It's remarkable to me how quickly my feelings for Ted have changed. I don't even care about him anymore—it almost feels as if a weight I didn't know I was carrying was lifted off my shoulders. Thank God, I didn't marry him.

"Have you spoken to him?" Eduardo winces.

"No. He keeps texting me and I keep ignoring. I did tell him I'd be by this evening to box up my belongings, but I didn't want to chance seeing him, that's why I decided to come this afternoon." I grin slyly at Eduardo who just shakes his head at me.

"When are the delivery guys coming?"

I look at my phone and smile. "In about fifteen minutes."

"Girl, you are sneaky." He whistles as he tapes up the box. "Good riddance, though. I was not sad to see this relationship end." Tossing the roll of packing tape on the floor, he walks over to me and pulls me into a gentle hug. "I don't mean to be so smug. I know this isn't easy...but everything happens for a reason, Frances. Seize this opportunity." He looks at me poignantly.

I wrap my arms around Eduardo in return and sink into his embrace as his truths hit me like a brick wall. It does feel good to be rid of Ted, and he's right—everything happens for a reason. "I plan to," I mumble against his chest.

SEVENTEEN

Cole

It's been three weeks since I left California and three weeks since I last spoke to Frankie. I texted her once to let her know I was thinking of her and loved her, but she never responded. I cannot even tell you the number of hours I've stared at the damn screen on my phone, waiting for anything from her...a call, a text, an email, anything.

My stomach twists and turns when every morning I still haven't heard from her. I'm trying to give her time to figure out her life—with or without me. But the morning I left Los Angeles, I felt we were headed in the right direction—back to each other.

"This car is unbelievable," Carter hollers at me from under the hood of the Corvette LS6. We got the Vanderbilt car delivered a week and a half ago and Carter is still giggling like a schoolgirl over it. We have a thirty-page list of every part we need to order, manufacture, or refurbish to get this car back to like-new condition in the next fourteen to sixteen months.

I swivel in my chair to find him walking toward me with a

huge grin on his face. "I still cannot believe you scored this car."
He slaps my shoulder and throws himself down into the chair
next to me. "In my entire life, I never expected to work on a
Corvette LS6."

"She's a beauty," I remark.

"Speaking of beauties, heard from Frankie?"

I shake my head and exhale loudly, releasing my frustration. "Nope."

"Well, you've got a lot going on the next few weeks. The
fewer distractions, the better." He cringes as soon as he says
that. I know he's just trying to make me feel better.

"Frankie would never be a distraction."

He sighs loudly. "I didn't mean it like that."

"Fuck, Carter, you were the one who kept telling me I
needed to talk to her. I did, I poured my damn heart out to her,
and now this." I push myself up from my chair and pace the
garage, raking my hands through my hair.

"Calm down," Carter says. "When has Frankie ever not
thought something through? She's taking her time and orga-
nizing her thoughts. That's what she does." As if Carter knows
a damn thing about her...except he's right.

"But what if she goes back to Ted?" My stomach turns at
the thought of this.

He laughs a deep belly laugh. "She's not going back
to Ted."

"But what if—"

He stands up and cuts me off. "She's not going back to him.
Stop stressing."

"But she's not coming back to me." My voice wavers.

"Yet. Give her time, man." He pats me on the shoulder
before heading back to the car to get to work.

I nod my head in agreement. Even though my gut tells me she's not coming back.

～

"Hang one picture on the wall over each booth," I instruct the handyman who's putting the finishing touches on The Fault Line Bar and Grill. We're scheduled to open on Sunday with an exclusive friends and family night the night before. I want to give everyone a dry run on what to expect when we open.

I stand back and look around, completely in awe of how this place has come together. The menu is the perfect mix of bar and pub food with touches of Mexican and Asian fusion to give it a nice flair. I've sampled everything on the menu and there isn't a damn thing I don't like.

We've got four homemade specialty craft beers and another twenty on draft, along with a full bar. Our focus will be on the happy hour and evening crowd, allowing Gus's diner to cater to the breakfast and lunch crowd. My intention was never to take out another small business, but to grow Crescent Ridge through more business and jobs. There's room for everyone in this town, and I love watching everyone be successful.

"Boss," Heather, our hostess, calls to me from the hostess stand near the front door. "Quick question on the app for seating." She points to the iPad that's propped on the hostess desk that shows the entire layout of the restaurant.

"Be right there." I grab the stack of freshly printed menus from the box that was just delivered and carry them with me to the hostess station. I help Heather figure out how to adjust servers' sections on the app and how to sign employees in and out for their shifts.

While Heather situates the stand, placing the menus in their holder and sorting other deliveries that have come in today, I step aside and admire how this once abandoned building has come together. This is the first time I've seen it in the evening. I appreciate how the wall sconces and small lanterns light up each individual booth, and the large metal and wood light fixture hangs perfectly over the bar, casting just the right amount of ambient light for that area. The metal, wood, leather, and brick all play off each other to give this place exactly what I was looking for. Modern, rustic, and old, all in one.

"Sorry, Ma'am, we're not open yet." I hear Heather say as the front door chimes.

When I turn, I see her bright blue eyes looking back at me. She's wearing a pair of worn jeans with a hole in the knee, a long sleeve black t-shirt, and a pair of black Converse sneakers. She's a vision from the past, only she's here now.

"Cole," she says my name hesitantly, but her feet betray her excitement and carry her toward me.

"You're here." I look at her in disbelief. "How'd you find me here?"

She stops in front of me with a sheepish grin. "Just got back to town a couple of minutes ago. Word on the street is you're revitalizing Crescent Ridge building by building on every block." Her eyes widen with awe as she looks around the place. "The Fault Line Bar and Grill," she says quietly, taking in the significance of the name.

The fault line means something to Frankie and me—it's where we went as kids and grew up together. Our first kiss was there and our first fight. Damn near every memory of our childhood happened at the fault line.

"Seemed fitting." I swallow hard as my heart pounds deep in my chest. I want to reach out and touch her, but I refrain. "Everything good to me revolved around that damn fault line." One side of my mouth quirks up.

Her blue eyes dance around the room, taking in all of the details, the pictures of the old Crescent Ridge and the change I want to bring to the new Crescent Ridge. When her eyes finally land on me, she pulls her bottom lip between her teeth. "Me, too."

She shifts from foot to foot nervously, and I finally invite her to take a seat with me in a corner booth, away from the hustle and bustle and chaos of the crew still working. I want to kiss her, devour her, and hold her—but I pull myself together as we get situated in the booth.

"I wasn't sure I was going to hear from you," I tell her honestly, rubbing my hands together nervously.

She offers me half a smile. "I'm sorry about that. I just needed some time to really think about what I want to do with my life." She picks at her thumbnail as she speaks. "I wanted to take the time to make sure I was making decisions not out of emotion, but from the heart. Decisions that'll change the course of my future." Her voice shakes slightly.

My throat tightens and my heart sinks as I see the look on her face—a face I've always been able to read. Her features tell me her future isn't here in Crescent Ridge. I feel every ounce of hope drain from my body. I swallow down the growing lump as I tell myself that I can't be angry at her. I feign a happy smile for her. "I'm sure whatever you decide, or wherever you go, it'll be because you've been thoughtful about your choices.

You never make irrational decisions, Frankie. That is one of the things I've always loved about you. You're a smart woman —" I stop because I feel my throat tightening up again. This is it. She's here to tell me no, and I have to accept that. And I will. It'll destroy me, but I'll let her go for good this time...the way I should have before.

She stares at me, fighting whatever it is she's here to tell me. I see the fear in her eyes and the contemplation written across her face. She's not here to choose me. For a long moment, we both sit in silence, not knowing what to say or where to begin.

"So where are you headed and what are you going to do?" I almost choke on the words as they come out, they're so painful.

Frankie inhales deeply, her eyes misting over. "The last case I tried really took a toll on me. I don't know if you heard anything about it, but I got a successful conviction on a man who raped and murdered two little girls."

I nod. "I did hear." Everyone in this damn town talked about that case because Frankie was trying it. She may have abandoned this town, but she's still the best thing Crescent Ridge has ever produced. And everyone here is so fucking proud of her, no one more so than me.

"That's why I went into law. I loved prosecuting. I got a high off putting the bad guys away and bringing justice to people." Her forefinger traces a nervous circle on the table. "But something about this case just..." She pauses, searching for the right word, "hurt." She licks her lips before continuing. "I was happy to get justice for the girls and their families, but something inside me broke. I lost the passion. The pain and hurt was too much and what used to fuel me finally broke me."

A stray tear slides from the corner of her eyes and rolls

down her cheek. It takes every ounce of self-control to keep from reaching across the table and swiping it off her cheek.

"You're a damn good lawyer, Frankie. I hope you know that."

She nods her head. "But being a good lawyer and having the passion to continue doing what I was doing was going to kill me." She takes a deep breath. "And then when everything happened with Ted, it gave me perspective. After I took some time to think about what I wanted with my life, it was almost a relief, a chance for a fresh start."

My heart skips a beat at her revelation about Ted. "How were you not on the same page as Ted?" I ask curiously. "You were going to marry him."

She shrugs. "I settled for what he wanted, because I didn't care enough to fight for what I wanted."

I frown because this sounds so unlike the Frankie I know.

"He didn't want a family, so I said fine, I don't want one, either—but the reality is, when I was here with Mom, and seeing Maggie and Matthew it made me realize I do want a family. And I want to slow down and enjoy life more, not work so much." Her blue eyes sparkle with unshed tears.

My stomach twists as I listen to her justify her decision—to follow her dreams and not choose me. And it's so fucking selfish of me to feel this way, because this girl, my Frankie, deserves the fucking world. She wants a life, a family, and a future—and for her that's not here in Crescent Ridge, it never has been.

"I'm not fully getting away from law," she continues with a small sigh. "I'm going to volunteer with several non-profits and teach some pre-law classes online. It allows me a more flexible schedule so that I can slow down a bit and just live. Maybe take a vacation once in a while, read some books, and maybe take some classes on teaching yoga." She cracks a small smile, and while my heart slowly breaks it simultaneously feels good to see her happy.

I choke back my emotion as I think about how brave she is, sitting here being honest with herself and me. I see the fear leaving her eyes as she builds her plan in her head and tells me about it.

"I'm proud of you, Frankie. I always will be." In this moment, I feel like I might vomit and I'm not sure I can handle her telling me she can't choose me...us. I respect her decision, but it hurts like a motherfucker to know I'm losing her.

My eyes sting with unshed tears as I stare at the beautiful woman across the table from me. Her long fingers are laced together as she watches me in return. The sight of her is almost too much to bear. Her lip twitches and her chin trembles ever so slightly as we just take each other in. I wonder when I'll see her again. If she'll keep in touch with me. If we've forged a new kind of friendship where she might call or text me now and again. Bile rises in the back of my throat as I think about saying goodbye to her.

I shift uncomfortably, not sure how to say goodbye to the only woman I'll ever love. I can barely speak as I blink back tears. "I should probably get back to work." I point my thumb over my shoulder toward the kitchen, where the staff is still unloading equipment and supplies that are being delivered.

"So you're just going to go back to work?" she asks, her brows furrowing.

"Frankie..." I close my eyes. I can't break here.

She leans in and places her hand on mine. "Did you not hear a word I said?"

I slowly open my eyes and look at her. "I heard everything. You're moving on—blah, blah, blah." I know I sound like a dick when I say it like that, but fuck..."I'm so goddamn proud of you, Frankie, but please try to understand this is difficult for me. This isn't what I wanted. I wanted you. And me. And I wanted a second chance with you." I look away from her, not able to bear looking at her perfect face a second longer.

She actually starts laughing at me. "You're a real pain in the ass, aren't you?" Her head tips back and she laughs harder.

"This isn't funny, Frankie," I snap at her, my emotions turning from sadness to anger.

She leans forward, pulling both of my hands into hers. "If you were listening to me, I'm choosing us." She smiles the sweetest fucking smile I've ever seen. "I'm choosing you, Cole."

My heart damn near stops beating. "Me?" Now I'm the one that's confused.

"You." She squeezes my hand. "I'm choosing us."

My whole body floods with relief and a spontaneous but cautious joy. I slide out from the booth and pull her from her seat, scooping her into my arms. I squeeze her tighter than I've ever hugged her before. I can feel her lips pressed against my neck as she hugs me in return. Everything I wanted is falling into place and I didn't have a clue. The restaurant, my auto business, but mostly Frankie...I feel like my life is finally coming together.

"Us," I say.

"Us," she repeats.

I don't know how long I hold her, but when I finally let her down, I see tears on her cheeks. "We're going to be okay this time," I tell her, wiping them with my sleeve. "I promise." I know words don't mean much, it'll have to be my actions that prove I'm committed to her and our relationship. "I'm never letting you go, Frankie."

She smiles as she lets out a deep breath and looks around the restaurant. "You finish up here. I'm going to head over to my mom's and check on her. I came straight here when I got back to town."

I glance excitedly at the time on my phone. "I'll be done here in about an hour. Come over to the house after you get settled and see your mom, but take your time. I know she'll be excited to see you." I lean in and kiss her, hard...like I've never kissed her before as a sense of hope takes up residence inside me.

EIGHTEEN

Frankie

"Hey, Mama," I announce quietly as I open her bedroom door. It's just after nine o'clock in the evening and she's tucked into bed, watching television.

"Frances," she whispers, reaching her arms out for me. I sidle up to her on the edge of her bed and lean in, allowing her to hug me. "You're back?" She sounds surprised. Her speech is noticeably better than it was a month ago, but still a bit slurred.

"I am." I smile at her and tuck a stray piece of hair behind her ear. "I think I'm going to stay a while if that's okay with you."

"Oh, Frances." She smiles crookedly at me and rubs my hand excitedly. "Does this have anything to do with Cole?" She winces a bit when she says his name and I'm not sure if it's because of her asking about Cole or if she's in some pain.

I shrug. "He's part of the reason, but not the only reason."

"Faith filled me in a little bit," she sighs. "Regardless of what happens with you two, I think you both need to resolve the past. It's the only way you can build a future." She gives me a knowing look, and I shake my head. She always hits me with honesty and I love her for it.

"Mama, sometimes there are things that need to stay in the past—"

She cuts me off by shaking her head, but I don't want to argue with her. I lean in, pressing a gentle kiss to her forehead. "Rest. We'll talk more tomorrow."

She closes her eyes and struggles to find the words she wants to say. Taking a deep breath, she finds them. "I'm so glad you're back, Frances."

"Me, too, Mama." I never thought I'd say that about being back in Crescent Ridge, but for the first time in my adulthood, it actually feels good to be home.

My phone pings with an incoming text message as I'm brushing my teeth and freshening up. I swipe the screen, hopeful it's from Cole telling me he's home. Instead, I find a message from Ted.

This isn't over. I will get you back.

He's delusional. Rolling my eyes, I delete the message and close the screen. Ted couldn't give a shit about getting me back. He hates to lose and that's what this is about. We didn't end on his terms; we ended on mine and he can't handle that. He expected me to forgive his indiscretion and continue on as if he didn't cheat and lie to me. As shocked as I was to find out the truth, it was the best thing that ever happened to me.

Peeking out the front window, I see Cole's Jeep in the driveway. I check on Mama once more before heading across the street. My heart races as it did all those years ago when I'd sneak over late at night to see Cole. I raise my hand to knock on the front door just as he opens it, startling me.

"There you are," he says with a big smile, one that shows the dimple in his left cheek. Butterflies dance in my stomach as I take in the sight of him, all six-foot-three of lean muscle. He changed from jeans and a thermal shirt into a pair of joggers and a gray t-shirt that hugs every rippling muscle on his arms and torso. His dark hair is damp from a shower and I can smell his woodsy body wash. I want to bury my face in his neck and drink in the scent of him.

"Do you want anything to drink?" he asks, closing the door behind us.

"Not right now, thanks."

"Are you sure? Wine? Beer?" He grins at me.

"Maybe later," I respond and he reaches for my hand, taking it in his.

"Let's go sit outside. I've got a fire going in the fire pit." He motions toward the set of French doors that lead out to the backyard. When we step through the doors, I'm taken aback by how beautiful this space is. When we were teenagers, this backyard was nothing but dirt with trees along the fence line.

Now those trees are huge and beautiful, draping a large canopy over the entire property. The backyard is now transformed from a dirt lot to a comfortable outdoor living space. A huge wood deck has been added that has built in seats along the perimeter and holds a large table and chairs. Just off the wood deck is another sitting area made from pavers that surrounds a fire pit. A huge pergola covers the entire outdoor space and it's covered in twinkling white lights.

Large plush chairs surround the fire pit that flickers in the dark and Cole leads us over to them.

"Cole, this is amazing!" I remark as I look around and take a seat in one of the oversized plush chairs.

"It's come a long way," he says with a smile, taking a seat in the chair next to me. "I had a vision of what I wanted this space to look like, and after Pops died I took some time away from the shop and just worked on the house. It was therapeutic."

His dad. My stomach drops. "I'm sorry to hear about your dad. I plan to visit the cemetery to pay my respects."

Cole nods his head and squeezes my hand, staring at the flames that flicker from the gas fire pit.

"He always loved you," Cole remarks.

"And I loved him. He was always a voice of reason and a great man. He helped my mom so much, and I'll always be appreciative of everything he did for us."

The mood is somber for a moment until Cole slaps his hand on his knee, as if he's done being sad. "So Saturday night is the soft opening of The Fault Line Bar and Grill." He grins at me. "Then we open for business on Sunday. Would you do me the honor of being my guest?" He reaches out and places his hand over mine as it sits on the arm of the oversized wicker patio chair.

"I'd love to! I still can't believe you named that place The Fault Line." I chuckle and he laughs in response.

"Frankie," he says my name intimately. "Stay with me tonight. I need you with me." He squeezes my hand a little tighter.

I swallow hard, already feeling myself caving. I'll never say no to him. I don't have the capacity within me to say no to this man, but I also don't want to rush things with us.

"My mom, I should probably go home," I whisper.

He shakes his head. "Melinda will occasionally help during the nights when and if needed. I extended her contract."

I tilt my head to the side and narrow my eyes slightly at him. "You shouldn't be making decisions on behalf of my mom. Faith and I are capable of doing that."

He stubbornly shakes his head as I speak. "I'm not. All the medical decisions are left to you and Faith. Faith was assigned her medical power of attorney. I'm just paying Melinda and Judy to help out—to give you and Faith a breather now and then. Plus, selfishly that means you'll have more free time for me." He smirks at me, a familiar, boyish cockiness in his eyes.

"Faith and I will be just fine, Cole." I'm not upset, but I also don't want him making decisions on behalf of Faith, my mom, and me.

"Goddammit, Frankie. Let me help. Please. Let me do this." He's not angry, but his tone is firm. "It's the one thing I can do to help."

I stare at him for a moment and see the look of helplessness on his face. I nod in understanding and agree that this is how he can help and I should be grateful.

"So stay with me," he pleads again.

My thoughts instantly go back to the hotel in Los Angeles and our time reconnecting with each other. The way he took his time touching me—the way his lips felt on my body. I inhale sharply as my body answers for me. "Okay."

He wastes no time jumping up and shutting off the gas to the fire pit. With an extended hand, he reaches out and takes mine, gently pulling me up from the chair and into his arms. There is a hunger in his eyes as he buries his face in my hair, wrapping his arms around me, and just holds me. We sway lightly under the twinkling lights and everything inside me calms. Every fear, every reservation, every questioning thought I had about coming back here dissipates in his arms.

"Welcome home," he says, pressing a kiss to my temple. And by home, I'm not sure if he means Crescent Ridge or him, but Cole was always home to me—and it feels so damn good to be back.

Cole holds my hand, leading me to his bedroom, and my stomach twists in anticipation of being with him again. I'll never tire of his touch—of him. I've barely crossed the threshold into the room when Cole spins around and presses me firmly against the wall. His lips capturing mine, hungry and needy. I can feel every muscle in his chest and abs through his thin t-shirt. But it's his erection pressing against me that causes me to gasp.

His hands reach for the hem of my shirt and my arms instinctively rise as he lifts it up and over my head. One of his hands palms my breast while the other works the button of my jeans. His thick erection shifts, pressing against my center, and I moan as I feel him grow harder.

I reach down, pushing his jogging pants and boxer briefs down as far as I can while he manages to remove my bra simultaneously. He bends forward, pulling a nipple into his mouth, and I gasp as he bites gently, causing a shiver to run down my body, stopping at my core.

"Fuck, Frankie," he groans, pulling me away from the wall and walking me backward toward his bed.

As the back of my knees hit the mattress, I drop to the soft carpet, pulling his pants and boxer briefs the rest of the way down. His thick erection hangs heavy and I wrap my hand around it, pulling it into my mouth.

"Fuck," he hisses as his hands tangle in my hair and he holds me in place. He's soft and hard and sweet and salty. Every inch of him is perfection. My tongue swirls around his large head as he tries to hold back from pressing farther in my mouth. "I'm not gonna last if you keep doing that, sweetheart," he murmurs as I suck him further into my mouth. I feel him pressed against the back of my throat and his dick hardens even more.

"Frankie," he warns me. I tighten my lips and pull back, but he manages to pull out of my mouth. His large hands pull me up off the floor and he holds me in place as he leans in and whispers, "As much as I want you to suck me off, I want to bury myself in that sweet pussy of yours and get lost inside of you. Any other time, you can suck my dick all night long."

My eyes widen at his vulgarity because he never spoke to me like this when we were younger, but it also sets me on fire. I shrug out of his grip and wrap my arms around his neck as his hands grip each of my ass cheeks, his fingers digging into the soft, tender flesh.

With one shift, he easily lifts me off the floor and my legs wrap around his waist, pulling him to me. His cock positions itself at my wet, throbbing center and without warning, he presses himself firmly into me.

My head falls back as I let out a guttural moan and he nibbles the base of my neck and the skin around my collarbone. "I plan to make love to you later...but Frankie, right now I need to fuck you."

I don't even have the energy to answer him as he lifts me

and I fall onto his thick, hard length. My entire body tingles and shudders with each rise and fall. He licks his bottom lip as he spins, pressing my back against the wall.

He's like a rabid animal, wild and hungry. With each thrust he buries himself deeper into my body, my heart, my soul. My fingers twist the hair at the nape of his neck, and I hold onto him, fighting for every breath as he drives himself into me.

"Cole!" I scream his name as I feel my orgasm building faster than I think it ever has.

"Come on me, Frankie. Let me feel you come on me," he mumbles against my lips.

In that moment, I let go...of the past, and the hurt, and I succumb to Cole Ryan.

NINETEEN

Cole

The sun is beginning to rise and just barely peeks through the blinds when Frankie finally falls asleep in my arms. Her breathing is soft and steady, and her body is listless after our marathon of lovemaking.

It was wild and passionate, and soft and loving, and everything in between. It was exactly what Frankie is to me. She's kind and loving, and strong and fierce. She's what I want us to be together—she's what I want our kids to be.

I press a kiss to her forehead and bury my face in her neck as I feel sleep finally coming to me. And for the first time in fucking forever, Frankie and I sleep together...in my bed.

~

I don't know what time it is when I wake up because the curtains have been pulled over the windows so the bedroom is dark. All I know is that the space next to me is empty and cold. I find my boxers on the floor and step into them before following the smell of something delicious cooking in the kitchen.

There I find Frankie wearing nothing but my t-shirt as she stands at the stove, stirring a pot of something delicious. Her hips shimmy as she shifts back and forth to the music she has playing from her phone. It's upbeat and Latin and she's loving it. I can't help but grin as I watch her. I want to wake up to this every day for the rest of my life.

I sidle up behind her and reach around, lacing my arms around her stomach. She startles when I touch her until she leans back into my embrace.

"You scared me," she says, looking over her shoulder, her blue eyes finding mine.

"Sorry." I lean in and press a kiss to her soft lips. "You looked so cute dancing and what are you making?" My stomach rumbles. "It smells amazing."

"I had to improvise with what you had." She chuckles as she stirs the pot. "I found veggies, noodles, and chicken, so it's homemade chicken soup. Healthy and perfect for today since it's getting cold." She looks out the window and I see the overcast skies and the trees blowing in the wind.

"Well, it smells amazing."

"It should be ready in about a half hour." She sets the spoon in the spoon rest and turns in my arms, wrapping hers around my neck. "Until then, I was thinking maybe we could grab a shower together."

At her suggestion, I instantly get hard and she feels it, eliciting a smile from her. "Or maybe we can just go back to bed for a little bit," she adds.

I smirk against her lips. "You're insatiable, Ms. Callaway."

"Only with you, Mr. Ryan." She opens her mouth and her tongue finds mine.

"I think I'll take the bed option," I mumble as I lift her into my arms. As I begin carrying her out of the kitchen, her phone starts ringing, stopping the music.

"I should get that. It might be Faith." She wiggles out of my arms and walks across the kitchen to her phone. After looking at the screen, her body tenses and she silences the ringer but doesn't answer it.

"Everything okay?" I ask and she turns around to show me the screen that's illuminated with Ted's name scrawled across the face of it. My hands immediately clench. "What the hell does he want?"

She shakes her head and shrugs her shoulders. The one thing we haven't discussed yet is Ted and how everything between them was ultimately severed. "Don't know and don't care." She looks at me and I can see the apprehension on her face. From what, I don't know.

"Let me go start a fire in my office and let's talk," I suggest, knowing we can always resume our bedroom activities later. It's important to me that Frankie is safe and comfortable moving forward with us and leaving that fucker Ted in the past. It's not a conversation I'm looking forward to, but it's necessary and now seems like an appropriate time.

She nods and I notice her white knuckles gripping the phone. I reach for it and gently pull it from her hands, setting it on the kitchen counter. "Come on." I lace her fingers through mine and walk her down the hall to the office. Our last conversation in this room didn't go as well as I wanted it to, but this room is comfortable and where I handle business. Ted is nothing more than business to me. Failed business if I'm being honest, but I'd like to clear the air and leave him behind us once and for all.

Frankie's right, there is a chill throughout the house from the changing weather outside and the fire feels amazing as we settle onto the couch. I pull her close, draping a blanket over her bare legs as she snuggles up next to me.

"So let's pick up where we left off in L.A.," I start.

She swallows hard before taking a deep breath. I can only imagine the last thing she wants to do is talk to me about Ted. However, I want to know what we're dealing with when it comes to this asshole.

"So after you left that morning, I stayed in the hotel for a few more days," she begins, her thumb stroking mine as she speaks. "I enjoyed the space and the time to think with no one else around. Then I moved in with Eduardo and Jeremy. It just made sense. Eduardo offered their spare room. We worked together, they had the extra space, and he was helping me put my plan in place." She looks at me and her lips twist into a half smile.

By plan, she means the plan to come back here...to me. My heart skips a beat knowing that she spent so much time planning her future here—with me.

I nod, encouraging her to continue.

"While I was exploring and finalizing the details, Eduardo helped me pack everything I had at Ted's house. It wasn't much, mostly clothes and a few personal belongings. We had them shipped to his house so that once I get settled here he can ship them here. I wanted to get what I needed from Ted's house and be done."

"So it was a clean break, no separation of property or anything? There's nothing left to take care of with him?"

She shakes her head rapidly. "No. Everything was either in his name or belonged to him with the exception of my clothes, my phone, and my car. I even left the engagement ring on the bathroom counter. I wanted nothing to do with him...there is no reason for him to reach out to me."

I exhale a breath, satisfied with this answer.

She sighs. "He contacted me by text message a few times before I left Los Angeles, and then I got another text from him last night that said this wasn't over and he'd get me back."

"Not happening," I say firmly, not for her benefit but to keep from punching a wall.

She forces a smile. "I know. There is literally no reason for he and I to communicate. There are no joint bills, no exchange of property...it's done between us."

My stomach begins to settle when she says that.

"The only reason he's reaching out is because he has to be in control. He didn't end the relationship, I did. He hates not being in control."

I scoff at that. Fucker thinks he's that great, does he? "He ended it when you caught him in bed with another woman, Frankie."

She shakes her head again. "No. He didn't. He thought I'd just forgive him and we'd move on."

"So this is a power trip to him."

She nods. "That's all this is. I'm going to block his number and we'll never hear from him again." She stares into the fire before turning to look at me. "Cole. I chose you. I want to be with you. Please don't think for a minute that Ted is a threat to us."

I've never been an insecure person, but when you put

down on paper everything Ted is that I'm not, it's hard not to compare us. I can't compete with him.

He's a Harvard graduated lawyer. He owns a prominent law firm. His money could buy this entire town while I try to rebuild it piece by piece. I'm just a local guy, who works hard for what I have...and I do well, but not Ivy League lawyer well.

"Cole," she says my name, snapping me out of my thoughts. "Look at me." Her soft hands pull my face toward hers. "I chose us. I chose you."

"Us," I say, reminding myself.

"Us," she repeats.

I knock on the front door of Frankie's house, just like I did when we were kids. I'm a grown ass man, but I'm still giddy with anticipation at seeing her. After our talk this afternoon, we spent some time in bed before she decided to head back across the street to her house to see her mom. We made plans for dinner this evening, and I told her I'd pick her up around eight o'clock. Now here I stand, on her doorstep at seven fifty-seven, three minutes early because I cannot fucking wait.

I shuffle the large bouquet of flowers from hand to hand as I wait for her to answer the door.

The door creaks open and there stands Maggie Winthrop with her hand propped on her hip. "What do you want, Ryan?"

I stifle a laugh. "Well nice to see you, too, Mags. Gonna let me in?"

She narrows her eyes at me and shakes her head. "Grams is already in bed—" she starts, as if I'm here to see Grams with a bouquet of flowers. This kid loves to bust my balls. She knows why I'm here and who I'm here for. Her feisty personality and desire to protect those she loves reminds me so much of a younger Frankie that I can't find it in myself to even be upset with her.

I cock my head to the side, matching her. "I'm here for Frankie, Maggie."

She leans forward and whispers loudly, "I know who you're here for and if you hurt her again, I'll burn your house down."

I actually throw my head back and bust out laughing. Because goddamn the women in this family are fierce, and because I know she probably would.

"Cole!" Frankie's voice interrupts my laughter.

"I don't know what you see in him," Maggie mutters loud enough for both Frankie and I to hear as she walks away. "I'll be in Grams's room," she tosses over her shoulder.

Frankie's eyes grow wide as she watches her niece disappear. "I don't know what's gotten into her," she says, ushering me into the house.

"I don't want to wake your mom. Just throw these in some water and let's get out of here." I hand her the bouquet of mixed flowers. Roses, peonies, and giant daises all in different shades of pink.

"These are beautiful." She leans in to press a kiss to my lips. I snake my arm around her waist and hold her close to me. I used to sneak kisses from her on this threshold every chance I got. Only I won't sneak now...I'll take. I'm never letting her go.

"I never thought I'd see the day," the frail voice says from behind Frankie. We both turn to see Martha moving slowly toward us with a walker.

"Mama," Frankie gasps.

"Always knew you two would work through your problems." Martha's voice is quiet and slower than normal, but better than I expected.

Frankie glances at me and I chuckle. "Martha." I walk over and try to help her, but she shoos me away and takes one slow step after another, moving her walker in perfect coordination with her steps. Melinda is right behind her in case she loses her balance.

"I've been working with those darn therapists," she mumbles just as she reaches the couch. She braces herself on the arms of her walker before she slowly lowers herself down.

"I can't believe how well you're moving," Frankie comments, sitting down next to her mom.

"Enough about me. What're you kids up to tonight?" She pats Frankie's leg and winks at me with the side of her face that doesn't have paralysis.

"Was going to take Frankie out for a bit—" I pause when I notice the twinkle in Martha's eyes. Except it's not a twinkle, it's unshed tears. Frankie rubs her mom's hand and I walk over and squat down in front of her. "I told you that no matter what happened...I'd always take care of her."

Martha nods her head slowly.

"I love her, and I will keep that promise to my last breath."

Her chin trembles and her thin arms reach out for me. I lean in closer and she wraps them gently around my neck. With a little squeeze, she whispers, "thank you," before releasing me.

"You kids go have fun. I'm going to call it a night." Melinda jumps in to help get Martha up off the couch and to her walker. It is nice to see her getting around, albeit slow, but she's a fighter. I know where Frankie gets her fighting spirit from.

"Night, Mama." Frankie kisses her mom's cheek and grabs

her jacket. "Ready?" She looks at me as I watch Martha make her way back down the hall toward her room.

I smile at Frankie, feeling so complete for the first time in years. "Ready."

Frankie locks up behind us and I walk her across the street to my Jeep. "I was going to make you dinner, but then I had a better idea." I open the car door for her and she climbs up into the Jeep.

"Better idea?" Her eyebrows shoot up.

I know what she's thinking. There isn't a damn restaurant in this town other than the American Legion and it's past dinner hours there and Gus's diner is closed for the night. So unless I want to take her to the Sonic Drive-In, there isn't much choice for dinner out here in Crescent Ridge.

"It's a surprise," I tell her, sliding into the driver's seat, "but first I want to show you something."

Frankie settles into the front seat of the Jeep, resting her head back against the headrest as she looks out the window. "Everything looks so different," she remarks quietly as I drive down our street and toward Main Street where most of the revitalization is happening. "I used to think everything here was so big, and it's not...it's so small." She turns her head to look at me. I still see the eyes of eleven and sixteen-year-old Frankie looking back at me and my heart swells that she's here with me.

"Bigger isn't always better," I say, pursing my lips. I'm not sure where she's going with this, so I don't pry.

"It's not. It's definitely not. In Los Angeles everything was so big. The buildings, the houses, the roads, but the details and the character were lost," she sighs. She's right, the homes here are far from luxury, but they're beautifully constructed and have lasted decades.

"It's really nice to see this town coming back," she huffs out a small laugh. "I never thought I'd say that."

I nod and drive as she really takes in all of the change that's happened around here.

"I can't believe you're responsible for this, Cole." I can feel her eyes on me as I focus on the road. I've been lucky to make good money and reinvest in Crescent Ridge, but I'm not responsible for this. It's the people that never gave up on this town. There are good people here who need jobs, and I'm just glad I can give that to them.

"I'm not responsible—"

"Yes, you are," she cuts me off. "You invested back into this town when everyone else abandoned it. Look at this place." She points to The Fault Line Bar and Grill as I pull up in front of it. "This place is like no other. This town needed a place like this; you saw that and made it happen."

I love her enthusiasm and my heart thrums as I can see how proud she is. I kill the engine and turn to face her. "Come with me, this is what I want to show you." I open the car door and walk around to open hers.

She steps down from the Jeep and reaches for my hand. "Where are we going?" she asks as we walk past The Fault Line Bar and Grill and down the dimly lit street.

The old streetlights barely cast enough light to see the buildings, the part of town that used to be full of businesses but has died slowly over time. What Frankie doesn't know is I bought every building on this street...and there's one in particular I want to show her.

"Where are you taking me?" she asks curiously as we come to a stop in front of the small red brick building.

"Do you remember what this was?" I look at the boards that

are nailed up to protect the large glass window. It's a non-descript square brick building with huge glass windows in front and a gorgeous custom-built wood door.

She squeezes my hand tighter as she remembers. "It was a second-hand thrift store. I remember it well."

"Good memory." I kick a rock off the sidewalk.

"I used to get my clothes here." Her voice becomes softer, and I can hear the emotion. "Faith and I used to get two outfits for every school year. God, I can't believe that's all we could afford." She presses her fingers on the rough, exposed brick.

I reach into my pocket and pull out a single key, squeezing it into the palm of my hand. "Here." I hold out my hand toward Frankie.

"What?" she asks, confused and looking at my closed fist.

"Open your hand."

She pulls her hand off of the brick and opens it slowly. I carefully drop the key into her palm and she just looks at it, perplexed. "What is this?"

I turn back and look at the building. "It's the key to your building." My heart soars, knowing I can give her a piece of the town she once so badly wanted to escape from. I want her to set up roots here, with me, in Crescent Ridge. I never want her to feel like she has to escape again.

"My building?" she asks, amused. "This isn't my building, Cole."

I turn back to look at her and I see a million things flash before my eyes. Memories from our past and visions of our future.

"It is now, Frankie. Open the door."

TWENTY

Frankie

"What in the world?" is all I can say when we step over the threshold and into the old brick building. "Cole!" I call to him as I tip my head back and look around. "There's nothing in here."

"It's a clean slate," he says, shoving his hands down into his pockets. It's dark and chilly in this drafty old building, and I have to use the light from my cell phone to take a quick look around. "Do whatever you want with the place."

"I don't even know what to say," I keep spinning in slow circles, looking at every wall, up to the ceiling, and down to the floor, "except, thank you." My heart races with the possibilities that could happen with this space. I race over to Cole and slide my arms around his waist.

"You're welcome," he says softly, leaning down and pressing a kiss to the top of my head. "Come on, let's lock up. I have surprise number two for you tonight."

We lock up and Cole wraps his arm around me as we walk back toward his car. But before we get to his car, he turns us left down the dark alley that runs next to The Fault Line. There's a small light above a side door casting a halo of light around the area and we walk toward that.

As we approach, I see a sign that says, 'Employee Entrance Only' and Cole slides a key into the handle before pulling the door open. When we step inside, we're instantly surrounded by warmth and greeted with the aroma of fresh food cooking.

"This is where employees will enter. There are lockers for their personal belongings and a tablet where they can sign in and out." Cole points to the wall lined with small lockers and an iPad secured to the wall for timekeeping.

"It smells amazing in here!" I remark, trying to peek outside of the employee room and into the attached kitchen.

"Mario?" Cole calls out as he pulls me through the gorgeous kitchen. Everything is shiny and new and so clean, and I can't believe that Cole built this place.

"Ciao!" I hear a deep male voice call out from somewhere behind the stoves.

Suddenly, an older gentleman steps out from behind a wall and rushes over to greet us. "Sir, Ma'am." He wipes his hands on his apron before reaching out to shake Cole's hand and mine.

"Mario, this is Frances." I notice how he uses my formal name to introduce me and not Frankie.

"Pleasure to meet you, Bella." Mario's Italian accent is thick and he pulls my hand to his mouth and kisses the top of it. He is a short, portly man with rosy red cheeks and a tuft of gray hair.

"Lovely to meet you." I smile at him and glance at Cole, who's grinning from ear to ear.

"Mario is going to be cooking a special dinner for us

tonight," he says to me, then glancing back to Mario, he says, "We're going to go to the private dining room, take your time."

Mario nods at Cole and kisses the top of my hand once again before scurrying back into the kitchen. Pots and pans clank together and I follow Cole out of the kitchen and into an area in the back of the restaurant that I couldn't see the other night.

"Back here are a few private dining areas." Cole gestures with his hand as we walk by two rooms, one larger with a table that probably seats twenty, and another smaller room with a large round table that seats ten.

"We're using this room tonight." He pauses at the entrance before stepping aside. The room is dim, lit only by the candles in the center of the table. Small, low standing vases full of white roses encircle the candle centerpiece.

"Cole, this is stunning." I step into the room and he follows closely behind me.

"Sit down," he encourages me, helping me out of my jacket. There is a large standing wine bucket next to the table with a bottle of wine that's already been corked. Cole sits next to me and pours us each a glass of white wine.

I lean in, pressing a kiss to Cole's cheek. "I didn't think this place was open for business yet."

He smirks at me. "I happen to know the owner. He's a pretty cool dude and decided to let me wine and dine my woman here tonight." His blue eyes dance in the soft light of the candles.

I'll never get enough of him. He is everything I ever wanted and my heart soars with happiness that we're getting our second chance.

Cole wraps his hand around mine and presses his lips to

mine, causing a warmth to spread throughout my body. My heart pounds wildly as I look at all he's done to redeem himself.

I stifle a laugh. "Sounds like you have pretty amazing friends."

"Only the best," he jokes. "In all honesty, I wanted an amazing night with you alone, Frankie. Tomorrow is the soft opening for friends and family, and Sunday is the grand opening. It's going to be a busy week and I wanted to do something special for just you and me."

"I love it," I whisper and take a sip of my Pinot Grigio.

"I love you." His words are barely above a whisper, but I hear them loud and clear. His hand sits comfortably over mine and his eyes hold an intensity I've never seen before.

Without a thought, I unbury my broken heart again. "I love you too." The words fall from my lips naturally. I don't have to think about whether I mean them or if I'm saying them just to appease him. I'm not. I buried those feelings and words for Cole so many years ago. Stuffed them down where I never thought I'd use them again. I somehow feel lighter now that I'm speaking the truth.

He raises his glass in a toast. "To us."

I raise my glass as well. "To us."

Cole left early this morning to get everything ready for tonight's soft opening of The Fault Line, but not before waking me up for an early morning love session. He left me with a kiss and orders to go back to sleep. Now I lay wrapped in his sheets, his masculine smell surrounding me. My body is tender in the most satisfying ways, and for the first time in a long time, I wake feeling content.

Throwing on Cole's button down shirt from last night, I roll the sleeves and head to the kitchen to make coffee. I send a reminder text to Faith about tonight's opening of the bar and grill and remind her to book a babysitter for the kids. As I'm pouring a cup of coffee, I hear the front door open and a huge smile spreads across my face.

"Hey, babe! I'm in here!" I yell from the kitchen.

"Hey, honey, I'm home." I hear in response. Only it's not Cole's voice I hear behind me. I whip around to see Carter stroll into the kitchen, stopping dead in his tracks. "Jesus Christ, woman! Put some damn clothes on." He turns around quickly and covers his eyes. Cole's white dress shirt is fortunately long enough to cover all the important parts, but leaves little to the imagination when only two buttons are buttoned and it hangs off my shoulder.

"What're you doing here, Carter?" I yell.

"Don't yell at me. I'm looking for your damn boyfriend. Got shit blowing up at the shop."

"Don't you know how to knock?" I bark at him, shifting nervously and tugging at the hem of the shirt.

"Never needed to knock before," he mutters under his breath.

"What in the hell is going on?" I hear Cole's voice boom as the front door slams closed.

Both Carter and I are trying to talk over each other and Cole's eyes grow wide when he walks into the kitchen and looks between the two of us. He looks at Carter first, whose back is turned to me with his hands pressed over his face and then Cole looks to me, standing in the middle of his kitchen, wearing nothing but his button down shirt from last night.

"Your friend needs to learn how to knock," I snap at Cole, narrowing my eyes at Carter. Not that he can see me glaring at him, but it makes me feel better.

Cole snorts, looking back to Carter who grumbles, "And your girlfriend needs to keep some damn clothes on. Doesn't she know people stop by here unexpectedly?"

Cole props his hands on his hips, shaking his head as Carter and I bicker.

"He just walked in here like he owns the place," I continue, pointing at Carter.

"Stop!" Cole barks and I take a step back. "Carter. Learn to fucking knock. There is no way I'm telling my woman to put on more clothes." He looks at me, licking his bottom lip. "This is exactly how I want to come home to her." His eyes grow darker and his lips twist into an evil grin.

Carter grumbles, knowing he's lost this argument and his hands drop from his face to his hips.

I yell at him, "Carter, don't you dare turn around!" And like that I take off from the kitchen, round the corner, and run down the hall to Cole's bedroom.

Cole hollers from behind me, "Don't change, Frankie. I'll be back there in a minute." I can hear Carter and Cole's muted voices for a moment before the front door opens and closes. The sound of Cole's heavy footsteps draw closer just as the bedroom door opens and Cole appears.

The darkness in his eyes has turned rabid, and the smile on his face is now gone. He breathes heavily and without hesitation, he lunges at me, scooping me up into his arms. "You have no idea how fucking sexy you are wearing nothing but my shirt." He buries his face in my chest, nudging his shirt down further and giving him access to my breasts.

I wiggle out of his grasp, wrapping my legs around his waist, my wet center pressed against him.

"Fuck, Frankie," he growls as he pulls one of my nipples into his mouth. "I have a million things to do, but the only thing I want to do is you."

I reach down between us and unfasten the button of his jeans just as he plunges a finger inside me. I gasp loudly and he chuckles knowing I'm a goner. "Just feel it, baby," he whispers in my ear.

He inserts another finger, curling it to hit that spot that sends me over the edge. My head falls back as I ride his hand and my entire body shudders around him.

"Good girl." He sets me down on the bed and pulls his t-shirt off. He makes quick work of removing his jeans and kneeling down between my legs. "I'm not done with you yet, though." He smirks and positions himself directly at my center.

In one swift movement, he's inside me and my entire body begins to shudder again. Everything about this man is paralyzing. His hands control me, and his heart owns me. My heart stammers and my skin prickles with goose bumps as he thrusts in and out.

Our bodies are a tangled web of limbs and the room is filled with the sounds of our moans as he brings me to the brink of another orgasm.

"Cole," I gasp in between breaths as he kisses me.

"I love you, Frankie," he mumbles against my lips as I feel him harden and spill his release into me. "God, I fucking love you." He presses his forehead to mine while I try to catch my breath. "I'll never get enough of you."

"I love you, too," I admit my feelings for him. It's real and raw and tears prick at my eyes as I let him all the way in.

He stays inside me, his hands laced through mine on either side of my head. "Marry me, Frankie. You're it for me. Always have been." His blue eyes search mine.

I feel a lump in my throat beginning to grow. "Cole," I barely manage.

"Don't answer now. I know you've been back for, what, two days? But I don't want to lose another day without you. Marry me. Be mine."

I close my eyes and let his words sink in. *Marry me.* Those are the words I've always dreamt of hearing him say.

"Think about it." He kisses the tip of my nose and carefully pulls himself out of me. "As much as I'd like round three for the day, I have to get back to work. We'll resume this tonight." He stands up and slides back into his jeans. A huge grin spreads across his face as he stands over me.

"What?" I ask, suddenly feeling self-conscious.

"You have no idea how fucking sexy you look lying on my bed looking thoroughly fucked. Round three. Tonight. Go get ready. I'll be back to get you in a couple of hours."

TWENTY-ONE

Cole

"You ready for this, boss?" Justin, our lead bartender, slaps me on the shoulder.

I take one last look around the transformed space. Everything looks like it's in place, but my nerves are still on edge. I want perfection. Tonight is a big deal for me.

I nod and roll my bottom lip between my fingers, hoping to calm myself. "Yeah, I think so. Ready as I'll ever be. Did the liquor arrive?" I mentally run through the checklist of things that we were still waiting on and liquor was number one on the list.

He wipes the counter, pausing to take a look around the bar area. "Everything is here, exactly as it should be. Go home and get ready. Relax for a bit. We've got everything under control here."

He's right. I need to relinquish control to the people I hired. They are fully capable of doing what they were hired to do.

"You got it." I run my fingers through my hair and check the time. "See you in a couple of hours."

When I get home, Frankie is standing in my bathroom, applying makeup. Not that she needs any, she's fucking perfection just the way she is.

"You're finally here." She spins around and kisses me as I wrap my arms around her waist, holding her tightly.

"Yep. Gonna shower quick before we go."

"Everything all set over there? Do you need help with anything?"

"Everything is under control. Your job tonight is to enjoy yourself." I press a kiss to her forehead before letting her go.

I step into the hot shower, allowing the water to ease some of the stress in my neck and shoulders. I have a lot riding on tonight between the restaurant and Frankie.

"I can't even begin to tell you how proud of you I am." Frankie beams as we pull up outside The Fault Line Bar and Grill, parking along the curb.

"This would mean nothing if you weren't here with me," I tell her, squeezing her hand in mine.

She shakes her head. "Stop," she says quietly.

"I'm serious. You always made me want to be a better man. It took letting you go for me to realize that—and now we've come full circle." I lean in and press a kiss to her lips. "I love you, Frankie. Thank you for being here with me." She smiles against my lips and rubs her hand over my cheek. "Now let's get inside before I change my mind and take you home and straight to bed."

She laughs and my heart instantly warms. I hold her hand tightly as we walk through the front door to see the place fully packed. Everything is exactly as I imagined it would be. The low lights accent the brick walls and complement the iron and wood touches throughout the restaurant. The staff's friends and family are spread out throughout the place, sitting at tables and bellied up to the bar. The space is full of conversation and laughter, and seeing it all finally begins to calm my nerves.

Faith and Carter are already sitting at the table I reserved for us tonight, and both stand up and greet us.

"Congratulations!" Faith squeals, surprising the shit out of me when she pulls me in for a quick hug. "This place is stunning."

Out of the corner of my eye, I see Carter give Frankie a one-armed hug and they both break out into laughter, presumably making up for this afternoon. As kids, they were always at each other's throats and then making up again. It seems nothing has changed with those two.

I feel my heart squeeze in my chest. Everything in my life feels like it's falling into place. The people who are the most important to me are here and that's what matters more than anything. One of the servers, Mireya, delivers a tray of drinks to the table and Carter reaches in, picking up the first glass.

"A toast." He lifts his glass, and Faith, Frankie, and I each grab a glass off the tray. "To new beginnings." He looks around the restaurant and then at me and Frankie. "And to second chances."

At 'second chances', my heart skips a beat when I see Frankie grin, her blue eyes beaming. "To second chances," she responds to him, but she's looking at me.

"Cheers!" Faith shouts over the noise and Carter wraps his arm around her shoulder as they both sip their drink.

"Cheers," Frankie and I respond and we take a sip of our drink in celebration.

~

Hours pass by and I've talked to just about everybody who's come in tonight. The feedback thus far, on everything from the atmosphere to the food and staff, have all by far exceeded my expectations. Everyone has loved everything. This is exactly what Crescent Ridge needed I heard time and again. A place that'll bring everyone together with food and drinks in a modern atmosphere without losing the history that is Crescent Ridge.

Frankie encouraged me to spend as much time talking to everyone this evening, building relationships and making sure everyone was comfortable while she sat with Carter and Faith.

I wanted nothing more than to never leave her side, but she knew what I needed to do and promised me we'd have our time together later this evening. Looking at her across the restaurant, her eyes beaming and her head tipped back in laughter, makes my entire night. Seeing her happy is all I want in life.

As the crowd begins to thin, I make my way back to Frankie's side and sidle up on the stool next to her. She wraps her arm around my waist, pulling me to her just as I lean down and kiss her soft lips.

"So what'd you guys think?"

Carter shakes his head and chuckles. "I never thought

you'd follow through on this, but look at this place." He gestures with his hand. "You're gonna fucking kill it!"

"It's everything this town needed, Cole," Faith jumps in. "It's perfect."

"It's not too much?" I ask, worried that maybe it's a little over the top for Crescent Ridge, regardless of the feedback I got tonight. If anyone would be honest with me, it's these people right here.

Frankie shakes her head. "No. It's rustic and homey and not overstated. The pictures of old Crescent Ridge really drive home the history of this town. You're bringing the old and new together." She grabs the collar of my shirt and pulls me down for another kiss. "I'm so goddamn proud of you," she mumbles against my lips.

"Well, isn't this fucking cute." A male voice cuts off our moment.

Frankie's head snaps away from me and Faith's eyes widen as a tall man with salt and pepper hair sets a drink on the table.

"Ted," Frankie says with a shaky voice. "What the hell are you doing here?"

"I should be asking you that." He smirks and takes a long pull of his drink before slamming it down on the table. "What the *fuck* are *you* doing here? All you ever talked about was what a little piece of shit town this was, and yet here you are." He looks around the table with disdain.

I step around Frankie in a protective nature, ready to let this fucker have it if I have to.

"Leave," Frankie snaps at him from behind me.

"Ted," I say his name as calmly as I can, meeting him eye to eye. He's the same height at me, but I easily have forty pounds of muscle on this guy. He's lean and, while he may have me beat in the brains and career department, I will kick his ass into next week if he moves one fucking inch closer to Frankie.

"Who the fuck are you?" he barks, talking down to me. His angry eyes look me up and down.

"Cole Ryan, owner of this establishment and you heard the lady—leave."

He snorts. "I don't take orders from you...or Frances." He steps closer, pressing his chest to mine. "I'm here for Frances—" I press a hand to his chest, backing him up as he continues. "And as soon as she gets her fucking head back on straight, we'll be out of your hair and this dumpster fire of a town." He rolls his fingers on the table as if he's genuinely going to wait for Frankie.

I take a deep breath, willing myself to calm the fuck down before I plant a fist through his face. I lean in closely. "She's done with you, Teddy." I pat his chest, hard enough for him to take what I'm saying as a warning. "You heard her. This is the last time I will ask you leave before I make you leave."

He blows a huff of air through his lips and leans around me to look at Frankie.

"So this is how this is going to go, huh?" His face is pure hatred, narrowed eyes and pursed lips. "You're just going to give up a career you worked so hard for, one that I helped you build, for this piece of shit ex-boyfriend who owns a 'bar and grill'," he says with air quotes. "You're just going to act like the little whore you are and jump back into bed with this nobody and make another baby with him, all while living happily ever after in Crescent Ridge?"

I feel Frankie's fingers digging into my back like she's holding on for dear life, and Faith reaches across the table faster than I've ever seen her, picking up Frankie's drink and throwing it in Ted's face.

Vodka tonic is dripping from his chin as he lets out a low chuckle. It's then that what he said registers with me. The entire restaurant grows quiet as the remaining customers turn their attention toward us.

"What do you mean make another baby?" I turn and look at Frankie as my stomach flips and my mind searches for understanding.

His head falls back with laughter as he wipes his face with his sleeve. "Oh, this is so fucking good." He laughs harder. "Frances. You didn't tell him about the baby?" He clicks his tongue in disapproval. I have never wanted to punch someone so fucking bad.

I look over my shoulder at Frankie, whose entire body is shaking. Tears are falling in a steady stream down her face. Carter is holding back a wild Faith, who is trying to get out of his grasp.

"You fucking piece of shit!" Faith screams at Ted as she becomes more erratic. "I will fucking kill you."

His lips twist into an evil grin and he laughs at Faith before turning his attention back to Frankie. "Frances, last chance. Come home with me." He holds out his hand as if he's reaching for her. "Your home is with me, in Los Angeles. Leave this shitty town and everyone in it in your past—where it belongs." He looks at me and smirks.

Confusion and understanding simultaneously smack me just as something inside me snaps. I don't even feel my fist leave my side, let alone connect with Ted's face, however a single punch sends him to the floor. Blood spurts from his nose as I shake my hand once before actually thinking about hitting him this time. I lean over his cowering figure and punch him again, this time my fist connecting with his jaw. Every ounce of hurt and anger I've pent up for ten years rises from within and I swing again. Out of the corner of my eye, I barely register Carter releasing Faith and running to me as Faith runs to Frankie.

I can hear Frankie's sobs as I stand over a bleeding Ted, deciding if he's worth a fourth blow. But my anger is bubbling over, and I know if I hit him again, I'll kill him. Because I won't stop. I'll finish this motherfucker right here on the floor of my restaurant.

Carter grabs my arm and pulls me back. "Let it go, man. Get Frankie out of here and go home."

I shake my head and stare at the piece of garbage groaning on my floor. Clenching my fists, I force myself to take a step back.

My lungs feel like they're collapsing as I struggle to breathe. "Is it true?" I ask Frankie, my voice hoarse.

Faith has her enveloped in her arms as both of them cry, their arms wrapped around each other protectively.

"Tell me the truth, Frankie." My voice breaks as I run a hand over my face. "We promised no lies."

With a whimper, she nods, and my heart fucking explodes. My mind is in a million places as I look around. Justin, the bartender is ushering the last customers out the door as quickly as he can, and Carter stands waiting for me to make my next move so he can intervene. He's always been the smart one.

We stare at each other for a moment, me breathing heavily as the rage builds again. How the fuck did Ted know and I never did? How could she have kept a secret so big?

Carter contemplates my next move and shakes his head at me.

"Make sure they get home safely," I finally grind out, nodding toward Faith and Frankie as I step over Ted. "And get the fuck out of my restaurant." For my own satisfaction, I reel my foot back and kick him in the ribs on my way out.

Fuck them all.

With a closed fist, I beat the steering wheel as I drive around town trying to burn off some of my anger. I'm not ready to face Frankie yet. My cell phone has been ringing non-stop for the last half hour and I finally shut the fucker off, tossing it on the passenger seat.

Normally, I'd end up at the fault line with a bottle of Jack Daniel's. But tonight I find myself on the opposite side of town, in another familiar place.

My Jeep is crawling down the narrow paved road and I kill the engine as I roll to a stop. Heartache overtakes me as my feet carry me across the neatly trimmed grass and I fall to my knees. I gasp for air as I look at the etched stone.

"God, I need your advice, Pops." And the dam of emotions breaks free as I scream at the top of my lungs.

TWENTY-TWO

Frankie

"Where the fuck is he, Carter?" I slap the center console of his beat up pickup truck.

He throws his hand up. "If I fucking knew that, I'd tell you; he's not answering his phone—so get off my nuts, Frankie."

I need to talk to Cole, now. I bounce my knee as Carter drives me around town, looking for any signs of Cole or his Jeep. "He's probably at the fault line," Carter says, making a sharp U-turn.

"He's not," I cry out, feeling my desperation clawing at me. I'm so worried about him. "His jeep would either be at home or parked by the entrance to the trail."

Carter sighs deeply because he knows I'm right, but mostly because he knows he's going to be driving my ass around until we find Cole. Suddenly swerving, Carter pulls over to the side of the road as he throws his truck in park.

"I don't know, Frankie. Maybe he doesn't want to be found," he snaps at me. "That was some pretty fucked up news your fiancé fucking threw at Cole tonight." He glares at me.

I swallow hard. "He's *not* my fiancé, and it wasn't his news to share." I inhale a ragged breath. "He did that to hurt me. He doesn't want me back. He wants to make me suffer, and if hurting Cole is a means to that end, Ted will do it. He's a vindictive asshole." I turn and look out the passenger window as I feel the tears burning in the back of my eyes.

Carter taps the steering wheel impatiently with his thumbs. "It's really none of my business, Frankie. But were you ever going to tell him?"

I can't look at Carter as I feel the tears threaten to spill from my eyes, so I just simply nod in response. My fingers are twisted together in a ball on my lap and I choke back a sob.

Carter wraps his hand over mine, giving me a gentle squeeze. "Give him time, Frankie. His world was just turned upside down."

"Kind of like mine was ten years ago when I came home to tell my boyfriend I was pregnant and found him kissing a pregnant Whitney Carson on his front porch?"

Carter stares straight ahead out and purses his lips. "Two wrongs don't make a right, Frankie. You should've told him."

"I was going to, it's just that everything with us was happening so fast, and this was big...I needed to find the right time."

"Not that I'm Dr. Phil or anything, but the right time would've been when he was in Los Angeles, pining for you."

I get ready to say something and then snap my mouth shut, because motherfucking Carter Richardson is once again the goddamn voice of reason.

"If we find him, Frankie, what're you going to do?"

I finally have the courage to look at Carter, not even embarrassed that I'm a snotty mess again. My voice breaks,

"Tell him the truth." I wipe my tears with the back of my hand and Carter hands me a napkin from the pocket in the side panel of his door to wipe my nose. "What he chooses to do with that truth is up to him."

"You gonna run again?" he asks softly.

Once upon a time, Carter's directness used to be annoying. Now it's welcome.

I shake my head as I wipe my nose. My voice is barely above a whisper. "Nah, I'm done running."

He offers me a tight smile. "Good." He reaches for the gearshift and throws the car in drive before making another U-turn and heading back in the direction we just came from.

"Where are you going?" I ask as Carter presses the gas pedal on his old truck and we speed up, the back wheels spinning for a moment on the loose gravel.

He turns to look at me with a mischievous look on his face. "Taking you to Cole."

Carter kills the lights on the pickup truck as we pull through the main entrance of Sacred Heart Cemetery. His truck is louder than a bulldozer, so I'm sure if Cole is here, he is acutely aware of our presence.

As we round the corner, I see Cole's Jeep parked alongside the narrow, paved road. Carter rolls up next to the Jeep and cuts the engine. I rub the palms of my hands on my thighs as I nervously look out the window for Cole. Carter's long arm reaches past me as I see exactly where he is pointing. Cole is sitting at the far end of a row of headstones, his back pressed against the last one.

"His dad," Carter says quietly. I swallow hard and nod in understanding. Reaching for the door handle, Carter's hand grips my arm firmly. "Be honest with him, Frankie. If he's here, he's hurting. Don't bullshit him." His large hand releases me and the truck door springs open.

The heels of my shoes poke at the firm ground as I walk briskly toward Cole. The air has turned cooler and with each ragged exhale I can see my breath in the air. As I approach, I see him slumped over, his arms resting on his propped up knees, his head fallen forward just as I found him in the hallway of the hotel in Los Angeles when he came back for me.

Now I'm coming for him.

"Cole," I say his name softly, even though I know he knows I'm here.

He doesn't move, but I see his hand flinch. I sit down next to him. My butt hits the cold ground and I tuck my legs under me. I'm careful to give him space, but I want nothing more than to reach out and wrap my arms around him.

We sit in silence for a few minutes before I finally gather the nerve to start my explanation. "I'm going to start from the beginning. I'm sure you'll have a million questions...questions you rightfully deserve the answers to. I'll tell you everything and I'll be one hundred percent honest with you, but please let me tell you everything before you lash out at me. Let me finish, please." I beg this of him, just as he begged this of me when he explained his reasons for what he did to us ten years ago.

"A week and a half before I came home and found you with Whitney on your front porch, I found out I was pregnant." I swallow hard, fighting back my tears as I remember how hurt and alone I felt, coming home pregnant and finding him and Whitney together. "I woke up one morning feeling like I had the flu, only it lasted twenty-four hours a day and for four days. At first, I thought it was because I was pulling such long nights studying and preparing for finals, but after a few days, I knew it had to be more."

I rub my arms, fighting back the chill in the air. "Ashley finally insisted I take a pregnancy test, because I had been home to visit you just over four weeks prior to all of my symptoms starting. It was our last time together..." My voice trails off.

Clearing my throat, I forge on. "The test was positive...and, God, Cole, I was such a mix of emotions. Initially I was scared. So scared...Then I was excited. We always used to talk about having kids and getting married, and then I got nervous. We were so young, so ignorant to the real world and all of its realities. I knew I wanted to finish my undergraduate degree and go to law school, and I didn't know what all of this meant for *us*." My fingers pick at the grass on either side of my legs while Cole remains still next to me.

"I decided to speak to my professors to see if I could finish my finals early so that I could get home to you as soon as possible. This wasn't a conversation to have over the phone."

Cole suddenly sits up straight, lifting his head, but he looks straight ahead and not at me.

I swallow hard and continue. "So I finished and rushed home to tell you. I was so nervous, Cole...but I always remember what you told me, that there wasn't anything you and I couldn't conquer together." I pause. "So when I pulled up that night and I saw you and Whitney, I broke. I'd heard the rumors floating around about you...and Mama told me to ignore them, but when Whitney ran across the street and I saw her swollen stomach...a little piece of me died."

He inhales sharply and I continue. "I called Ashley that night and she asked me to spend the summer in Malibu with her and her family. She promised to help me with whatever I decided to do with the baby." I pause, taking a deep breath and to get my emotions under control again.

I hear Cole clear his throat and it startles me. "Did you have an abortion?" His head finally turns and he looks directly at me, his blue eyes rimmed with red, his cheeks damp from tears, and a world of hurt etched across his face.

I shake my head. "No. I didn't."

His shoulders fall slightly, in partial relief.

"I thought about it, I'm not going to lie," I admit. "So that next morning I drove to Malibu, not sure what I was going to do with my life. I had a million decisions to make. Would I keep the baby? Have an abortion? Give it up for adoption? And then I had to think about the consequences of each of those decisions. If I kept the baby, I'd have to quit school, or at least not go full-time. I'd possibly lose my scholarship and I couldn't afford USC on my own. There were so many decisions I had to make, *alone*, Cole."

I'm not blaming him, but he is also not free of the hurt he caused me. He put into motion a series of events that led me to making the decision I had to. I was an asshole for not telling him, but almost eleven years ago, I was a hurt kid whose world had just been shattered.

"I was a scared kid who moved in with her college roommate that summer. Ashley's parents were nothing short of saints. I had nothing. Literally. I had no job, a shitty, unreliable car, and no money. They helped me with everything.

They made sure I had the best doctor, they fed and clothed me, and supported me with whatever decision I made. They cancelled their summer European vacation to make sure that I was taken care of. I was Ashley's best friend and they treated me like a daughter." I will never be able to repay them for the kindness they showed me. I was nothing more than Ashley's best friend and roommate and their unwavering support changed my life.

I take a deep breath and choke back another wave of emotions. "One night, I was sitting on their patio and Joe and Anne approached me with an offer."

Cole shifts and slides his legs out as he listens to me.

"When Anne had Ashley, she had a terrible pregnancy. They had to do an emergency hysterectomy and she was never able to have more children. For years they jumped through hoops trying to do a domestic adoption and nothing ever panned out for them. They spent thousands on attorneys and with agencies praying for another child. A year prior to all of this, they finally began the process of trying for an international adoption. Part of their summer vacation was going to be spent touring international orphanages. They made a proposal and I accepted it."

I see a single tear fall down Cole's cheek and I feel my chin begin to tremble as I see how this is affecting him. "Anne and Joe asked to adopt our baby. They'd cover my medical expenses and they gave me money for law school."

"You sold our baby?" Cole snaps.

I gasp. "It wasn't a sale, Cole. Joe hired an attorney for me, to make sure that I understood my rights, that I was protected, and what birth mothers are entitled to...such as medical care, compensation for expenses, etc."

His face twists with anger. "What the fuck are birth fathers entitled to? Sounds like a fucking sale to me."

My temper flares. "It wasn't a goddamn sale, Cole. They also offered me an open adoption. Meaning at any time, they'd let me see our baby. They promised me they'd be honest with the baby about the adoption—"

"It was all about you, wasn't it, Frankie?" he says bitterly, his eyes full of disgust. "Just stop talking. I think I'm going to be sick to my stomach." His lips curl in hatred. I slide back further away from him as he tips his head back and inhales deep breaths.

"I'm not done," I tell him, doing my best to stay strong. He has no idea what it's been like living with this for all these years.

"I can't hear any more of this." He pushes himself up and stands over me. His large form is intimidating and daunting. Hurt has been replaced by anger on his face and he clenches his fists. "I don't even know who you are. The Frankie I fell in love with would've never done what you did." He steps over my legs and walks toward his Jeep.

Anger and hurt course through me and I snap back at him, "And the Cole I fell in love with would've never set into motion the lie that made me do that." At that, he suddenly stops but doesn't turn around. "I'm not running this time, Cole. I'm done running. You don't have to forgive me, but at least have the courtesy to hear me out."

I hear him mumble something under his breath, but he walks away. This time, he's the one running.

～

Carter brought me home and for the last two hours I've been peeking out the front window, hoping to see Cole's Jeep parked across the street in his driveway. He still hasn't returned home and my heart thrums nervously as I wonder where he's at and if he's okay.

It's six in the morning and sleep won't come to me, so I decide to throw on my workout clothes and tennis shoes and go for a run. I hit the pavement with one goal in mind...to clear my head. I warm up with a slow jog, but before long I'm at a full sprint. My legs move quickly, carrying me across the old concrete streets of Crescent Ridge. I run past The Fault Line Bar and Grill and thoughts of Ted and the whole fucked up situation last night make me nauseous. I wonder for a moment if Ted is still in town, but knowing him, after getting his ass beat he's back in Los Angeles tending to his bruised ego and his broken nose.

I slow down my pace as my heart beats wildly in my chest and I finally come to a stop, resting my hands on my knees as I bend over trying to catch my breath. My ponytail hangs over my shoulder and sweat drips off my nose and onto the pavement. My ears sting from the cool morning air and I take deep breaths of it, feeling the sting deep in my lungs.

I hear a car pull up next to me before I hear Cole's voice. "Get in," he orders.

Frowning, I stand up and look over at him. He's still in the same clothes as last night and looks as though he hasn't slept either. Swallowing hard, I press my hands into my hips and take in the beautiful sight of him.

Thick forearms grip the steering wheel as he waits for me to move, and I wonder how our worlds could be turned upside down so many times and if we'll ever be able to get beyond our past.

He rubs his eyes slowly with the heel of his palms as he patiently waits for me. I hesitate only because I'm angry at him for walking away last night, but I've never feared Cole. My feet finally move and I pull the handle on the Jeep and step up into the passenger seat. He takes off before I even have time to buckle my seat belt.

We drive in silence for about twenty minutes, out past the edge of town to a secluded, wooded area. I remember camping out here once as a teen with Cole and Carter and some of the other kids from high school.

"What are we doing here?" I ask when he finally kills the engine. I can tell his mood has shifted back to something more resolute and less angry. I find this an odd place to bring me as my eyes search for any reason he'd bring me here.

He shrugs and rubs his cheek. "Used to come here after you left, just to think or get drunk." He turns and looks at me. "Never felt right going back to the fault line without you, but this place kind of reminded me of it so this is where I'd come."

"I shouldn't have cut you off last night, Frankie," he starts, clearing his throat. "I want you to finish, you deserve my attention, just as you gave me yours. I won't interrupt you this time."

For some reason, probably the lack of sleep, or maybe talking about our past and the deepest, saddest secret I've ever held on to...something inside me breaks. My anxiety is at an all-time high and I literally lose it. Burying my face in my hands, I sob. My entire body shakes and I struggle to catch my breath.

"Hey, hey..." I feel Cole's hand on my shoulder. It's gentle and comforting, but I can't stop the flood of tears. "Talk to me," he says as I wipe my tears with the back of my hand. "Finish your story."

It takes me a minute to gain my composure, but I nod and swallow back the large lump in my throat. With a staggered breath, I continue where I left off last night.

"I accepted the open adoption as it was proposed by Ashley's parents." I turn to look at Cole as he sits somberly, chewing on his bottom lip. "It was the best option for all of us," I tell him weakly. I will always regret not telling him about being pregnant, for allowing him a voice in my decision, but I was so broken and lonely and simply...scared.

"Was it a boy or a girl?" he asks, his voice cracking.

I turn my body to face him. "A girl."

He closes his eyes and his head drops back against the headrest. His fingers grip the steering wheel, his knuckles turning white.

My voice wavers with emotion as I speak. "She was born on December twenty-seventh, over the holiday break of my sophomore year. She was a week early. She weighed five pounds, ten ounces. She was tiny and beautiful...and perfect," I barely manage to choke out. "I'll never forget her tiny pink face, even though she was so small her cheeks were full and round. The love I felt for our little girl is what got me through the worst time of my life—knowing I was making the right decision for her—for us."

Tears flow freely from Cole's eyes and down his cheeks. He turns his head and opens his eyes, looking at me through his tears. "They were with you at the birth?"

I shake my head and clear my throat. "They were at the hospital, but I was alone for the birth. I needed to do that alone and I needed those moments right after birth with her and only her. I held her for an hour, that's it." My shoulders shake violently as I begin to crumble completely, remembering my daughter's perfect little nose, fingers, toes, arms...and those bright blue eyes that perfectly matched Cole's.

I can barely get out the next words. "I held her hand and promised her this was what was best for her...that the Whites would give her the life we couldn't."

Cole cries openly. It's something I've never seen from him...ever. He hits his fist against the steering wheel and I decide to give him a moment alone. I step out of the Jeep and walk toward the tree line. There's a large tree that's fallen over and I head toward it, taking a seat on it once I reach it.

I give him his space to deal with his emotions, as I've had ten years to deal with mine. Opening this wound was painful, and he may never forgive me for the choices I made—but for the sake of all involved, I did what I felt was best.

Both of us mourn the obvious—our baby, but there was so much loss between us ten years ago, I wonder if we'll ever recover. I'll never get over letting her go, but there is peace and comfort in knowing she's safe, she's loved, and she's happy.

After a few minutes, Cole slides out of the driver's seat and walks around to the front of his Jeep. He leans against the hood and stares at me. While I'll never understand exactly what he's feeling, I have a pretty good idea of what he's going through. All I can do is ask for his forgiveness, just as he asked of me.

I push myself up on wobbly legs and walk through the thick grass over to Cole. His hands are shoved deep in his pockets and his beautiful jaw ticks as I stop in front of him.

"I'm sorry, Cole," I barely manage above a whisper. "You deserved better and you deserved to know."

He shakes his head and looks down at the ground where

we stand toe-to-toe. He sounds so broken, I almost can't take it. "I'm the one that's sorry. I shouldn't have lied to you. I should've been there for you—I should've been a better man—"

I interrupt him. "We were kids, Cole. There are so many things I think we both wish we could take back."

He nods and looks up at me. His voice trembles when he speaks. "You deserve better, Frankie. You always did..."

His words feel like a goodbye. My heart races and blood rushes through me, fogging my hearing. This is how we will end. This is how we will crumble and dissolve, and my heart drops to my stomach. I can't go through this again. I can't lose him again.

"I think we both bear the fault lines for the hurt between us," I say, looking up into his blue eyes.

"I have a million more questions, Frankie. But right now I just need to digest all of this." He looks away from me and back toward the road we came in on. "Come on, I'll take you home." He pushes himself off the hood of the Jeep and walks over to the passenger door, opening it for me.

Cole isn't in a rush to get home. He drives slowly, lost in his thoughts. As he pulls onto our street and parks in his driveway, he turns to look at me. Something unspoken passes between us—an understanding, or maybe a goodbye. We both step down from the Jeep at the same time and meet behind it at the end of his driveway.

"Bye, Cole." I barely manage to say, not sure if it's temporary or not. All I know is my heart feels like it's breaking into a million little pieces. This feels like the end—and while my heart is breaking, a sense of peace is also present. There are no more secrets. There are no more lies between us. Whether I ever see Cole again or not, one thing is certain—we're both living in the truth.

"Bye, Frankie."

And just like that, he saunters up his driveway, onto his front porch, and through the front door—not once looking back at me.

TWENTY-THREE

Cole

When I finally wake up, it's seven o'clock in the evening and my head is pounding to the beat of my pulse. I grumble and push myself out of bed, stumbling into the bathroom. Two Tylenol and a hot shower is exactly what I need right now.

I swallow down two capsules and step into the warm spray. As the hot water stings my face, I inhale the steam and let it burn my lungs. My stomach turns when I think about my child, my own flesh and blood, and Frankie keeping that from me. I draw in a deep breath and pinch my eyes closed as I envision what my little girl might look like, what she might be into these days, if she plays sports, if she loves music. Does she have my eyes and Frankie's dark hair? Does she have Frankie's fighting spirit? So many things roll around in my mind.

Yesterday I was filled with anger and hurt, and today I'm just numb. I believe everything Frankie told me. I could see her pain written across her face as she recounted the decisions she made based upon her life in those moments.

To think about how life may have turned out had I not

gone through with my plan to push Frankie away...I can't even think about it; it makes me fucking sick to my stomach. Is there a feeling deeper than regret? Because regret doesn't seem to even touch how I'm feeling for the part I played in all of this.

Feeling lower than I've ever felt in my life, I finish my shower and throw on some clothes before heading over to the shop. Planning to lose myself in Jack Vanderbilt's vehicle is a much better choice than what I used to lose myself in—booze and pussy.

When I get to the shop, Carter's truck is parked at the curb and the exterior lights shine bright against the dark sky. Carter has gotten good at reading my mood over the years, and with my current state of mind, I fully expect him to leave me the fuck alone.

When I push the door open and step into the large garage, I find Carter standing next to a rolling cart, holding a laptop. He does this when parts start coming in for restoration vehicles, ensuring every part ordered is correct. This is how we keep inventory and maintain accurate records of every part ordered for the vehicles we're restoring. Carter has always been the one to maintain organization in this place. I've always been the creative mind, the chaos, while he keeps the ship afloat.

He looks up from the computer, giving me a onceover. His face hardens yet he says nothing, just as I expected. I toss my sweatshirt on the chair and push the power button on the car lift. As Vanderbilt's car rises, I mentally break down where we'll start with this thing.

I run my fingers over the rusted muffler, feeling the old, rough metal under my fingertips. As I poke around under the car, I can see Carter powering down the computer and beginning to stock parts that have come in. He works quietly while I make noise. That's just how we work.

Hours pass when I finally see him shrug on his jacket and toss the last cardboard box he's unloaded over in the corner. He walks over slowly, resting both of his hands on side panel of the Corvette I'm still standing under. "You know, this car has seen better days." He runs the palm of his hand over the large dent in the door. "When it was new, it used to be perfect." His eyes almost smile as he looks over the car. "But like everything else in life, wear and tear and abuse beat it down."

I stop poking at the lines underneath and prop my hands on my hips, wondering where he's going with this.

"Sometimes we get cars with a history so bad I wonder if we'll ever get it back to its original condition." I narrow my eyes as he builds on his story. "And then I remember, we don't want it to be new. These cars have a history, and stories, and we're taking away all of the outside damage to make it look new, and work like new—but we can't erase that car's history."

He clears his throat and his hands fall to his sides. "Kind of like you and Frankie."

Resentment burns inside me as he speaks of us. I clench my jaw, my heart squeezing in my chest at the sound of her name.

"Back in the day, you two were perfect." He looks down at his feet, avoiding my death glare. "But then wear and tear happened...nothing that can't be restored. Pull off the damaged pieces and start building a new relationship. The history will always be there—you don't get to erase that—but you can put it back together better than it was." He raises his head to look at me. His eyes hold mine and I swallow hard against my dry throat.

"Don't let this destroy you two," he says quietly before turning around and grabbing his car keys off the rolling cart. "Just like you, Cole, she deserves a second chance, too." He pushes the shop door open and steps outside. I hear the click of the lock moments before I hear his old truck roar to life. Fucking Carter Richardson, always dropping wisdom when I least expect it.

The past week has been a time of reflection and mourning for me. I haven't spoken to Frankie since that night a week ago. I see her come and go, and a few days ago she had Maggie return the key I gave her to the old thrift store. She assumes that I want it back. I don't. It's hers. It always will be.

I hate to admit it, but I've learned that there is nothing that time can't or won't heal—it's about learning to let go of the past and not becoming a hostage to it. The last ten years I've been a hostage to the choices I made that led to Frankie making choices that have held her hostage. We've been in an endless cycle of living our present based on consequences of the past.

I'm done with that.

Two days ago, I placed a lumber order, printed the building plans off my computer, and hired a construction crew to help me with one goal in mind—tear down the past and rebuild the future.

So here I stand, on a Saturday morning at seven o'clock, with two cups of coffee, a sledgehammer, and a plan. The old front porch is flimsy and it takes only a couple of swings for the sledgehammer to bring the entire damn thing down. A part of me hurts watching an important part of my past descend into a pile of rubble, while another part of me understands that letting the past go is critical to building a future.

Frankie and Faith stand in the large picture window, each juggling a mug in their hands while watching the crew work with a look of confusion on their faces. Faith looks pissed and Frankie looks...sad. I cleared the demolition and construction with Martha a long time ago; I just didn't have the heart to let go before now.

Ten minutes later, Frankie rounds the corner of the house all bundled up in a large cream sweater. Her hair is piled on top of her head and a few loose strands hang down, framing her perfect face. Her bright blue eyes shine in the morning sun.

"What the hell are you doing?" she yells over the sounds of saws and hammers.

"What I should've done a long time ago." I turn and look at the pile of old wood sitting in a large construction dumpster. "Letting go of the past." I manage to say without getting emotional. I'm tucking those memories deep inside my heart. I'll never forget the days and nights Frankie and I spent sitting on this porch—every conversation we had here, and every dream we conveyed to each other. I'll carry those memories, and also the pain of some of those memories, with me forever. However, I decided it's time to focus on moving forward.

Frankie tilts her head and narrows her eyes at me as I begin to speak. "If you thought for a single second I was going to walk away after getting you back, you are sorely mistaken."

I toss the sledgehammer onto the frost-covered ground and hold Frankie's gaze. "I needed to take some time to process everything." I look away from her and to the ground where I kick at the brown lawn. "I needed to think about how my choices and decisions impacted yours." I look back to her. "And I needed time to get my head put back together."

Frankie shivers and rubs her arms with her hands. She pulls her lips in between her teeth as she watches me.

"I'm sorry," I tell her. I seem to always be apologizing. "I don't know that I'll ever agree with the decision you made, but I do understand why you did it."

I see tears forming in the corner of her eyes and her chin trembles.

My voice grows hoarse with emotion as I tell her, "It's time for us to move forward, Frankie...if you still want me."

The tears that were pooling in her eyes finally spill over and she lunges forward, colliding with my chest. Her arms wrap tightly around my neck and I pull her closer, breathing in the scent of her. She smells like coconut and coffee, and while our story is far from perfect, it's also far from over.

"I love you, Frankie," I whisper against the top of her head.

"I love you, too." I hear her say as the final piece of our past is loaded into the dumpster and driven away.

TWENTY-FOUR

Frankie

ONE MONTH LATER

I walk the perimeter of the vacant building Cole gave me, pointing out ideas with the construction foreman of what I'd like to do to transform the space. I have an entire vision board with pinned transformation ideas incorporating the brick industrial feel of the building, along with modern office conveniences. While these ideas are far from final, I want his expert opinion on whether they're feasible within the space we have before I have an architect draft up the plans.

He listens intently as I describe collaborative workspaces, individualized offices, and small business workstations that anyone in the community can rent for a minimal fee. This allows me a place to have my office for teaching while also providing a much-needed place where students or other members of the community can utilize a desk or meeting room without ongoing rental commitments. In addition, I envision satellite classrooms for a local community college and community meetings all having a place for the residents of Crescent Ridge.

As Brian, the foreman, points out a corner in the building that'll work better for conference room space, the front door swings opens with a large squeak and Cole steps inside, closing the door behind him. He watches us from a distance, however he won't offer his thoughts on this space as he wants it to be mine. Every decision about this building and renovation, he wants me to make—from the design, to the decorating, even the marketing. Even though I've asked him a million times for advice, he wants me to own it all.

"Hey, babe!" I call out to him and he smiles, leaning up against the door. He waits patiently while Brian and I finalize our walkthrough and Brian makes notes on paper before wrapping up our meeting. I collect my purse from the corner while Cole sees Brian out with a handshake.

"So how'd it go?" he asks, meeting me in the center of the vacant space.

"Awesome. He's really brilliant, ya' know. So smart and has a good vision for my ideas."

Cole nods. "He's phenomenal. His entire crew has transformed this town." He reaches out and pulls me to him, wrapping his arms around my waist. "When did he think they'd have the space complete?" He nuzzles himself into my neck and presses his lips to that spot right behind my ear that drives me crazy.

I catch my breath and sink into his touch. "Once the plans are drawn up and permits approved, he thought no more than twelve weeks."

Pulling away, he looks at the space without releasing me. "Sounds about right. You both on the same page?" He looks at me with concern, his way of offering help. Making sure I'm happy with Brian.

"Yep. He really brought my vision to life."

"Good, good." He rubs his thumb over my bottom lip. "Hopefully the plans and permits won't take too long. Until then, the office at the house is yours for your classes. Anything you need, just say the word."

I've basically moved into Cole's house. This gives my mom more space in the house for the physical and occupational therapy she's receiving. Her therapists visit a couple of times a week and there is equipment all over the house. She's making great progress and, since I'll be just across the street, it made sense to move in with Cole.

I press a quick kiss to his lips and thank him.

"Are you done for the day? Because I'd like to steal you for the afternoon." He grins slyly at me. That's code for he wants to spend the afternoon in bed with no clothes on.

I let out a happy sigh. "I am done for the day, Mr. Ryan. What did you have in store for us?"

He taps his finger on my nose. "You're just going to have to wait and see. But first, we're getting lunch. You're going to need your energy." He pulls me toward the door and laughs. I swear, this man is trying to kill me with his sex Olympics.

He holds my hand all the way down the street until we get to The Fault Line Bar and Grill. Inside we settle into a corner booth and enjoy all of our favorite appetizers. I chew on a fried pickle as I lean into Cole and rest my shoulder up against him. We've come a long way in the last few weeks. Uncertainty loomed over us due to both of our choices in the past, but we've been able to come out of the fire stronger than we've ever been before.

"Ashley called," I casually mention as I take a sip of my iced tea.

"Oh, yeah?" He glances at me out of the corner of his eye.

"She wants us to visit." I squeeze the lemon wedge that was resting on the rim of my glass into the tea. "She said her parents would love to meet you."

He shifts in the booth and lets out a small sigh.

"Honestly, I think it's so she can meet you." I let out a small laugh.

"I just don't want to disrupt Libby's routine," he starts before I hold up my hand, stopping him.

"This isn't about meeting Libby. Libby wouldn't even know we're there. It's just so you can meet Joe and Anne. And you'd get to see Libby, but not meet her. Libby already knows she's adopted. When and if she ever asks about her birth parents, then they'll tell her and we can meet her at that time. This is just an opportunity for you see her—"

He cuts me off. "From a distance, right?"

I nod my head. "Yeah. No interaction. That'd be confusing to her."

He nods his head in agreement, seemingly relieved.

"But only if you're comfortable," I add. "I think it would be great for you to meet Joe and Anne, though. I think you'll understand how they made this decision much easier for me."

He exhales loudly. "I don't know if I'm ready—"

I swallow the lump in my throat. "Then we won't go. I just want you to know that anytime you are ready, they're willing to talk to you."

"You've had access to her all this time—" he says.

"No, Cole, I haven't. I've had pictures of her, and I get updates through Ash about her—but for the sake of normalcy for their family, and for me, I've kept my distance. Everyone felt like that was the best approach."

We're both silent for a moment.

"But, Cole..." I choke down the growing lump in my throat. "She's happy, and healthy, and the last thing I want to do is disrupt her life. I know where she's at, and I know she's safe and loved and so my love for her has been ensuring that her life stays as normal as possible, which means I've had to let her go. Cole, I've had a lot of time to deal with all of the emotions that came with this decision. This was a very difficult decision for me, but I've had the time to work through it." I pause and take a deep breath to still my emotions. "I gave birth to her. She'll always be *our* biological daughter—but she's also Joe and Anne's daughter. They're the ones who raised her. They deserve that normalcy and no disruptions from us."

Cole traces a wood knot on the table with his forefinger and nods his head slowly. "How many times have you seen her?" he asks, his voice low.

"Outside of pictures or on social media, just once." My voice trails off when I remember driving to Malibu that day. It was the only day I ever took a day off work. I had just started working at Ted's office...I didn't tell Ted where I was going and no one knew where I was. It felt so good to just disappear, to see my daughter and have this private moment to myself.

"It was about six years ago," I begin. My heart races as I remember seeing her in the flesh. Her little round face with bright pink cheeks. The experience was beautiful and heartbreaking all at the same time. I knew the second my eyes landed on her she was mine. Her dark hair and bright blue eyes spoke to me and my heart—a connection you can't deny.

Shaking off the memory, I continue. "I drove to Malibu to

see her ballet recital. She was little, just about four years old. Anne had mentioned in an email that Libby had started ballet class and that her first recital was the weekend before Christmas. They were doing The Nutcracker."

Cole listens intently while I tell him my story. "It sounds a little creepy now, but she gave me just enough information to do some investigating. The Internet is an amazing tool. I found the dance studio online and their website told me where the recital was. I bought a ticket online and picked the last row in a corner where no one would see me."

I take another deep breath as those old feelings surface. I wonder if this is what Cole might be feeling. The intense need to see her coupled with the actual fear of seeing her. Emotions are a crazy thing. One second you're just needing to see someone, get a glimpse of their life, and the next minute you're doubled over in grief and despair.

"I didn't go there to meet her. I just felt a maternal need in that moment to see her." I close my eyes and remember the memory of seeing her for the first time since I gave her away.

I squeeze the ticket in my fingers and walk into the auditorium and I see the lights are still on. I waited in the parking lot until the last minute in hopes of sneaking in when it was dark, hoping not to be seen by anyone. An older gentleman in an usher's vest takes my ticket and guides me over to the last row. I slide into the aisle seat in the far corner, slinking down as I shrug off my coat.

My hands tremble as I lay my jacket neatly across my lap and the lights begin to fall. I use the light from my phone to read the program, with each recital number listing the class name and dancer's name. My eyes stop at Elizabeth White. Libby. I see her name listed in the beginning ballet number, which is the third performance.

The opening number seems to last forever as my heart races in anticipation of seeing her. The lights stay dark between each performance as one group shuffles off the stage and the other takes their positions. I wipe my hands on my skirt when I realize they are drenched in sweat. The second performance is a solo, a teenage girl, tall and lean, floating around the stage on pointe shoes. She's graceful and everyone claps wildly for her when she finishes.

I sit up straighter, feeling my throat tighten as the lights slowly come up. The stage is covered in a soft amber light as the little girls take their positions. There are ten girls, but it's the front row, far left, where I see Libby.

Her dark hair is pulled into a tight bun on the back of her head and I can see her striking blue eyes from the back of the auditorium. Her chubby cheeks are pink and a huge smile is plastered to her face.

She stands in position, but her eyes wander until she finds Joe and Anne in the second row, straight in front of me. Anne has her arm laced through Joe's, who has a small handheld video camera in the other hand, recording Libby.

She gives them a little wave before promptly lifting her arms above her head and holding her position. Libby glides across the floor, and I know I hold my breath the entire time she dances. I take in every detail of her, from her fair skin to her long legs. When the lights fall, I stay seated, wiping tears from my cheeks.

My daughter.

I choke back a sob and try to gain my composure.

However, in this moment, a sense of peace takes over me—knowing that I made the right decision, that she is living a life she deserves with a family that can give it to her. Neither Cole nor I were ready to raise a child, we were barely managing to take care of ourselves. I'm just barely starting my own life and she deserves the time that the Whites can devote to her.

The lights fall and she disappears behind the curtain as I burn the memory of her sweet face into my mind and I make a quick exit to avoid being seen by the Whites. I needed this moment tonight, to know she was okay, to know that she was happy, and to allow me to heal.

My heart was never the same when I handed her over—and tonight was the first step in healing those wounds. Sure I saw pictures and I got updates, but seeing her in the flesh was what cemented everything I've been told or seen from a distance.

Cole stares past me at the wall. I can't tell if he's angry, hurt, or just trying to keep it together. "What was it like...seeing her?"

I smile and take a deep breath. "It was everything." I pause. "That's why when you're ready, you should do it."

He just nods his head slowly. "Someday," he says quietly and I reach my hand out and cover his.

"Whenever you're ready."

After lunch Cole drives me across town and parks in the parking lot of the only elementary school in Crescent Ridge.

"What are we doing here?" I ask as I look around. I remember the bus dropping me here every day. Nothing seems to have changed. The windows are the same, and the red brick is beginning to fade with age.

"See that over there?" Cole points to an empty dirt lot.

"There's nothing to see," I remark, squinting my eyes in hopes of seeing something I'm missing.

"What happened to your creative vision?" Cole smirks at me. "That right there is the future home of a YMCA."

"What?" I snap my head back and look at the lot again.

"Yep. We've been working on getting one for three years. We built the business case and met all of their prerequisites. We got approval last week. I didn't say anything right away because I wanted to be sure," he says proudly.

"Cole!" I bounce up and down in the seat of his Jeep. "How the hell do you do it all?"

He amazes me. Years ago, all I thought Cole's life would be was running his dad's auto shop. Instead, he's transformed that business and built so many other businesses from his willingness to never give up. He never gives up on anything he sets his mind to.

He sighs with satisfaction. "When I want something bad enough, I won't let anything get in my way." He turns those sparkling blue eyes to me, and I see the meaning in them.

"I'm so proud of you." I sit back in the seat as tears sting my eyes with pride.

After a minute, he throws the Jeep in drive and heads back toward the other side of town. "I've got one more thing to show you," he says as he rolls up to the hidden trailhead that leads to the fault line.

"At the fault line?" I ask as I hop down out of the Jeep.

"Yep." He grabs my hand and laces his fingers through mine. He maneuvers the trail with ease, pushing branches out of the way for me as we forge our way deeper through the woods and closer to the edge of the valley.

When we pass that last set of trees and step into the clearing that appears before the fault line, Cole drops to a knee.

"Frankie," he says my name, his voice shaking. "Everything began for us at the fault line. We were here the first time I knew I loved you. Our first kiss happened here—everything good about my life with you happened here."

My entire body trembles as he pulls a velvet box from the front pocket of his jeans.

"Marry me." He flips the box open and there sits a huge cushion-cut diamond flanked by smaller diamonds.

My heart leaps in my chest, not because of the stunning ring, but because this is what it feels like to know I'm about to say yes to spending the rest of my life with the only man I've ever really loved.

Tears spill from my eyes and I drop to my knees in front of him.

"Please say yes," he begs.

I nod my head frantically. "Yes. Yes, I'll marry you."

With a huge grin, Cole slides the ring on my finger before pulling me into his arms. It's here, the only place I've ever felt at home—safe in Cole's arms.

Cole

EPILOGUE

NINE MONTHS LATER

Her waist-length, dark brown hair whips around in the breeze and her feet stumble through the sand as she runs toward the ocean. I'm sitting a hundred yards away, watching her. Just far enough to not look creepy, but close enough to hear her squeals and laughter as Joe and Anne White playfully chase her.

She does flips and cartwheels, a bellowing laugh erupting at the end of her flipping, and a lump grows in my throat, making it hard to swallow. Tears sting the back of my eyes as I see my daughter double over in laughter as Joe tackles her into the sand and tickles her stomach. She's just about the age Frankie was when I met her—and she is the spitting image of Frankie.

I hear light voices approach from behind me as Frankie plops down next to me in the sand, Ashley sitting on the other side of me.

"You okay?" Frankie asks, placing her hand on my forearm.

I swallow hard, trying to push the lump down, but I can't. I just focus on Libby—my daughter.

"She's happy," Ashley says quietly and I nod my head.

She is happy. I can tell Joe and Anne have given her a good life. A life that I'm not sure I could've ever given her—but I would've liked to have tried.

"My parents are totally open with her about the adoption. Anytime you want to meet her or she wants to meet you, they'll make it happen." Ashley is so sincere, and I appreciate it.

"She's still so young," I choke out and clear my throat. "I think it would be confusing for her right now, but someday..."

Frankie laces her fingers through mine and rests her head on my shoulder.

Ashley pushes herself up. "I'm going to go say hi to my parents. I'll see you guys at dinner tonight. Reservations are at seven. Don't be late."

Ashley jogs through the sand, down the beach toward Joe, Anne, and Libby, and Libby runs to her when she sees her approach. Frankie swipes tears from under her eyes, and we sit in silence, watching our daughter from afar with her family. *A great family.*

For the rest of my life, I'll regret my actions that set off a series of events that damn near destroyed me. But as I watch my daughter laugh and smile, I know she's happy and that brings me some peace from the past.

"She looks so much like you did at that age," I remark, squeezing Frankie's hand. "It's like I'm looking at my past."

Frankie digs her toes further into the sand and tips her head back, allowing the sun to reach her face. I lay back in the sand and Frankie rests her head against my shoulder. Contentment falls over me as the woman I love lies wrapped in my arms on a sunny beach with the sounds of Libby's laughter blanketing us.

It isn't the life we planned, or the broken one we thought we'd always have. It's somewhere in between, and I have to trust that it's the one we were supposed to have.

"You ready, man?" Carter asks as he rolls up the sleeves of his white dress shirt to his mid-forearm.

"Ready as I'll ever be," I say, taking a deep breath. I'm not the type of guy who gets nervous or emotional very often, but my nerves are on edge today and nothing will put them at bay until I see Frankie.

"Calm down, man. She'll be there." He lets out a small laugh. "I never thought I'd see this day—all the booze, the ladies—"

"Carter," I bark, stopping him mid-sentence, and he lets out a hearty laugh.

Once he composes himself, his expression shifts to something more serious.

"I'm happy for you guys—but if you do anything to fuck this up, I'll take you outside of town and kill you myself."

I huff and straighten my tie in the mirror. "Not gonna happen, man. Never letting her go this time." I know our breakup was hard on Carter, too. He respected Frankie and he didn't like what I did—because for nearly ten fucking years he had to pick up the pieces of my wreck of a life. When I finally pulled my shit together, I saw the toll it took on him.

It wasn't easy being my friend, but he stayed. He picked

my drunk ass up off the floor more times than I can count. He drove me home. He punched me in the face when I'd fuck up, but mostly he was just there for me. Whether it was his silent presence at the shop, or listening to me bitch like a little girl, he was always there for me, and I'm grateful.

He claps his hand on my shoulder and gives it a squeeze. "Good. Now let's go get you married!"

Who knew a vineyard in Temecula, California, would be the place that I'd get married? Frankie found this place and it's perfect for our small, casual bunch. The chapel sits out in the middle of the vineyard, surrounded by green vines full of grapes. It's simple yet beautiful with its twinkling lights and rustic feel.

This isn't a traditional ceremony—the only one walking down the aisle will be Frankie. Faith is standing to my right and Martha is sitting in the front row with Melinda, who we hired to come with her to make sure she's well cared for.

Faith is holding a small bouquet of flowers and wearing a simple navy dress. Frankie wanted causal and comfortable and that's exactly what she got. Aside from Faith, Carter, Martha, and Melinda, there are only a handful of other people in the chapel. Ashley and her husband, Maggie and Matthew, Frankie's niece and nephew, and Eduardo's husband, Jeremy, all sit with smiles on their faces. It's small and intimate, just what we wanted.

There's no music, but it doesn't matter because it's as if I've gone deaf when I see Frankie at the back of the chapel. She's gripping Eduardo's arm and holding a larger bouquet of cream roses with greens filling it out. Eduardo looks down at her and presses a sweet kiss to her forehead. Normally I'd want to rip the man's head off, but once I met him and knew he wasn't a threat, I actually found his relationship with Frankie endearing. He's been a great friend and mentor to her, and I'm thankful she has him.

They begin to walk the short aisle, and it's as if time stands still. A million little moments flash before my eyes—Frankie at the fault line, her hair blowing in the wind; Frankie kissing me on her front porch as she sits with her head in my lap.

When her mouth stretches into a large smile, my heart stops.

Everything I feared I'd lost is walking down the aisle toward me, and I can't keep the tears at bay. Eduardo gives me a little wink as Frankie and he come to a stop right in front of me.

The pastor clears his throat and takes a deep breath before he starts. "Who gives this woman to be married to this man?" Eduardo squeezes Frankie's hand and leans in to give her cheek a quick kiss.

Martha stands with Melinda's help and answers, "I do."

As Frankie reaches for my hand and steps up to me, everything else in the world becomes non-existent. Tears openly fall from my eyes, and she reaches up and swipes them away with her finger before she rests her hand on my cheek for a brief moment.

The entire ceremony maybe lasts seven minutes. As much as I'd like to say I remember every second, I don't. I only remember looking into Frankie's eyes, knowing she's mine. Forever.

Today is a new beginning for us. For the rest of our lives,

we'll be bonded in love and marriage. This is exactly how I wanted our story to end—together, us against the world. Mr. and Mrs. Cole and Frankie Ryan. Except it's stubborn Frankie we're talking about here...so she's actually Mrs. Frances Callaway-Ryan.

Frankie

EPILOGUE

FOUR MONTHS LATER

"Babe," Cole mumbles against my neck as he nibbles the sensitive flesh. I was sleeping until he woke me up, his hard erection pressing against my back.

"So tired." I manage as he rolls me to my back and inspects me.

"You okay?" He presses his hand to my forehead, checking for a temperature.

I curl into a ball, my entire body aching. "Everything aches."

He gently massages my neck for a minute. "Let me go run a bath for you and then I'll make coffee and breakfast. We'll just relax today and watch some movies in bed." He kisses my forehead and slides out of bed.

Suddenly, my stomach flips and nausea hits me. I inhale sharply, drawing a deep breath into my lungs. I mentally tick off every symptom as I recall them. Nausea, check. Exhaustion, check. Tender breasts...check.

We've been unsuccessful in getting pregnant the last three months and I was beginning to worry. With a hopeful smile, I push myself up from the bed, careful to steady myself as my head spins from the nausea. Hearing the bath water running, I slowly make my way to the bathroom.

Cole is sitting on the edge of the tub, pouring bubble bath into the running water when he catches me come in. "Get in," he says as he stands up and places the bubble bath on the bathroom counter. "I'll bring you some coffee and toast."

"Tea," I tell him.

He nods. "You got it, babe. Tea and toast, coming right up!" He takes off for the kitchen and I grab a pregnancy test from my drawer.

I stockpiled these from the pharmacy last month right before my period arrived. I was three days late and was so hopeful that I'd be pregnant, only to be disappointed by my monthly visitor.

With a bit of nerves, I slide the test from the box and tear open the foil packaging. My hands are trembling with anticipation of what I already know. Needing privacy, I close the door to the private toilet room and sit down on the toilet. Following the directions on the box, I place the test in my stream and wait.

It takes less than fifteen seconds for the test to display a giant plus sign and my heart leaps in my chest. A baby. Ours.

Tears prick the back of my eyes as relief washes over me. I know people wait much longer than we have to get pregnant, but after it happening so unexpectedly for us so many years ago, it was becoming worrisome that it might not happen again.

Cole has reassured me that, regardless of what happens, we'll be fine. That we'll always be fine as long as we're together. I agree with him, but now we don't even have to worry about it.

Hiding a grin, I tuck the test under the towel on the bathroom counter and slip into the hot bath that Cole drew for me. Bubbles surround me and my body begins to relax in the hot water.

I rest my head against the back of the tub and close my eyes, my hands running over my lower stomach under the water. We're going to have a baby...So many emotions hit me all at once—happiness, relief, and a tinge of sadness that it wasn't like this with my last pregnancy, the feelings of happiness and relief.

"Tea and toast, madam," Cole says, pushing through the bathroom door with a large wood serving tray with tea and a plate of wheat toast. He's wearing nothing but his boxer briefs and every defined muscle in his abs and arms are on full display. Pushing the towel with the pregnancy test under it aside, he makes room for the tray, and my heart leaps in hopes that he doesn't see the test yet.

"Sip," he says, handing me the small porcelain tea glass. "It's hot, though."

I nod and pull the glass to my lips, drawing in the hot Earl Grey tea.

"Mmmmm..." I hum as the tea makes its way down my throat and into my belly. "Thank you for taking care of me." I look up, my eyes meeting Cole's.

He leans against the bathroom counter, his arms crossed against his chest.

"Always, Frankie. I'll always take care of you."

I hand him the tea glass and sit up, getting nervous. "Can you hand me that towel?"

I watch him set the tea glass down and reach for the large towel. Unplugging the drain, I stand up, the bath water whirling around my legs. When he lifts up the towel, he notices the test stick on the counter, then hands me the towel without even looking at me. His eyes are fixed on the giant plus sign staring him down.

I wrap the towel tightly around me, tucking the edge so that it stays put. Cole's shaky hand reaches for the test stick and he picks it up before turning to me. My eyes fill with tears, happy tears, when Cole lunges at me and scoops me out of the tub, spinning me around.

My arms wrap tightly around his neck, and he hugs me tighter than he's ever hugged me before.

"We're having a baby?" he asks, his mouth pressed against my neck. I can feel his heart racing against my chest as his entire body quakes in excitement.

"We are," I answer as he sets me down.

"Is that why you've been so tired?"

I nod and readjust the towel as it starts to slip off of me. Cole stops me, flicking the edge of the towel and watching it fall to a pile on the floor.

With a grin, he lifts me into his arms, carrying me back to our bedroom and setting me carefully in the middle of our bed. He pushes his boxers off and kicks them aside before nudging his way between my thighs.

His hand trails a soft line from my hip up to my ribs, finally stopping as he cups my breast, giving it a gentle squeeze. My breasts are sensitive, but Cole handles them with care, pulling a nipple into his mouth and gently sucking, causing my core to instantly react.

His cock probes my entrance before sliding right in, accepting him fully. I gasp at the outburst of emotions my body is feeling right now. All of my senses are heightened and Cole knows how to expertly work every single one.

I wrap one of my legs around Cole's lower back, allowing my other leg to fall open as I pull him further into me. I'll never have enough of him. Our lovemaking is slow this morning, attentive and emotional. So many unspoken emotions and words pass between us, but mostly love.

A single tear falls from the corner of my eye as Cole brings me to release. This is what we always dreamed of, and while we took a long, bumpy road to get here, we made it. This is what home will always be to me, Cole and our baby—and Libby someday. But no matter where we're at, with him and our family by my side, I have everything in the world.

ACKNOWLEDGMENTS

It takes a village to write a book, from the sacrifices my family makes, to the help and support I get from my friends, family, and peers along the way. I could not have written Fault Lines without the following people:

Mi Familia. I love you dearly. Thank you for supporting my dreams even when it means sacrifices for you...like shitty takeout instead of home cooked meals. There aren't words adequate to express my love for you.

K.L. Grayson. Your help and encouragement pushed me to the finish line. Thank you for helping me plot, forcing me to write when I wanted to quit, and reading and finessing Fault Lines. I love you.

Sarah Arndt. Your help, opinions, and critical eye made Fault Lines better. Thank you for your help.

A.L. Jackson. Thank you for always being there...to listen to me bitch, pushing me to write when I just want to sleep, and to lend your eye and opinion to my stories. They are better because of you.

To my "Fab Four". Your laughing keeps me going in this crazy business. I love us.

ALSO BY REBECCA SHEA

Bound & Broken Series

Broken by Lies – Book 1

Bound by Lies -Book 2

Betrayed by Lies - Book 3

Unbreakable Series

Unbreakable -Book 1

Undone -Book 2

Unforgiven - Book 3

Dare Me - Standalone title

CONNECT WITH REBECCA SHEA

Website
www.rebeccasheaauthor.com

Sign up for Rebecca Shea's newsletter for updates on new releases
http://tinyurl.com/h8mfya2

Sign up for Rebecca Shea's new release and sale alerts
http://www.subscribepage.com/j1m3c5

Follow Rebecca Shea on Facebook:
www.facebook.com/rebeccasheaauthor

Follow Rebecca Shea on Twitter:
@beccasheaauthor

Follow Rebecca Shea on Instagram:
https://www.instagram.com/rebeccasheaauthor/

Email: rebeccasheaauthor@gmail.com

CPSIA information can be obtained
at www.ICGtesting.com
Printed in the USA
LVOW12s2320011117
554606LV00002B/513/P